J. T H

The Second War With England
Volume 1

J. T Headley

The Second War With England
Volume 1

1st Edition | ISBN: 978-3-75233-176-9

Place of Publication: Frankfurt am Main, Germany

Year of Publication: 2020

Outlook Verlag GmbH, Germany.

THE SECOND WAR
WITH
ENGLAND.

BY J. T. HEADLEY

VOL. I.

PREFACE.

More books, probably, have been written on the War of 1812 than on any other portion of our history. The great political leaders of that time were so vindictive in their animosities, and took such strong and decided ground on all political questions, that the success of one or the other afterwards in public life depended very much on his conduct during the war. Hence, much detached and personal history has been written in order to clear up or illustrate some particular event. A candidate for public office was often chosen for his services in the war; hence, every portion of it in which he took part was thoroughly investigated by both friends and foes. So if one had failed in that trying period of the country, the world was sure to hear of it when he came up for the suffrages of the people. The war proved very unfortunate for some of the leaders, and court martials and disgrace closed the career of many which had hitherto been bright and prosperous. These men have written long pamphlets and books in self-defence, or they have been written by their descendants, so that if hearing both sides would aid the reader in coming to a correct conclusion, he was pretty sure to reach it. When so many quarrels are to be settled the public will not fail to be informed all about the origin of them. Another class of works have been written, designed only to furnish a synopsis of the war, and scarcely reach to the value of histories. Others have been confined solely to the military and naval movements—others still are devoted almost exclusively to political matters of that period; so that notwithstanding the large supply of works on the War of 1812, I know of none in which all these different topics are even attempted to be combined in proper proportions. The present work is an effort to accomplish that end without being too voluminous on the one hand, or too general on the other. I have endeavored to give impressions as well as facts—to trace the current and depict the phases of public feeling, rather than inflict on the reader long documents and longer debates, in which everything that gave them life and interest was carefully excluded by the reporter.

The effects of the fierce conflict waged between the Federalists and Democrats during the war have not yet passed away, and many of the actors in it are still living, who retain their old prejudices and hatred. Their near descendants and relatives, though so many of them are found in the ranks of democracy, still defend the memory of those whose names they bear, and endeavor to throw discredit on the writer who would rob them of reputation, and consign them to the obloquy they deserve. In a war like the late one with Mexico, where almost every officer was a hero, and in narrating the progress of which the historian is called upon only to eulogize, his task is an easy one. But in one like that of 1812, in which the most conspicuous leaders met with signal defeat and disgrace, and instead of winning reputation, lost that which had illustrated them in the revolutionary struggle, the historian necessarily recalls feuds and assails character, which is sure to bring down on him the maledictions and open condemnation of friends and relations. A noble man and true patriot, like General Dearborn, will never want friends who will deny his incompetency as commander-in-chief, while one who had won so brave a name in the revolution, and was so estimable a man in social life as General Hull, must always be defended by those in whose veins his blood flows. The inefficiency and blunders of the government remain to this day to many a sufficient apology for the conduct of Wilkinson, Hampton and others.

Having no animosities to gratify, and no prejudices to favor, I have set down nought in malice, but have endeavored to ascertain, amid conflicting testimony, the exact truth, without regarding the friendly or hostile feelings the declaration of it might awaken. In many cases I have withheld much that was personal, because it was not necessary to my purpose, and useless only in self-defence. That I should reconcile difficulties which have never yet been healed, and please rivals who have ever hated each other, was not to be expected. I have attempted also to give a clear impression of the political and social feelings of the times, and make the reader, as far as lay in my power, live amid the scenes I depict.

Two new features have been introduced into the present work, which I though necessary to a complete history of the war, viz., privateering and the Dartmoor Prison.

It would be impossible to give all the authorities to which I am indebted. State papers, records, journals, Gazettes of the time have been consulted, as well as histories, while I have earnestly sought for information from the survivors of the war. In many cases I have omitted references to books in which facts I state are found recorded, because I came across them in old pamphlets, letters, and newspaper paragraphs, where, probably, the original compiler also obtained them. I cannot omit, however, acknowledging the vast aid I have derived from Niles' Register. A more valuable periodical was never published in this country. Ingersoll's History also, though very deficient in arrangement, contains more valuable material than any other work embracing the same period.

    — army, <u>319</u>

CHAPTER I.

A REVIEW OF THE CAUSES LEADING TO THE SECOND WAR

WITH ENGLAND.

Duplicity and oppressive acts of the British Government contrasted with the forbearance of the United States — Character of Madison — Debates in Congress on War measures — Declaration of War.

The peace which closed our revolutionary struggle was like a wound healed only at the surface, and which must be opened anew before a permanent cure can be effected. The desire for territory had become the ruling passion of the British Empire, and the loss of the most promising part of her vast possessions could not, therefore, be borne with equanimity. The comparatively barren and inhospitable tract lying north of the St. Lawrence and the lakes, which still belonged to her, was but a sorry substitute for the rich alluvial bottoms that stretched along the western rivers, while the mouth of the St. Lawrence furnished but a meagre outlet compared with the noble rivers and capacious harbors that seamed the inland and indented the coasts of the Atlantic slope. Some have supposed that England had never abandoned the design of recovering a part, if not the whole of the possessions she had lost on this continent. If this be true, that purpose was doubtless a very vague one, and it depended entirely on circumstances whether it ever assumed a definite form. One thing, however, is certain, she had determined to narrow down our limits wherever it was practicable, and to the fullest extent of her power. This is evident from the eagerness with which she urged us to acknowledge the various Indian tribes on our frontier, as independent nations. She wished to have them placed on a footing with other sovereign States, so that they could form treaties and dispose of territory to foreign governments. Numerous and powerful tribes then roamed undisturbed over vast tracts which have since become populous States. Could Great Britain have purchased these, or had them colonized by other foreign powers, nearly the whole line of lakes and the territory west of Lake Erie would have presented an impenetrable barrier to our growth in the north-west. Not succeeding in this policy, she determined that the Indians should retain possession of the land as her allies. This is evident from the constant disturbance kept up on our north-western frontiers—from Lord Dorchester's speeches instigating the Indians to war, and from the fact that an English fort was erected within the territory of the republic. So resolved was the British Government on this course that it for a long time refused to carry out the stipulations of the treaty of 1783, and still retained American posts captured by its forces during the revolutionary war. The defeat of General Harmar, in 1790, and of St. Clair, in 1791, were not wholly owing to our inefficiency or to Indian prowess, but to British interference and encouragement.

The victory of Wayne, which followed these disastrous expeditions, proved this true. Canadian militia and volunteers were found in the Indian armies, while the battle that completed their overthrow ended under the walls of a British fort standing on American ground. These violations of a sacred treaty, and undisguised encroachments upon our territory on the frontier, were afterwards surpassed by still greater outrages at sea.

The French revolution exploding like a volcano in the heart of Europe, followed by a republic whose foundation stones were laid in the proudest blood of France—the extinction of the Bourbon dynasty, and the loud declaration of rights which startled every despot from the Archangel to the Mediterranean like a peal of thunder, had covered the continent with hostile armies. The European powers who rejoiced in the success of the revolutionary struggle on these distant shores, because it inflicted a blow on their proud rival, saw with consternation the principle that sustained it at work in their midst. Like the first crusade against the infidels, which at once healed all the animosities of the princes of Europe, a second crusade, harmonizing powers hitherto at variance, was formed against this principle of human rights, and the allied armies moved down upon the infant republic of France. The devastating flood of feudalism would soon have swept everything under but for the appearance of that strange embodiment of power, Napoleon Bonaparte. Rolling it back from the French borders, he commenced that long and fearful struggle which ended only at Waterloo. England rashly formed a coalition with the continental powers, anticipating an easy overthrow to the plebeian warrior, but soon found herself almost alone in the conflict; and instead of treading down her ancient rival, began to tremble for her own safety. The long and deadly strife that followed exhausted her resources and crippled her strength. Her war ships stretched from Copenhagen to the Nile, and to supply these with seamen, she resorted to impressment not only on her own shores, amid her own subjects, but on American ships, among American sailors. Our merchant vessels were arrested on the high seas, and men, on the groundless charge of being deserters, immediately coerced into the British service. To such an extent was this carried, that in *nine months* of the years 1796 and '97, Mr. King, the American minister at London, had made application for the release of *two hundred and seventy-one seamen,*[1] most of whom were American citizens.

At first the British Government claimed only the right to seize deserters; but its necessities demanding a broader application to right of search, her vessels of war arrested American merchantmen to seek for *British seamen*, and later still, for British subjects—finally, every sailor was obliged to prove himself a citizen of the United States on the spot, or he was liable to be forced into British service. American merchants were thus injured while prosecuting a lawful commerce, and worse than all, great distress was visited on the friends and relatives of those who were illegally torn from their country and pressed into the hated service of a hated nation. Over six thousand were known to have been thus seized, while the actual number was much greater.

Not content with committing these outrages on the high seas, English vessels boarded our merchantmen and impressed our seamen in our own waters. That line which runs parallel to the sea coast of every nation, and which is considered its legitimate boundary, presented no obstacles to British cruisers.

In 1804, the frigate Cambria boarded an American merchantman in the harbor of New York, and in direct opposition to the port officers, carried off several of her seamen. To complete the insult, the commander declared, in an official letter to the British Minister, that he "considered his ship, while lying in the harbor of New York, as *having dominion around her within the distance of her buoys.*" Not long after a coasting vessel while going from one American port to another, was hailed by a British cruiser, and, refusing to stop, was fired into and one of her crew killed. Thus an American citizen was murdered within a mile of shore, and while going from port to port of his own country.[2]

These aggressions on land and insults at sea continued, at intervals, down to 1806, when our commerce received a more deadly blow from the British orders in council, and Napoleon's famous Berlin and Milan decrees. To annoy and cripple her adversary, England declared the whole coast of France, from Brest to the Elbe, in a state of blockade. Napoleon retaliated by the Berlin decree, in which he declared the British Islands in a state of blockade. The next year the English government issued other orders in council, blockading the whole continent, which were met by Napoleon's Milan decree.

These famous orders in council, so far as they affected us, declared all American vessels going to and from the harbors of France and her allies, lawful prizes, except such as had first touched at, or cleared from an English port. The Berlin and Milan decrees, on the other hand, pronounced all vessels that had so touched at an English port, or allowed themselves to be searched by a British cruiser, the property of France, while British goods, wherever found, were subject to confiscation. In short, if we did not confine our commerce to England, the latter would seize our merchantmen, wherever found, as lawful prizes, while if we did trade with her, or even touch at her ports at all, France claimed them as her property.

England, without the slightest provocation, had commenced a war against France, and irritated at her want of success, declared her coast in a state of blockade—thus violating an established law of nations. The principle has long been admitted and acted upon by the principal maritime nations of the world, that neutral flags have a right to sail from port to port of the belligerent powers, to carry any merchandise whatever, except those contraband of war, such as arms, munitions of war, or provisions for the enemy. The only exception to it is an actual blockade of a port where neutrals are forbidden an entrance. This principle is founded in common justice; otherwise two strong maritime nations might make a third neutral power the greatest sufferer from the war. Besides, if the right to create paper blockades is allowed, no restrictions can be placed upon it, and in case of another war with England, she could declare the whole coast of America, from Maine to Mexico, and that portion of our territory on the Pacific, in a state of blockade, while the naval force of the world could not maintain an *actual* one.

The injustice of these retaliatory measures was severely felt by our government. They placed us, a neutral power, in a worse attitude than if allied to one or the other we had been at open war with the third, for in the latter case our war ships could have defended our commerce, which would also have been under the protection of the cruisers of our ally. But now our men-of-war were compelled to look silently on and see American merchantmen seized, while two nations, instead of one, claimed the right to plunder us. Our commerce for the last few years had advanced with unparalleled strides—so that at this time our canvass whitened almost every sea on the globe, and wealth was pouring into the nation. Suddenly, as if the whole world, without any forewarning, had declared war against us; the ocean was covered with cruisers after American vessels, and the commerce of the country was paralyzed by a single blow.

But the most extraordinary part of the whole proceeding was, that while England, by her orders in council, shut the Continent from us and confiscated as a smuggler every American vessel that attempted to enter any of its ports, she herself, with *forged* papers, under the American flag, carried on an extensive trade. The *counterfeit* American vessel was allowed to pass unmolested by British cruisers, while the real American was seized. It was estimated that England made fifteen thousand voyages per annum in these disguised vessels, thus appropriating to herself all the advantages to be gained by a neutral nation in trading with the Continent, and using our flag as a protection.

These were the prominent causes of the war, sufficient, one would think, to justify the American Government in declaring it. One-hundredth part of the provocation which we then endured, would now bring the two governments in immediate and fierce collision.

But, notwithstanding England's desires and necessities, she would never have committed these outrages, had she not entertained a supreme contempt for our power, and cherished an inextinguishable hatred of the nation, rendering her utterly indifferent to our rights. The treaty of 1783, by which our independence was acknowledged, was wrung from her by stern necessity. It was not an amicable settlement of the quarrel—a final and satisfactory adjustment of all difficulties. On the part of England it was a morose and reluctant abandonment of a strife which was costing her too dear—the unwilling surrender of her best provinces under circumstances dishonorable to her flag, and humbling to her national pride. This hatred of the rebel colony was mingled with contempt for our institutions and national character, exhibited in a proud assumption of superiority and disregard of our rights and our demands. A nation sunk in helpless weakness may submit to tyrannical treatment, but one rapidly growing in strength and resources, is sure to have a day of reckoning, when it will demand a swift and complete settlement of the long-endured wrongs.

Our wisest statesmen, aware of this state of feeling, foresaw an approaching rupture. The elder Adams, as far back as 1785, says, in writing from England: "Their present system (the English) as far as I can penetrate it, is to maintain a determined peace with all Europe, in order that they may war singly against America."[3] In 1794, Washington, in a letter to Mr. Jay, after speaking of the retention of posts which the British Government had, by treaty, ceded to us, and of the conduct of its agents in stirring up the Indians to hostilities, says: "Can it be expected, I ask, so long as these things are known in the United States, or at least firmly believed, and suffered with impunity by Great Britain, that there ever will or can be any cordiality between the two countries? I answer, No. And I will undertake, without the gift of prophecy, to predict, that it will be impossible to keep this country in a state of amity with Great Britain long, if those posts are not surrendered." Still later, Jefferson, writing home from England, says: "In spite of treaties, England is our enemy. Her hatred is deep-rooted and cordial, and nothing with her is wanted but power, to wipe us and the land we live in out of existence."

Having scarcely recovered from the debility produced by the long revolutionary struggle—just beginning to feel the invigorating impulse of prosperity, the nation shrunk instinctively from a war which would paralyze her commerce and prostrate all her rising hopes. The Government hesitated to take a bold and decided stand on its rights, and urge their immediate and complete acknowledgment. This forbearance on our part, and apparent indifference to the honor of the nation, only increased the contempt, and confirmed the determination of the British Government. Still, remonstrances were made. Soon after the arrival of the British Minister, Mr. Hammond, in 1791, Jefferson stated the causes of complaint, followed up the next year by an able paper on the charges made by the former against our Government. This paper remained unanswered, and two years after Jefferson resigned his secretaryship.

The next year, 1794, the British Government issued an order of council, requiring her armed ships to arrest all vessels carrying provisions to a French colony, or laden with its produce. The American Government retaliated with an embargo, and began to make preparations for immediate hostilities. In a few months the order was revoked, and one less exceptionable issued, that calmed for awhile the waters of agitation, and Mr. Jay was sent as Minister to England, to negotiate a new treaty, which was to settle all past difficulties, establish some principles of the law of nations, especially those affecting belligerents and neutrals, and to regulate commerce. This treaty removed many of the causes of complaint, but like all treaties between a weak and strong government, it secured to England the lion's portion. But with all its imperfections and want of reciprocity, it was ratified in the spring of 1796, and became a law. Met at every step by a determined opposition, its discussion inflamed party spirit to the highest point, while its ratification was received with as many hisses as plaudits. Still, it brought a partial, hollow pacification between the two governments, which lasted till 1806, when the orders in council before mentioned were issued. Great Britain, however, hesitated not to impress our seamen and vex our commerce during the whole period, with the exception of the short interval of the peace of Amiens. In 1803, with the renewal of the war between her and France, impressment was again practiced, though met at all times by remonstrance, which in turn was succeeded by negotiation.

Those orders in Council seemed, at first, to preclude the possibility of an amicable adjustment of difficulties. The country was on fire from Portland to New Orleans. Cries of distress, in the shape of memorials to Congress, came pouring in from every sea port in the Union. Plundered merchants invoked the interposition of the strong arm of power to protect their rights, and demanded indemnity for losses that beggared their fortunes. Scorn and rage at this bold high-handed robbery, filled every bosom, and the nation trembled on the verge of war. Jefferson, however, sent Mr. Pinckney as envoy extraordinary to cooperate with Mr. Monroe, our minister to England, in forming a treaty which should recognize our maritime rights.

In the spring of the next year Jefferson received the treaty from London. It having arrived the day before the adjournment of Congress, and containing so much that was inadmissible, he did not submit it to that body.

In the first place, there was no provision against the impressment of seamen; and in the second place, a note from the British ministers accompanied it, stating that the British government reserved to itself the right to violate all the stipulations it contained, if we submitted to the Berlin decree, and other infractions of our rights by France. This reservation on the part of England was an assumption of power that required no discussion. To declare that she would annul her own solemn treaty, the moment she disapproved of our conduct towards other nations, was to assume the office of dictator.

In the mean time, the death of Fox, whose character and conduct the short time he was in power had given encouragement that a permanent peace could be established, and the election of the dashing and fiery Canning to his place, involved the negotiations in still greater embarrassments. To indicate his course, and reveal at the outset the unscrupulous and treacherous policy England was henceforth determined to carry out, he had ready for promulgation long before it could be ascertained what action our government would take on that treaty, those other orders in Council, blockading the continent to us. He declared, also, that all further negotiations on the subject were inadmissible; thus leaving us no other alternative, but to submit or retaliate. Thus our earnest solicitations and fervent desire to continue on terms of amity—our readiness to yield for the sake of peace what now of itself would provoke a war, were met by deception and insult. England not only prepared orders violating our rights as a neutral nation while submitting a treaty that protected them, but plundered our vessels, impressed our seamen, and threatened the towns along our coast with conflagration.

We could not allow our flag to be thus dishonored, our seamen impressed, and our commerce vexed with impunity, and declared common plunder by the two chief maritime nations of Europe. Retaliation, therefore, was resolved upon; and in December of 1807, an embargo was laid upon all American vessels and merchandize. In the spirit of conciliation, however, which marked all the acts of government, the President was authorized to suspend it soon as the conduct of European powers would sanction him in doing so. This embargo prohibited all American vessels from sailing from foreign ports, all foreign ships from carrying away cargoes; while by a supplementary act, all coasting vessels were compelled to give bonds that they would land their cargoes in the United States.

This sudden suspension of commerce, threatening bankruptcy and ruin to so many of our merchants, and checking at once the flow of produce from the interior to the sea-board, was felt severely by the people, and tried their patriotism to the utmost. Still the measure was approved by the majority of the nation. New England denounced it, as that section of the republic had denounced nearly every measure of the administration from its commencement. The effect of the embargo was to depress the products of our own country one half, and increase those of foreign countries in the same proportion. There being no outlet to the former, they accumulated in the market, and often would not bring sufficient to pay the cost of mere transportation, while the supply of the latter being cut off, the demand for them became proportionably great. Thus it fell as heavy on the agricultural classes as on the merchant, for while a portion of their expenses were doubled, the produce with which they were accustomed to defray them became worthless. But ship owners and sailors suffered still more, for the capital of the one was profitless, and the occupation of the other gone. It is true it helped manufacturers by increasing the demand for domestic goods; it also saved a large amount of property, and a vast number of American ships, which, if they had been afloat, would have fallen into the hands of French and English cruisers.

But, while the embargo pressed so heavily on us, it inflicted severe damage also on France and England, especially the latter. The United States was her best customer, and the sudden stoppage of all the channels of trade was a heavy blow to her manufactures, and would, no doubt, have compelled a repeal of the orders in council to us, had not she known that we were equal, if not greater sufferers. But while the two nations thus stood with their hands on each other's throats, determined to see which could stand choking the longest, it soon became evident that our antagonist had greatly the advantage of us, for the embargo shut ourselves out from the trade of the whole world, while it only cut England off from that of the United States. Besides, being forced to seek elsewhere for the products she had been accustomed to take from us, other channels of trade began to be opened, which threatened to become permanent.

A steady demand will always create a supply somewhere, and this was soon discovered in the development of resources in the West Indies, Spain, Spanish America, and Brazil, of which the British Government had hitherto been ignorant.

The loud outcries from the opponents of this measure, especially from New England, also convinced her that our government must soon repeal the obnoxious act.

Under the tremendous pressure with which the embargo bore on the people, New England openly threatened the government. John Quincy Adams, who had sustained the administration in its course, finding his conduct denounced by the Massachusetts Legislature, resigned his seat, declaring to the President that there was a plan on foot to divide New England from the Union, and that a secret emissary from Great Britain was then at work with the ruling federalists to accomplish it. Whether this was true or false, one thing was certain, an ominous cloud was gathering in that quarter that portended evil, the extent of which no one could calculate.

1809.

Under these circumstances the embargo was repealed, and the non-intercourse law, prohibiting all commercial intercourse with France and Great Britain substituted.

While these things were transpiring an event occurred which threatened to arrest all negotiations.

The Chesapeake, an American frigate, cruising in American waters, had been fired into by the Leopard, a British 74, and several of her crew killed. The commander of the latter claimed some British deserters, whom he declared to be on board the American ship. Capt. Barron denied his knowledge of any such being in the Chesapeake; moreover, he had instructed, he said, his recruiting officer not to enlist any British subjects. The captain of the Leopard then demanded permission to search. This, of course, was refused, when a sudden broadside was poured into the American frigate. Captain Barron not dreaming of an encounter, had very culpably neglected to clear his vessel for action, and at once struck his flag. An officer from the Leopard was immediately sent on board, who demanded the muster-roll of the ship, and selecting four of the crew, he retired. Three of these were native Americans, the other was hung as a deserter. This daring outrage threw the country into a tumult of excitement. Norfolk and Portsmouth immediately forbade all communication with British ships of war on the coast. July 2.
The war spirit was aroused, and soon after Jefferson issued a proclamation, prohibiting all vessels bearing English commissions from entering any American harbor, or having any intercourse with the shore.

1808.

The act of the Leopard was repudiated by the English Government; but the rage that had been kindled was not so easily laid, especially, as no reparation was made. Mr. Monroe, our Minister to England, and Canning could not adjust the matter; neither could Mr. Rose, the English Minister, afterwards sent over for that especial purpose. The British Government would not consent to mingle it up with the subject of impressment generally, and refused to take any steps whatever towards reparation, until the President's hostile proclamation was withdrawn. Jefferson replied that if the minister would disclose the terms of reparation, and they were satisfactory, their offer and the repeal of the proclamation should bear the same date. This was refused and Mr. Rose returned home.

March.

In the midst of this general distress and clamor, and strife of political factions, Mr. Madison, who had been elected President, began his administration.

Jefferson had struggled in vain against the unjust insane policy of England. Embargoes, non-intercourse acts, all efforts at commercial retaliation, remonstrances, arguments and appeals were alike disregarded. Proud in her superior strength, and blind to her own true interests, she continued her high-handed violation of neutral rights and the laws of nations. In the mean time, the republic itself was torn by factions which swelled the evils that oppressed it. It was evident that Madison's seat would not be an easy one, and it was equally apparent that he lacked some most important qualities in a chief magistrate who was to conduct the ship of State through the storms and perils that were gathering thick about her. The commanding mind overshadowing and moulding the entire cabinet, the prompt decision, fearless bearing and great energy were wanting. His manifest repugnance to a belligerent attitude encouraged opposition and invited attack. Small in stature and of delicate health, with shy, distant, reserved manners, and passionless countenance, he was not fitted to awaken awe or impart fear. Still he was a thorough statesman. His official correspondence, while Jefferson's Secretary of State, his dissertation on the rights of neutral nations and the laws that should govern neutral trade, are regarded to this day as the most able papers that ever issued from the American cabinet. His knowledge of the Constitution was thorough and practical, and his adherence to it inflexible. The exigencies of war, which always afford apologies, and sometimes create demands for an illegal use of power, never forced him beyond the precincts of law or provoked him to an improper use of executive authority. His integrity was immovable, and though assailed by envenomed tongues and pursued by slanders, his life at the last shone out in all its purity, the only refutation he deigned to make.

But Madison possessed one quality for which his enemies did not give him credit, and which bore him safely through the perils that encompassed his administration—a calm tenacity—a silent endurance such as the deeply-bedded rock presents in the midst of the waves. Men knew him to be in his very nature repugnant to war, and when they saw him go meekly, nay, shrinkingly into it, they expected to laugh over his sudden and disgraceful exit. But while he was not aggressive and decided in his conduct, he boldly took the responsibilities which the nation placed upon his shoulders, and bore them serenely, unshrinkingly to the last. His hesitation in approaching a point around which dangers and responsibilities clustered prepared the beholder for weak and irresolute conduct, but he was amazed at his steadiness of character. This apparent contradiction arose from two conflicting elements. Incapable of excitement and opposed to strife, he naturally kept aloof from the place where one was demanded, and the other to be met. Yet, at the same time, he had a knowledge of the right, and an inflexible love for it which made him immovable when assailed.

On the whole, perhaps the character he possessed was better fitted to secure the permanent good of the country than that of a more executive man. A bold, decided chief magistrate, possessing genius, and calming by his superior wisdom and strength, the disturbed elements about him, and developing and employing the resources of the country at the outset, would probably have ended the war in six months. But the knowledge the country gained and communicated also to other governments of its own weakness and power, was, perhaps, better than the misplaced confidence which sudden success, obtained through a great leader would have imparted. In the vicissitudes of the war, we worked out a problem which needs no farther demonstration.

Madison's administration was based on those principles which had governed that of Jefferson, and the same restrictive measures were persevered in to compel England to adopt a system more conformable to our rights and the laws of neutrality. In the mean time Mr. Erskine was appointed Minister on the part of Great Britain to adjust the difficulties between the two countries. April 19, 1809 At first this seemed an easy task, for he declared that his government would revoke the orders in council on condition the non-intercourse act was repealed. The proposal was at once communicated to Congress when it assembled in May, and accepted by it. The 10th of June was agreed upon as the day on which commercial intercourse should recommence between the two countries, and the President issued a proclamation to that effect. In July, however, it was ascertained that the British Government repudiated the agreement entered into by its Minister, declaring that he had exceeded his instructions. A second proclamation reestablishing non intercourse was instantly issued, and the two countries were farther than ever from a reconciliation.

The conduct of Great Britain, at this period, presents such a strong contrast to her loud declarations before the world, or rather stamps them as falsehoods so emphatically, that the historian is not surprised at the utter perversion of facts with which she endeavored to cover up her turpitude, and quiet her conscience. Without any provocation, she had declared war against the infant republic of France. In order to shield herself from the infamy which should follow such a violation of the rights of nations, and waste of treasure and of blood, she planted herself on the grand platform of principle, and insisted that she went to war to preserve human liberty, and the integrity of governments. In this violent assault on a people with whom she was at peace, she made a great sacrifice for the common interests of states, and hence deserved the gratitude, and not the condemnation of men. With these declarations on her lips, she turned and deliberately annulled her agreements with the United States, and invaded her most sacred rights. She impressed our seamen, plundered our commerce, held fortresses on our soil, and stirred up the savages to merciless warfare against the innocent inhabitants on our frontier. While with one hand she professed to strike for the rights of nations, with the other she violated them in a hardihood of spirit never witnessed, except in a government destitute alike of honor and of truth. So, also, while sacrificing her soldiers and her wealth, to prevent the aggressions of Napoleon; nay, sending a fleet and troops to Egypt, for the noble purpose of saving that barbarous state from a reckless invader; her armies were covering the plains of India with its innocent inhabitants, and robbing independent sheikhs of their lawful possessions, until, at last, she tyrannized over a territory *four times* as large as that of all France, and six times greater than her own island. Such unblushing falsehoods were never before uttered by a civilized nation in the face of history. The most unscrupulous government does not usually cover up its tyranny and aggressions by pharisaic mummeries. There are all shades of hypocrisy, but to do the most damning acts under pretence of religious principle, has generally been considered the sole prerogative of the Spanish inquisition.

The disavowal of Mr. Erskine's treaty by the English government, and the consequent renewal of the non-intercourse act, threw the country into the fiercest agitation. The conduct of Great Britain appeared like mockery. Forcing us into conciliation by promises, and then withdrawing those promises; proposing to settle all difficulties by negotiation, and yet, in the progress of it, refusing to touch one of them, she determined to try the patience of the American people to the utmost. The disavowal of a treaty made by her own minister, which buoyed up the nation with the hope of returning peace and prosperity, well nigh exhausted that patience; and there is little doubt but that an immediate declaration of war would have been sustained by a large majority of the American people. In passing from town to town, the traveller saw groups of angry men discussing and denouncing the tyranny of England. The shout of *"Free trade and sailors' rights,"* shook the land, while flashing eyes and clenched fists told how aroused the national feeling had become.

Mr. Jackson was sent, in the place of Mr. Erskine, to negotiate a treaty; but his proposals were the same as those which the administration had already rejected, while his insulting insinuation that the President knew when he made the arrangement with Mr. Erskine, that the latter was acting without authority, abruptly terminated all intercourse, and he was recalled.

1810.

On the first of May, Congress passed an act which revoked the restrictive system, yet excluded British and armed vessels from the waters of the United States.[4] It provided, however, that it should be renewed in March against the nation, which did not before that time so revoke or modify its edicts, as to protect the neutral commerce of the United States. This was regarded as the ultimatum, and beyond it, war against which ever government refused our just demands, was the only resort. Messrs. Pinckney and Armstrong, our ministers at the courts of England and France, were urged to press the repeal of those obnoxious orders in council and decrees, in order that such a catastrophe might be prevented. France receded, and Mr. Armstrong was notified that the decrees were to cease to have effect after the first of November, provided England withdrew her orders in council; or, if she refused, that the United States should force her to acknowledge the rights that France had, in a spirit of kindness, conceded. This glad intelligence was made known by the President in a proclamation, in which he also declared, that unless the British government repealed her orders in council, within three months from that date, the non-intercourse law should be revived against it.

In the mean time Mr. Pinckney urged, with all the arguments in his power, the English Cabinet to recede from its unjustifiable position. The latter endeavored, by prevarication and duplicity, to avoid coming to a definite understanding, but being closely pushed, it at length gave our minister to understand that the United States must force France to take the first step in revoking those odious acts against which we complained. But as England had been the aggressor, this was plainly unjust and impossible, and all hope of a peaceful settlement was given up, and on the 1st of March, 1811, he took a formal leave of the Prince Regent. At the same time Congress had passed an act, authorizing the President to arrest the non-intercourse Act at any moment that England should revoke her orders in council April, 181. On the 38th of the next month, Napoleon definitely revoked his Berlin and Milan decrees, so far as they related to us—the repeal to be ante-dated November 1st, 1810. This decree was forwarded by our minister, Mr. Barlow, who had succeeded Armstrong, to the English Government, but it still refused to repeal its orders in council on the ground that the decree did not embrace the continental

16

states, and affected only the United States. It soon became apparent, therefore, to every one, that war was inevitable. The American Government had placed itself, where it could not recede without disgrace, while England was evidently resolved not to change her attitude.

1811.

Another collision at sea between two armed vessels inflamed still more the war spirit that was pervading the land. On the 16th of May a British sloop of war, the Little Belt, fired into the frigate President, thinking doubtless to repeat the outrage committed on the Chesapeake, but found her fire returned with such heavy broadsides that in a few minutes thirty-two of her crew were killed or wounded. The commander of the English ship declared that the American frigate fired first. This Rodgers denied, and his denial was sustained by all his officers.

The election of members of Congress, which took place in 1810 and 11, had given a majority to the administration, so that there could be harmony of action between the Legislature and the Executive. Beset with difficulties, treading on the brink of a war, whose issues could not be foreseen, anxious and uncertain, the President, by proclamation, called the Twelfth Congress together a month before the appointed time. It met Nov. 8th, and Henry Clay was chosen speaker. From the outset he had been a warm supporter of the Administration, and his eloquent voice had rung over the land, rousing up its warlike spirit, and inspiring confidence in the ability of the nation to maintain its rights. James Fisk, of Vermont, Peter B. Porter, and Samuel L. Mitchell, of New York, Adam Leybert, of Penn., Robert Wright, of Md., Hugh Nelson, of Va., Nathaniel Macon, of N. C., Calhoun, Langdon, Cheeves, and Wm. Lowndes, of S. C., Wm. M. Bibb and George M. Troup, of Ga., Felix Grundy, of Tenn., and Wm. P. Duval, of Ky., rallied round the young speaker, and presented a noble phalanx to the anxious President. On the other side were Josiah Quincy, of Mass, and Timothy Pitkin and Benjamin Talmadge, of Conn.

In the Senate the democratic leaders were Samuel Smith, of Md., Wm. B. Giles, of Va., Wm. H. Crawford, of Ga., George W. Campbell, of Tenn., and George M. Bibb, of Ky. Leading the opposition were James Lloyd, of Mass., and James A. Bayard, of Del.[5]

The great accession of strength which the democratic members had received, showed clearly the state of public feeling, especially south and west, and the doubtful, hesitating policy of the last four years was thrown aside. The tone of the President's Message was also decidedly warlike, and no hope was held out of an amicable adjustment of the difficulties with England. They were invoked as the "Legislative guardians of the nation," to put the country "into an armed attitude, demanded by the crisis." The halls of Congress resounded with the cry of "to arms." The nightmare of fear and doubt which had weighed down its councils was removed, and bold and fearless speakers called aloud on the nation to defend its injured honor and insulted rights. The might of England had ceased to be a bugbear—the Rubicon of fear was passed. Mr. Madison, deprecating precipitate measures, saw with alarm the sudden belligerent attitude which Congress had assumed. The democratic leaders however told him the nation was for war—that timidity would be his ruin—that those who were resolved to make Mr. Clinton their candidate at the next presidential election were taking advantage of his hesitation. In the mean time bills providing for the enlistment of twenty-five thousand men in the regular army; for repairing and equipping frigates and building new vessels; authorizing the President to accept the services of fifty thousand volunteers, and to require the Governors of the several States and territories to hold their respective quotas of a hundred thousand men in readiness to march at a moment's warning,[6] were rapidly pushed through Congress. Nov. 7, 1811. The brilliant victory, gained three days after Congress met by Harrison, over the Indians at Tippecanoe, helped also to kindle into higher excitement the martial spirit of the West and South-west, and for a while opposition seemed to be struck powerless before the rising energy of the nation.

The bill authorizing the President to accept and organize certain military corps to the number of 50,000, reported by Mr. Porter, Chairman of the Committee on Foreign Affairs, called forth a long and exciting debate. Mr. Grundy, one of the committee, defended the resolution in a bold and manly speech. Referring to the Indian hostilities on our north-western frontier, he unhesitatingly declared that they were urged forward by British influence, and war, therefore, was already begun. Some of the richest blood of the country had already been shed, and he pledged himself for the western country, that its hardy sons only waited for permission to march and avenge those who had fallen. He was answered by Randolph, who denied that Great Britain had stimulated the Indians to their merciless border warfare—stigmatized the war to which this resolution looked as a war of conquest—declared it was another mode of flinging ourselves into the arms of Bonaparte and becoming "the instruments of him who had effaced the title of Atilla 'the scourge of God.'"

He ridiculed the idea which had been started of conquering Canada, as an insane project, and useless if accomplished. "Suppose it is ours," he exclaimed, "are we any nearer to our point? As his minister said to the king of Epirus, "may we not as well take our bottle of wine before as after the exploit? Go march to Canada—leave the broad bosom of the Chesapeake and her hundred tributary rivers—the whole line of sea-coast from Machias to St.

Mary's unprotected. You have taken Quebec—have you *conquered England*? Will you seek for the deep foundations of her power in the frozen depths of Labrador?

> 'Her march is on the mountain wave,
> Her home is on the deep.'

Will you call upon her to leave your ports and harbors untouched only just till you can return from Canada to defend them? The coast is to be left defenceless whilst men in the interior are revelling in conquest and spoil." He pronounced the country to be in a state wholly unfit for war.

Mr. Clay answered him in an eloquent speech. He defended the character of our troops, and expressed his full confidence in the loyalty and bravery of the country. "Gentlemen," he said, "had inquired what would be gained by the contemplated war? Sir, I ask in turn, what will you not lose by your mongrel state of peace with Great Britain? Do you expect to gain anything in a pecuniary view? No sir. Look at your treasury reports. Yon now receive only $6,000,000 of revenue annually, and this amount must be diminished in the same proportion as the rigorous execution of the orders in council shall increase. Before these orders existed you received *sixteen millions*." He declared that war was inevitable unless we tamely sacrificed our own interests, rights and honor. In answering the objection that we ought only to go to war when we were invaded, he exclaimed in thrilling tones, while the house gazed in breathless silence on his excited features, "*How much better than invasion is the blocking of your very ports and harbors, insulting your towns, plundering your merchants and scouring your coasts? If your fields are surrounded, are they in a better condition than if invaded? When the murderer is at your door will you meanly skulk to your cells? or will you boldly oppose him at his entrance?*"

Every part of his speech told with tremendous effect. Many of the members opposed the bill, which continued the subject of debate for several days. Mr. Williams of South Carolina, defended it in a fearless speech. In reply to a remark made by one of the members, that it was unjust to go to war with England, as she was fighting for her existence, he exclaimed in a loud sonorous voice that pealed through the chamber, "*If her existence, sir, depends upon our destruction, then I say down let her go. She is contending* for the liberties of the world too, it seems. I would as soon have expected to hear that the devil had espoused the cause of Christianity. Sir, we may trace her progress for years through blood. Did she raise the standard of liberty in India? Was it for liberty she offered up so many human hecatombs on the plains of Hindostan? Was it to plant the standard of *liberty* in this country that she immolated even infant innocence during the war of the Revolution? Is it to extend or secure the blessings of freedom to us that the fireside and the cradle are exposed to savage incursions in the west at this time?" This part of his speech created a marked sensation.

The bill finally passed by 44 to 34.[7] The winter passed in exciting debates, both in Congress and in the State Legislatures, while every hamlet in the land was agitated with the notes of hostile preparations. March 9. In the midst of this excitement, the country was startled by the transmission of documents to Congress showing that a man by the name of Henry had been sent by the Governor of Canada to sound the disaffected New England States and endeavor to form some connection with the leading federalists.[8]

Apr. 8.

In the mean time, Jonathan Russell, of Rhode Island, who had been appointed *chargé d'affaires* to the English Court on the return of Mr. Pinckney, wrote home that there was no prospect that the British government would revoke its orders in council; and the President, therefore, on the first of April, recommended an embargo to be laid on all vessels in port, or which should arrive, for the term of sixty days. The message was received with closed doors, and the house felt that this was preparatory to a declaration of war. When Mr. Porter, in accordance with the recommendation of the message, brought in a bill to lay this embargo, there was great sensation in the house. In reply to the interrogation, whether this was a peace measure or preparatory to war, Mr. Grundy, one of the committee, arose and said, "it is a *war* measure, and it is meant that it shall lead directly to it." Mr. Stow, of New York, said, "if it was a precursor to war, there were some very serious questions to be asked. What is the situation of our fortresses? What is the situation of our country generally?" Mr. Clay then left the chair, and, in a short speech, made it apparent that after what had passed, to shrink from this because it was a war measure, would cover the nation with disgrace. Randolph, in reply, said, that he was so impressed with the importance of the subject, and the solemnity of the occasion, that he could not keep silent. "Sir," said he, "we are now in conclave—the eyes of the surrounding world are not upon us. We are shut up here from the light of Heaven, but the eyes of God are upon us. He knows the spirit of our minds. Shall we deliberate on this subject with the spirit of sobriety and candor, or with that spirit which has too often characterized our discussions upon occasions like the present? We ought to realize that we are in the presence of that God who knows our thoughts and motives, and to whom we must hereafter render an account for the deeds done in the body." He spoke at some length and earnestly. Clay seeing the effect of his solemn adjurations on some members of the house, left the speaker's chair and replied, that the gentleman from Virginia need not have reminded them in the manner he had, of the presence of that Being who watches and surrounds us. He thought that consciousness should awaken different sentiments from those which had been uttered. It ought to inspire us to patriotism, to the display of those qualities which ennobled man. God always was with the right, and extended his protection to those who performed their duty fearlessly, scorning the consequences. The discussion of the bill continued through several days, and exhibited, in a striking manner, the different effect of an event so momentous and fearful as war on different characters. In one, the overwhelming responsibility and direful results of adopting a measure leading to it, shut out all other considerations. To another, its chances and calamities were a matter of mere calculation to be taken and met by any nation that expected to exist; while many hailed it with the delight of true patriotism, feeling that the country had, at last, risen from its humiliating attitude. Mr. Bleecker addressed the house more like a clergyman than a statesman, warning the members to desist from the perilous course. On the other hand, Mr. Mitchell, from New York, declared, that the country was not to "be frightened by political screech-owls;" and, alluding to the profligate character of the Prince Regent, said, "he did not think any one should be afraid to face a nation, at whose head stood such a man—one who was some years since expelled a jockey club, and who was lately turned out of doors for his unworthy conduct to his neighbor's wife. The power with which we are to contend is not so terrific and almighty as is imagined."

Apr. 4.

The bill finally passed, 69 to 36. In the senate, 17 to 11.[9] About the same time another dispatch was received from Mr. Russell, closing with, "I no longer entertain a hope that we can honorably avoid war."

This was the feeling of the majority of the nation. In establishing certain fixed limits beyond which it would not go, and erecting certain barriers over which it would not allow England to pass, the American Government had taken a position from which there was no receding, with honor. While every thing was thus rapidly tending to war, and the public was eager with expectation, waiting for the next movement that should precipitate it, with all its horrors, on the land, a despatch, received by the British Minister, Mr. Foster,[10] from Castlereagh, closed at once every avenue towards a peaceful adjustment of the existing difficulties. In it he declared "that the decrees of Berlin and Milan must not be repealed singly and specially in relation to the United States, but must be repealed, also, as to all other neutral nations, and that in no less extent of a repeal of the French decrees, had the British Government ever pledged itself to repeal the orders in council."[11] This was saying, that unless the United States instituted herself lawgiver between France and all other European powers, and through her own unaided efforts obtained that which England, with all her maritime strength could not enforce, the latter would consider herself perfectly justified in withholding from us our national rights. This awkward attempt to cover up under the mask of diplomacy, duplicity and falsehood, from which an honorable mind would have shrunk, was perfectly characteristic of the man who carried the English and Irish Union by the most stupendous frauds and bribery and corruption that can be found in the annals of modern civilization.

I know the quasi denial of Mr. Foster, that this construction was a just one, yet the language used can convey no other. To place it beyond dispute, Lord Castlereagh, as late as May 22d, 1812, declared as British Minister, to the House of Commons, that as the Berlin and Milan decrees "were not unconditionally repealed, as required by his Majesty's declaration, but only repealed so far as they regarded America, he had no objection to state it, as his own opinion, that this French decree, so issued, made no manner of alteration in the question of the orders in council."[12]

It is rare to find such unscrupulous conduct on the part of a Ministry, protected by so miserable a subterfuge. It could not be supposed that the American Government would be deceived for a moment by it, but the belief that we could not be *forced* into a war, rendered ordinary care and cunning superfluous. Occupied with continental affairs alone, England looked upon the American Republic as only a means to accomplish her ends there. The administration, at Washington, was thus *compelled* by the arbitrary conduct of its enemy, to declare war, or forfeit all claim to the respect of the nations of the earth, and all right to an independent existence.

Under these circumstances, Mr. Madison no longer hesitated, but on the 1st day of June transmitted a warlike message to Congress. After recapitulating, in a general way, the history of past negotiations and past injuries, he says: "Whether the United States shall continue passive under these progressive usurpations and accumulating wrongs, or opposing force to force in defence of their natural rights shall commit a just cause into the hands of the Almighty Disposer of events, avoiding all connections which might entangle it in the contests or views of other powers, and preserving a constant readiness to concur in an honorable reestablishment of peace and friendship, is a solemn question, which the constitution wisely confides to the legislative department of the Government. In recommending it to their early deliberations, I am happy in the assurance that the decision will be worthy the enlightened and patriotic councils of a virtuous, a free and a powerful nation." This message was referred at once to the Committee on Foreign Relations, who reported ten days after in favor of an immediate appeal to arms. The deliberations on this report were conducted with closed doors.

A bill drawn up by Mr. Pinckney, and offered by Mr. Calhoun, declaring war to exist between Great Britain and the United States, was rapidly pushed through the House, passing by a vote of 79 to 49. In the Senate, being met not only by the opposition of the Federalists, but by the friends of De Witt Clinton, who voted with them, it passed by a majority of only six.[13] Congress, after passing an act, granting letters of marque, and regulating prizes and prize goods, authorizing the issue of Treasury notes to the amount of $5,000,000, and placing a hundred per cent. additional duties on imports, adjourned. July 8. In accordance with a resolution of Congress, the President appointed a day of public humiliation and prayer, in view of the conflict in which the nation had entered.

CHAPTER II.

The proud and sensitive American of to-day can scarcely comprehend how, under the heavy and protracted provocations which I have traced in the preceding chapter, the country could have been kept for so long a time from open hostilities. It would seem that the most arbitrary exercise of executive and legislative power, could not have prevented the people from rushing spontaneously to arms, and demanding their rights at the bayonet's point. He is still more astounded, when he remembers that this declaration of war was received with a storm of indignation by a large party in the Union—that all New England, with the exception of Vermont, anathematized it. The pulpit and the press thundered forth their maledictions, and the wrath of heaven was invoked on the heads of its authors. The flags of the shipping in Boston harbor were hoisted at half-mast, in token of mourning, and the spot rendered immortal by the patriots of the revolution, became the rallying place of the disaffected, and the hope of the enemy. A common welfare and a common country, could not allay this hostility, which strengthened instead of diminishing to the last, and which was so fanatical and blind in its violence, that it exhibited itself in the most monstrous forms. Our defeats were gloried in, and the triumphs of our oppressors hailed as an evidence that God was on their side, while downright insubordination, plots, and incipient rebellion, crippled the efforts of an already weak government, and swelled the disasters on which they fattened.

But to one who knows to what a height the spirit of faction will reach, nothing in all this unnatural hostility will seem strange. The country, at this time, was divided into Federalists and Democrats, who were scarcely less vindictive in their animosities, than the Whigs and Tories of the revolution. New England was the furnace of Federalism, and Boston the focal point from which issued incessant and bitter assaults on Jefferson's, and afterwards on Madison's administration. Thus, in the most trying period of our existence since the adoption of the constitution, the country was divided and torn by the fiercest spirit of faction with which it has ever been cursed.

I shall not enter into a history of the feuds of these two parties. The principle which originally divided them was plain. One was for a consolidated government, and more power in the executive; the other for a larger distribution of power among the separate states of the confederacy; one was strongly conservative, and the other tending to radicalism; one was for putting the strictest construction on the constitution, the other for giving it the greatest possible latitude. These two parties had grown up with the republic. Their germs were seen in the first convention that met after the achievement of our independence, to settle the form of government. On one point all were agreed —that our mutual safety and welfare depended on a confederacy, but a difference of opinion arose on the amount of power the separate states should confer on the Federal head. The constitution which was finally adopted was not stringent enough to suit the Federalists; but as a compromise, it was on the whole the best that could be secured. Besides, by standing firmly with the general government in all conflicts with the separate states, and with the executive when brought in collision with Congress, and by the great patronage of the President, that power which they preferred to see directly delegated might practically be obtained. This party numbered among its leaders, the first statesmen of the land.

Nor should these views be considered strange, nor the patriotism of those who held them be assailed. Some of the noblest men who offered their lives and fortunes to the cause of liberty, looked upon the British Government as the best in the world, and stripped of some of its peculiarities, and purged of its corruptions, would be the best that human ingenuity could devise. They did not originally war against a form of government, but to be free from its oppressive acts. They did not hate, they admired the British constitution, and took up arms not to destroy it, but to enjoy the rights it guaranteed to its subjects. The government, in the principles of which they had been educated, was the most prosperous and the strongest on the globe, and common wisdom dictated that all its good points should be retained and incorporated into our own. Why enter on an entirely new experiment when we had so much to build upon in the experience of the mother country? One of the grand features of that government was the central power lodged in the throne; so ours should be characterized by a strong executive. The very reason, the force of which was felt by all, and that made a confederacy indispensable, viz., that a number of independent states, separated by only imaginary lines, would, inevitably, lead to frequent collisions and final civil war, operated they thought with equal force against a *loose* confederacy. The same results would follow. The wisdom of these fears is seen at the present day, in the separate power demanded by some of the states, and alas was soon exhibited by the Federalists themselves in the spirit of disobedience they instilled into the people against the general government.

The Democrats, on the other hand, saw in all this a decided leaning towards a monarchy, and afterwards boldly accused their adversaries of conspiring to erect a throne in the midst of this republic. They were taunted with sycophancy to England, and a craving after English distinctions and aristocratic preeminence. The *principles* on which the two parties rested had their birth in true patriotism, and their effect on the character of the Constitution was, doubtless, healthful. Nor was there anything in their nature adapted to awaken such vindictive hate. But like a strife between two individuals, the origin of which is soon lost sight of in the passion engendered by the conflict, so these two factions, in the heat of party rancor, forgot in the main the theories on which they split. In the proposition of every measure by either party for the welfare of the state, some secret plot was supposed to be concealed.

The embarrassments in which this fierce hostile spirit placed the administration, rendering it timid and cautious, was increased by the form it took. The levelling and radical notions of the French revolution, followed as they were by such atrocities, disgusted the federalists, while the democrats, though they denounced the violence, sympathized with the people, and saw in the commotion the working of their own principles amid the oppressed masses of France. They not only loved France, as their old ally, but they sympathized with her in her efforts to hurl back the banded oppressors who sought to reestablish a hated throne in her midst. So while the former party stood charged with hating republics and wishing the domination of England, the latter was accused of seeking an alliance with the usurper Napoleon.

Many of the reasons given by the Federalists for their opposition, furnish another exhibition of the blinding power of party spirit. As to the simple question between England and America, it would seem that no sane man could doubt, that sufficient provocation had been given to justify us in a resort to arms. The impressment of six or seven thousand seamen, most of them American citizens, the destruction of nearly a thousand merchantmen, and the insults every where heaped upon our flag, were wrongs which could not be justified. They therefore endeavored to cover them up, by saying that the Democrats were assisting Bonaparte, whom they regarded as a monster in human form, and whose success would be the downfall of all liberty. The wrongs we suffered were thus lost sight of, in the greater wrong of crippling England in her desperate struggle with this modern Attila. Rather than endanger the success of that conflict, they would suffer for a time from the effect of her odious measures. They felt that England, in her conduct, was not governed by hostile feelings towards this country—that the evils she inflicted on us, were only incidental to the war she was waging against a tyrant. Placed in imminent peril, as the champion of freedom, she was compelled to resort to extraordinary measures, which though they injured us, were intended only to crush a common enemy. Hence the absurd interrogatory so incessantly urged by wise statesmen: "Why do you not declare war against France as well as England?"—as if the neglect to protect the interests and honor of the country in one quarter, rendered it obligatory on the government to neglect them in all quarters. The law which would redress one wrong, is none the less right, because he who administers it refuses to apply it to a second wrong. The injustice is in the person, not in the deed. Besides, when a nation is insulted and outraged by two powers, it has a perfect right to choose which it will first assault and chastise. And yet the false doctrine was constantly promulgated, that we had no right to declare war with England, without including France, because she was equally criminal. In other words, the nation was bound to bear quietly the evils under which it groaned, or embrace in the contest, France, which stood ready to do us justice the moment that England would.

It seems incredible that so absurd a dogma was soberly defended by clear-headed statesmen. Strictly applied, it would require a nation, for the sake of consistency, to submit to wrongs that degrade and ruin her, or enter on a war equally ruinous, from its magnitude, when there was a safe mode of procedure. Besides, all the circumstances pointed out England as our antagonist. She harassed our frontiers—had taken the first step against our commerce, and impressed our seamen. France was guilty only of violating the laws of neutrality, while she always stood pledged to recede from her position, if England would do the same, and finally did recede, leaving no cause for war. The seizures under the Rambouillet decree, were matters for negotiation before a declaration of war could be justified.

As Jefferson was the head of the Democratic party, the Federalists bent all their energies against his administration, and on his retirement transferred their hostility to that of Madison.

But the Federalists were not all opposed to the war. The elder Adams, the noblest chief of Federalism, was too clear-headed and high-minded a statesman to let party spirit come between him and his country's good, and he firmly advocated it, which brought down on him the condemnation of many of his friends. Said he—"It is utterly incomprehensible to me that a rational, social, or moral creature can say the war is unjust; how it can be said to be unnecessary is very mysterious. I have thought it both just and necessary for five or six years." His son, John Quincy, deserted the party to uphold the war. On the other hand, many friends of the administration and several members of the cabinet were wholly opposed to it. There seemed to be an awe of England oppressing our older statesmen that rendered them insensible to insult, and willing to see the country the scorn and contempt of the world, for its base submission under the unparalleled indignities heaped upon it, rather than risk a conflict with that strong power. Many of the merchants, also, who saw that their own ruin would inevitably follow hostilities, were averse to it—indeed, the learning and intelligence of the land was against it—but the people of the South and West, between whom and their country's honor and rights selfish interests and bitter party hate did not come, nobly sustained it.

The gloomy prospect with which a nation always enters on an unequal war, was in our case saddened by these divided feelings of the people, and by the open animosity of several of the States. In order to paralyze us still more, and render our complete humiliation certain, provided England would strike a bold and decided blow, no preparation had been made for the struggle. Although we had been for many years on the verge of war, we had done comparatively nothing to meet its exigences, but stood and stupidly gazed into its fearful abyss.

The income from the customs, in 1811, was $13,000,000. This, of course, the Government knew would decrease in time of war, as it did, to $9,500,000. Our debt at this period was $45,000,000. Yet a loan of $11,000,000, five millions of Treasury Notes, and the revenue from the imposts, which were doubled, was all the money furnished to carry on a war, which was to cost over thirty millions a year. Congress, however, did, as a last act of wisdom, appropriate $100,000 to the support, expense, exchange, &c., of prisoners of war. The utter blindness which had fallen on the Government was exhibited more fully in its neglect of the Navy. Under the "peace establishment" of 1801, our navy had been reduced, and from that time to 1812, "a period of eleven eventful years, during which the nation was scarcely a day without suffering a violation of its neutral rights, *not a single frigate* had been added to the navy." Gun-boats had been built for the protection of our harbors, and the marine corps increased by seven hundred men, and $200,000 per annum was appropriated to rebuild three frigates that had been suffered to decay. Beyond this, nothing was done, and with but nine frigates and a few other cruising vessels of less rate, while seven thousand of our merchant ships were scattered over the ocean claiming our protection, we plunged into a war with a nation that had a hundred ships of the line in commission, and more than a thousand vessels of war which bore her flag of defiance over the deep.

Superadded to all, the President, commander-in-chief of the army, was utterly ignorant of war, and by nature and in principle wholly repugnant to it. Conscious of his high and responsible position, he resolved to press it with vigor. But he was unfortunate in his Cabinet. Mr. Monroe, Secretary of State, had seen a little military service, but only in a subordinate capacity. Mr. Gallatin, Secretary of the Treasury, first opposed the declaration of war, and afterwards insisted that the only hope of the country lay in a speedy peace.

Hamilton, Secretary of the Navy, and Eustis, Secretary of War, were both ignorant of the duties of their respective departments. Pinckney, the Attorney-General, shook his head at our prospects, while Gideon Granger, Postmaster-General,[14] openly declared that the war could not but end in failure, while Madison conducted its operations. To complete the climax, a General wholly unfit for his position, was to open the campaign. At this critical juncture, too, we had scarcely any representatives abroad to enlist sympathy with us in our struggle. Mr. Adams had been sent to Russia, and Joel Barlow was our Minister to France. The latter, however, died in Poland a few months after he received the news of our declaration of war, leaving us with scarcely a representative in Europe.

It is not a matter of surprise that such a commencement to the war was disastrous; the wonder is, that five, instead of two years of defeat, were not meted out to us, as a just punishment for such stupidity and neglect. Nothing but the momentous events transpiring in Europe, distracting the attention of England, and rendering the presence of her armies necessary at home, prevented her from striking us a blow, from which it would have taken years to recover. May our Government never be left to try such an experiment again!

CHAPTER III.

In determining the course to be pursued in carrying on hostilities the administration selected Canada as the only field of operations promising any success. The navy was to be shut up in port, leaving our seven thousand merchantmen to slip through the hands of British cruisers, and reach home as they best could. It was to be a war on land and not on the sea, and the conquest of Canada would undoubtedly be the result of the first campaign. General Dearborn, who had served in the revolution, was appointed commander-in-chief of the northern forces, and soon repaired to Plattsburgh, while General Van Rensalaer, of the New York militia, and General Smith were stationed on the Niagara frontier.

In anticipation of the war, General Hull, Governor of Michigan, had been ordered to occupy his territory with an army of two thousand men, for the purpose of defending the north-western frontier from the Indians, and in case of war to obtain the command of Lake Erie, and thus be able to cooperate with Dearborn and Van Rensalaer in the invasion of Canada. The command naturally descended on him as Governor of Michigan. Having, also, been an officer of merit under Washington, the appointment was considered a very judicious one.

With part of the first regiments of United States infantry, and three companies of the first regiment of artillery, the balance made up of Ohio volunteers and Michigan militia, and one company of rangers, he left Dayton, in Ohio, the first of June, just eighteen days before the declaration of war. On the tenth, he was joined at Urbana by Colonel Miller, with the fourth regiment of infantry, composed of three hundred men. Here the little army entered the untrodden wilderness, and slowly cut its way through the primeval forest, two hundred miles in extent, to Detroit. It reached Maumee the latter part of June, where, on the second of July, Hull received the news of the declaration of war. The letter of the Secretary of War had been *fourteen days* reaching him. The British officer, at Maiden, had been officially notified of it *two days before.* "On this occasion, the British were better served. Prevost received notice of it, on the 24th of June, at Quebec. Brock on the 26th, at Newark. St. George on the 30th, at Malden; and Roberts on the 8th of July, at St. Joseph's. But, a fact still more extraordinary than the celerity of these transmissions, is, that the information thus rapidly forwarded to the British commanders, at Malden and St. Joseph, was received under envelopes, franked by the Secretary of the American Treasury."[15] But, if the Secretary of the Treasury had been the victim of a shrewd trick, the Secretary of War had commenced his career by a most egregious blunder. On the day of the declaration of war, he wrote two letters to General Hull, one announcing the fact, and the other making no mention of it. The latter despatched by a special messenger, reached the General on the 24th of June. The former being intrusted to the public mail as far as Cleveland, thence to be forwarded as it best could, did not arrive at head quarters till the 2nd of July, or two days after the news which it contained had been received by the British officer at Malden.[16] By this unpardonable carelessness of the Secretary of War, General Hull not only lost all the advantage to be derived from having the knowledge of the declaration of hostilities six days before the enemy, but he had to suffer from the preparations which this previous information gave the latter time to make.

The first disaster that resulted from this culpability of the Secretary of War, was the loss of General Hull's baggage, "hospital stores, intrenching tools, and sixty men," together with the instructions of the government, and the returns of the army. Having received a letter from the Secretary of War, dated as late as the 18th of June, in which he was urged to march with all possible despatch to Detroit, and containing no announcement of a rupture, he naturally supposed that the two governments were still at peace, and so to carry out the instructions of the secretary, and expedite matters, he shipped his baggage, stores, &c., to go by water to Detroit, while he took his army by land. But the day previous the British commander, at Malden, had received official notice of the declaration of war, and when the packet containing the stores, &c., attempted to pass the fort, it was stopped by a boat containing a British officer and six men, and its cargo seized.

This first advantage gained over him so unexpectedly, by the enemy, had a most depressing effect on the General. Instead of rousing him to greater exertion, it filled him with doubt and uncertainty. He had a dozen subordinates, either of whom, with that army, would in a few days have seized Malden, and recovered all he had lost, and inflicted a heavy blow on the enemy.

At length, however, he seemed to awake to the propriety of doing something to carry out the objects of the campaign, and on the 12th crossed the Detroit River and marched to Sandwich, only eighteen miles from Malden. But here, with an unobstructed road leading to the enemy before him, he paused and issued a proclamation to the Canadians, and sent out detachments which penetrated sixty miles into the province. The friendly disposition of the inhabitants was apparent, while the Indians were overawed into a neutral position.

Four days after crossing the river, General Hull sent Colonels Cass and Miller, with a detachment of two hundred and eighty men, towards Malden. These gallant officers pushed to the river Canards, within four miles of the fort, and driving the British pickets who held the bridge from their position, took possession of it, and immediately dispatched a messenger to General Hull, announcing their success. They described the occupation of the post as of the utmost importance in carrying out the plan of the campaign, and begged that if the army could not be moved there, that they might be allowed to hold it themselves—the General sending reinforcements as occasion demanded. Instead of being gratified at this advantage gained over the enemy, General Hull seemed irritated, condemned the attack as a breach of orders, and directed the immediate return of the detachment. These brave officers persisting in their request, he gave them permission to retain the position, provided they were willing to do so on their own responsibility, and without any aid from him.

This he knew they would not do. Such a proposition, from the commanding officer, indicated a weakness of judgment, and a willingness to resort to the most transparent trickery to escape responsibility, that no apology can excuse. From the statements of the British afterwards, it appeared that the approach of this detachment filled the garrison with alarm; the shipping was brought up to the wharves, and the loading of baggage commenced, preparatory to flight. On two sides the fort was in a dilapidated state, while seven hundred men, of whom only one hundred were regular troops, constituted the entire garrison. From the panic which the approach of Cass and Miller created, there is no doubt that the appearance of the whole army, of two thousand men before the place, would have been followed by an immediate surrender. One thing is certain, if General Hull supposed that a garrison of seven hundred men behind such works, could make a successful defence against nearly three times their number, he had no right to regard his strong position at Detroit, when assailed by only an equal force, untenable. Either Malden could have been taken, or Detroit was impregnable. The troops felt certain of success, and were impatient to be led to the attack, but he pronounced it unsafe to advance without heavy artillery; besides, he wished to wait the effect of his proclamation on the enemy. The Indians and Canadian militia, he said, had begun to desert, and in a short time the force at Malden might be "materially weakened." Two thousand men sat quietly down to wait for this miserable garrison of seven hundred, six hundred of whom were Canadian militia and

Indians, to dwindle to less force, before they dared even to approach within shot. The army was kept here three weeks, till two twenty-four pounders and three howitzers could be mounted on wheels strong enough to carry them, and yet a few weeks after, behind better works than those of Malden, and with a force fully equal to that of his adversary, he felt authorized to surrender, though the largest guns brought forward to break down his defences, were six pounders.

The cannon at length, being mounted, were with the ammunition placed on floating batteries, ready to move on Malden, when the order to march was countermanded, and the army, instead of advancing against the enemy, recrossed the river to Detroit, over which it had passed a few weeks before to the conquest of Canada. General Hull had issued a proclamation, sent out two detachments, mounted two heavy cannon and three howitzers, and then marched back again. Such were the astonishing results accomplished by the first grand army of invasion.

The gathering of the Indian clans, and reinforcements pouring into the British garrison, had alarmed him. The news seemed to take him by surprise, as though it for the first time occurred to him that during these three or four weeks in which he remained idle, the enemy might possibly be active.

The surrender, at this time, of Fort Mackinaw, situated on the island of the same name in the straits between Lakes Huron and Michigan, was a severe blow to him, for it opened the flood-gates to all the Indians, Canadians and British in the north-west. This fort was the key to that section of the country, and the grand depôt of the fur companies. By its position it shielded General Hull from all attack in that direction. Lieutenant Hanks commanded it, with a garrison of sixty men. As soon as the British commander of St. Joseph's, just above it, received news of the declaration of war, he took with him some two hundred Canadians and British, and four hundred Indians, and suddenly appearing before the fort demanded its surrender. This was the first intimation to Lieutenant Hanks of the commencement of hostilities. He capitulated without offering any resistance, and the Indians at once rallied around the British standard. Here was another blunder, a double one. In the first place, private enterprise had outstripped the action of Government. The British officer at St. Joseph's, though more remote than Mackinaw, received the declaration of war *nine* days before it reached the American commander at the latter place, or rather, Lieutenant Hanks did not receive it at all, either from the Government or General Hull. Colonel Roberts, of St. Joseph's, with his band of Canadians and Indians, was kind enough to convey the information.

It is surprising that General Hull, after his experience, did not at once provide that a post so vital to him, should not become the victim of the same criminal negligence which had paralyzed his efforts. *Fifteen days* intervened between his receiving the notification of war, and the taking of Fort Mackinaw, and yet no messenger from him, the Governor of the Territory, and commander-in-chief of the forces in that section, reached the garrison. Were it not for the calamitous results which followed, the whole campaign might be called a "comedy of errors."

Three days previous, however, to the retreat of Hull from Canada, he committed another error which increased his embarrassments. Proctor, who had arrived at Malden with reinforcements, threw a small detachment across the river to Brownstown, to intercept any provisions that might be advancing from Ohio to the army. Captain Brush, who was on the way with the mail, flour and cattle, was thus stopped at the River Raisin. To open the communication and bring up the provisions, Major Van Horne was dispatched with two hundred volunteers and militia. But the detachment, marching without sufficient caution, was led into ambush, and utterly defeated. Only about one-half returned to the army. Both Gen. Hull and Major Van Horne were to blame in this affair—the former for not sending a larger detachment, when he knew the enemy must be on the march, while at the same time he was ignorant of his force. This error is the more culpable, because he did not expect an immediate attack; for, after the detachment was despatched, he remained quietly in Canada, and then crossed at his leisure to Detroit. He therefore could, without danger, have spared a larger force, and should have done so, especially when the want of provisions was one of the evils he would be called upon to encounter. On the other hand, Major Van Horne should have heeded the information he received, that the enemy were in advance, in position, and not allowed his little army to rush into an ambuscade.

General Hull's position had now become sufficiently embarrassing. "The whole northern hive was in motion." Reinforcements were hastening to the support of Malden; his communications on the lake were cut off by British vessels, while the defeat of Van Horne announced that his communications by land were also closed. The latter he knew must be opened at all hazards, and Colonel Miller was dispatched on the route which Van Horne had taken with four hundred men to clear the road to the river Raisin. Leaving Detroit on the 8th of August, he next day in the afternoon, as he was approaching Brownstown, came upon the enemy covered with a breast work of logs and branches of trees, and protected on one side by the Detroit river, and on the other by swamps and thickets. The British and Canadians were commanded by Muir, and the Indians by Tecumseh. Captain Snelling leading the advance guard approached to within half musket shot, before he discovered the enemy. A fierce and deadly fire was suddenly opened on him, which he sustained without flinching, till Colonel Miller converting his order of march into order of battle, advanced to his support. Seeing, however, how destructive the fire of the enemy was, while the bullets of his own men buried themselves for the most part in the logs of the breastwork; perceiving, also, some symptoms of wavering, Miller determined to carry the works by the bayonet. The order to charge was received with loud cheers; and the next moment the troops poured fiercely over the breastwork, and routing the British and Canadians pressed swiftly on their retiring footsteps. Tecumseh, however, maintained his post, and Van Horne, who commanded the right flank of the American line, supposing from his stubborn resistance that it would require more force than he possessed to dislodge him, sent to Colonel Miller for reinforcements. The latter immediately ordered a halt, and with a reluctant heart turned from the fugitives now almost within his grasp, and hastened to the relief of his subordinate. On arriving at the breastwork, he found the Indian chief in full flight. He then started again in pursuit, but arrived in view of the enemy only to see him on the water floating away beyond his grasp.

He, however, had established the communication between the army and the river Raisin, and dispatched Captain Snelling to Detroit with the account of the victory, and a request for boats to remove the wounded, and bring provisions for the living, and reinforcements to supply the place of the dead and disabled. General Hull immediately sent Colonel McArthur with a hundred men and boats, but with provisions sufficient only for a single meal. [17]

Colonel Miller was some twenty miles from the supplies, but not deeming it prudent with the slender reinforcements he had received, and the still scantier provisions, to proceed, remained on the battle field, and sent another messenger declaring that the communication was open, and it required only a few more men and a supply of provisions, to keep it so. The next evening, the messenger returned, bringing instead of provisions a peremptory order to return to Detroit. It is doubtful whether Colonel Miller ought not to have advanced without waiting for further reinforcements, and formed a junction with Captain Brush, who had an abundance of provisions, and a detachment of a hundred and fifty men. But, after the communications were established, he did not probably see so much necessity for dispatch as for security. But General Hull seemed to be laboring under a species of insanity. After sending forth two detachments to open his communications, and finally succeeding, he deliberately closed them again, and shut from his army all those provisions, the want of which he a few days after gave as a reason for surrendering. The rapid concentration of the enemy's forces, in front of him, might have been given as a sufficient cause for suddenly calling in all his troops to defend Detroit, had he not two days after sent Colonel McArthur, accompanied by Cass, with a detachment of four hundred men, to obtain by a back, circuitous and almost wholly unknown route through the woods that which Colonel Miller had secured, and then been compelled to relinquish.

Aug. 7.

When General Hull recrossed the river to Detroit, he left some hundred and fifty, convalescents and all, "to hold possession of that part of Canada," which he had so gallantly won, "to defend the post to the last extremity against musketry, but if overpowered by artillery to retreat."[18] In the mean time, General Brock, the commander of the British forces, approached, and began to erect a battery opposite Detroit to protect his army, and cover it in crossing the river. Not a shot was fired to interrupt his proceedings, no attempt made to destroy his shipping which had arrived. Daliba offered "to clear the enemy from the opposite shores from the lower batteries," to which General Hull replied, "I will make an agreement with the enemy, that if they will not fire on me I will not fire on them." Major Jessup asked permission to cross the river and spike the guns, but this was considered a too desperate undertaking. In short, every project that was proposed was rejected, and the twenty-four pounders and the howitzers slept dumb on their carriages, in the midst of these hostile preparations of the enemy.

At length, on the morning of the 15th, a messenger arrived from General Brock demanding an immediate surrender of the town and fort. To this summons Hull replied in a decided and spirited manner; but this did not seem to daunt the British commander. He immediately opened his fire from a newly erected battery, which, after knocking down some chimneys, and disabling a few soldiers, finally ceased at ten o'clock in the evening. The next morning it re-commenced, and under cover of its harmless thunder the British, in broad daylight, commenced crossing a river more than three thousand feet wide. This presumptuous attempt succeeded without the loss of a man. The troops then formed in column twelve deep, and marching along the shore, soon emerged into view, about five hundred yards from the fort. The opposing forces were nearly equal, but the position of the Americans gave them vastly the advantage. The fort proper was of great strength, surrounded by a deep, wide ditch, and strongly palisaded with an exterior battery of two twenty-four pounders. It was occupied by four hundred men, while four hundred more lay behind a high picket fence, which flanked the approach to it. Three hundred more held the town. Against this formidable array, General Brock, preceded by five light pieces of artillery, boldly advanced. He did not even have a vanguard, and rode alone in front of his column. To the most common observer, they were marching on certain and swift destruction. The militia who had never been under fire, were eager for the conflict, so confident were they of victory. On swept the apparently doomed column upon which every eye was sternly bent, while every heart beat with intense anxiety to hear the command to fire. In this moment of thrilling excitement, a white flag was lifted above the works, and an order came for all the troops to withdraw from the outer posts and stack their arms. Such a cry of indignation as followed, probably never before assailed the ears of a commander. Lieutenant Anderson in a paroxysm of rage, broke his sword over one of his guns and burst into tears. The shameful deed was done, and so anxious was General Hull that all should receive the benefit of this capitulation, that he included in it Colonels McArthur and Cass, and their detachment whom he had sent to the river Raisin, together with that entrusted with the supplies.

To enhance the regret and shame of this sudden surrender, it was soon discovered that McArthur and Cass, having heard the cannonading twenty-four hours before, had returned, and at the moment the white flag was raised were only a mile and a half from the fort, and advancing so as to take the enemy in rear. The result of a defence would have been the entire destruction of the British army. Ah! what a different scene was occurring on this same day, in another hemisphere. On this very morning Napoleon crossed the Dnieper, on his way to Moscow, and Murat and Ney, at the head of eighteen thousand splendid cavalry, fell on the Russian rear guard, only six thousand strong. Yet this comparatively small band, composed like most of the troops under Hull, of new levies, never thought of surrendering. First in two squares, and then in one solid square they continued their retreat all day—sometimes broken, yet always re-forming and presenting the same fringe of glittering steel, and the same adamantine front. Forty times were the apparently resistless squadrons hurled upon them, yet they still maintained their firm formation, and at night effected a junction with the main army, though with the loss of more than one-sixth of their number. It was to be left to Scott and Brown and Miller and Jessup and Jackson, to show that Russian serfs were not braver troops than American freemen.

It sometimes happens that events widely different in their character, and presenting still wider contrast in the magnitude and grandeur of the circumstances that attend them, are in their remote results alike, both in character and in their effect on the destiny of the world. Thus, six days after our declaration of war, Napoleon crossed the Niemen, on his march to Moscow. This first step on Russian territory was the signal for a long train of events to arise, which in the end should dash to earth the colossal power of Napoleon, while our movement was to break the spell which made Great Britain mistress of the seas; and two nations, one an unmixed despotism and the other a pure republic, from that moment began to assume a prominence they never before held, and from that time on, have been the only powers which have rapidly increased in resources and strength, till each threatens, in time, to swallow up its own hemisphere.

Much has been written of this campaign of Hull, and in the controversy, statistics differ as widely as opinions. He was tried by Court Martial, of which Martin Van Buren was Judge Advocate, acquitted of treason, but found guilty of cowardice and sentenced to be shot. Being pardoned by the President, his life was saved, but he went forth a blighted and ruined man.

On many points there is room for a diversity of judgment, but one thing is certain, General Hull was unfit for the station to which he was assigned. He had been a gallant subordinate officer in the revolution, but a man may be a good major, or even colonel, but a bad commander-in-chief. There are many officers who are fit only to act under orders, whom personal danger never agitates, but who are unnerved by responsibility. Let the latter rest on some other person and they will cheerfully encounter the peril. Hull may have been one of these, at least it seems more rational to attribute a portion of his conduct to some mental defect rather than to cowardice. It is hard to affix such a stain on a man who moved beside Washington in the perilous march on Trenton—stood firmly amid the hottest fire at Princeton—gallantly led his men to the charge at Bemis' Heights, and faced without flinching the fiery sleet that swept the column pressing up the rugged heights of Stony Point. Gray hairs do not make a coward of such a man, though they should render him imbecile.

It is not easy at this remote period to appreciate the difficulties of the position in which Hull eventually found himself. At first he refused to take command of the expedition, but being urged by the government, accepted, though with the express understanding that in case of hostilities, he was to be sustained both by a fleet on Lake Erie, and an army operating on the northern and western frontier of New York. He knew that the conquest of Canadian territory would be of slight importance, if the lake and river communication was controlled by the enemy, for they could pass their troops from one point to another with great rapidity, cut off his supplies and reinforcements, and hem him in till a force sufficient to overwhelm him was concentrated.

On arriving near Malden, he was astounded to hear that the enemy had received notice of the war before him, and hence had time to make more or less preparations. The second blow was the loss of hospital stores, intrenching tools, army baggage, private papers, &c. The third came in the fall of Mackinaw, thus removing the only barrier that kept back the northern hordes. He knew the enemy had possession of the water communication, and were therefore able to threaten his retreat. Dearborn, who ought to have been pressing the British on the Niagara frontier, and thus attracted their forces from Malden, had entered into an armistice with the Governor of Canada, leaving the latter at full liberty to reinforce the troops opposed to Hull, a privilege of which he was not slow to avail himself. There was not a gleam of sunshine in the whole gloomy prospect that spread out before the American commander. His own army diminishing, while that of his adversary was rapidly increasing—behind him a wilderness two hundred miles in extent, his situation was disheartening enough to make a strong man sad. The difficulties in which he found himself environed must always produce one of two effects on every man—either rouse him to tenfold diligence and effort and daring, or sink him in corresponding inactivity and despondency. There can be no middle state. That the latter was the effect produced on General Hull, there can be no doubt. He proved plainly that he was not one of those whom great emergencies develope into an extraordinary character worthy to command and worthy to be obeyed. The very first misfortune unmanned him, and from that hour to the sad close of the campaign, when he acted at all he did nothing but heap blunder on blunder. His mind having once got into a morbid state, his position and his prospects appeared to his diseased imagination ten times more desperate than they really were.

With the failure of General Dearborn to invade Canada from the New York frontier, and more especially with the lakes entirely under the control of the enemy, his campaign, according to all human calculations, must prove a failure. Detroit must fall, and Michigan be given up to the enemy. The only chance by which this catastrophe could have been prevented, was offered by General Brock when he crossed the river to storm Detroit. If Hull had possessed a spark of genius or military knowledge, he would have seen in this rash movement of his enemy, the avenue opened for his release, and the sure precursor of his fortunes. With that broad river cutting off its retreat, the British army would have been overthrown; provisions and arms obtained, and the enemy received a check which in all probability would have enabled Hull to sustain himself till reinforcements arrived. But he had made up his mind to surrender, and thus save Detroit from the cruelties of the savage, and the enemy could not commit a blunder of sufficient magnitude to arouse his hopes and spur him into resistance; and having scarcely heard the report of his guns from first to last, he veiled the banner of his country in the dust.

This explanation of his conduct would correspond more with his former life, than to admit the charge of either treason or cowardice, and be perfectly satisfactory, but for the *mode* of his surrender. There is a mystery here, that neither General Hull nor his friends have ever cleared up. After having shown the imbecility of government, by which failure became inevitable, they stop as though their task was done. But the criminality of government being conceded, and the fall of Detroit acknowledged to be an inevitable consequence, it does not follow that the surrender of the army was necessary. Why, after Colonel Miller opened the communications with supplies and reinforcements, did not General Hull retreat at once? The enemy would not have attempted a pursuit through that wilderness. With a rear guard left to man the works, he could have gained two days' march, while Detroit was able to make as good terms without him as with him. He could have had no reason for staying, except the determination to hold his position and defend Detroit to the last. If he had not fully resolved to do so, the way of retreat was open, and he was bound to occupy it; if he *had*, why did he not keep to that determination? No new elements had entered into the struggle—no unforeseen events occurred to affect the conclusions he had adopted. The enemy was not in greater force than he imagined, but on the contrary, in less. He understood the strength of his own position; his troops were never in greater spirits; why then did he so suddenly and totally change his purpose? It is impossible to reconcile this grievous inconsistency in his conduct. Nor is this all that is dark and mysterious; supposing new conditions had occurred to alter his determination, and affect the relative position of the armies—an entirely new order of things had taken place, requiring another mode of procedure than the one adopted by himself and the army; why did he not call a council of war, and submit those new features to its consideration? When his troops wished to attack Malden, he considered the question so momentous as to require a council of his officers. When a simple repulse was the only misfortune that could happen, he regarded it his duty to take advice from his subordinates; but when it came to an absolute surrender of his whole army, no such obligation was felt. This man, who was so afraid to compromise his force, lest it should meet with a repulse, did not in the end hesitate to surrender it entire, and cover it with dishonor on his own responsibility. Military history rarely records such an event as this, and never unless either treason or cowardice was apparent as noonday. Not a faltering word—not a doubtful movement—not a sign of flinching, till the white flag was seen flaunting its cowardly folds before the banner of his country. No general has a right to assume such a responsibility, at least, until the question has been submitted to his officers. He may peril his troops in an unsuccessful attack, but never *dishonor* them without consulting their wishes. The act was that of a timorous commander, or of a bold and unscrupulous man, like Gorgey. The rash and unmilitary advance of Brock, which notwithstanding its success, met the disapproval of his superior, seems wholly unaccountable, except some one, in the confidence of Hull, had whispered in his ears, that the latter intended no defence.

The *manner* of surrender, conflicts with the explanation of the act itself, and involves the conduct of Hull in a mystery. To tell us he was neither a traitor nor a coward, and yet leave those violations of military rules and contradictions of character unexplained and unreconciled, is to leave the same painful doubt on the mind as though no defence had been attempted. A morbid state of mind equivalent to insanity, thus changing for a time the whole character of the man, is the only charitable construction.

The blame, however, was not distributed impartially. The Secretary of War should have been immediately removed from office, Dearborn withdrawn as commander-in-chief, and the whole administration thoroughly overhauled, and its policy changed. As it was, the swelling curses of the land smote the single head of General Hull. The news of his surrender fell on the country like a thunderbolt at noonday. The march of his army had been watched with intense interest, but with scarcely any misgivings. So large a force appearing with the declaration of war in their hands on the weak and unprepared posts of the north-western frontier was expected to sweep everything before it. Its defeat was considered impossible, its entire, shameful surrender, therefore, could hardly be credited. The nation was stunned, but with surprise, not fear, at least that portion west of the Alleghanies. Indignation and a spirit of fierce retaliation swelled every bosom. But eastward, where party spirit and divided feelings and views, had rendered the war party cautious and timid, the effect was for a time paralyzing. If defeated at the outset, while England could bring into the field scarcely any but her colonial force, what would be our prospects of success when her veterans drilled in the wars of the continent should appear? The government, however, awoke to the vastness of the undertaking, but still remained ignorant of the means by which it was to be accomplished.

To save the north-western frontier, now laid open to the incursions of savages, Kentucky, Ohio, Pennsylvania and Virginia, sent forth crowds of volunteers, eager to redeem the tarnished reputation of the country. Several members of Congress from Kentucky enlisted as private soldiers—the young and ardent Clay was seen at the musters, thrilling the young men who surrounded him, as though he wielded the fiery cross in his hands. Ten thousand men were raised in an incredible short space of time, and placed under General Harrison, the hero of Tippecanoe. To these were added portions of the 17th and 19th regiments of regular infantry and two regiments from Kentucky and Ohio, for government was apparently determined to make up for the insufficient, niggardly expenditures of the first campaign by its useless prodigality in preparing for the second.

Four thousand men raised by order of Gov. Shelby, of Kentucky, all mounted on horseback, were put under Major General Hopkins, of the militia, who, jointly with three regiments already sent to Vincennes by Harrison, were to defend the frontiers of Indiana and Illinois.

Oct. 10.

Reaching Fort Harrison, which Captain, afterwards General Taylor, with scarcely thirty efficient men, had gallantly defended against the attacks of four or five hundred Indians, this motley crowd of horsemen started on the 14th for the Indian villages which lay along the Illinois and Wabash rivers. But the long and tedious march and the uncomfortable bivouacs by night, obscured the visions of glory that had dazzled them, and the fourth day, the enthusiasm which from the first had been rapidly subsiding, reached zero, and open mutiny seized the entire body of the troops. A major rode up to General Hopkins and peremptorily ordered him to wheel about. The General refusing to obey, he was compelled next day to constitute the rear guard of this splendid corps of cavalry, whose horses' tails were towards the enemy and their heads towards Fort Harrison.

Sept. 12.

In the mean time, Harrison, with about 2,500 men reached Fort Deposit, and relieved the garrison composed of seventy men who had gallantly withstood the attacks of hordes of Indians. Here he paused till the arrival of other troops, and occupied the time in sending out various detachments against the Indian villages, all of which were successful.

On the 18th, Harrison returned to Fort Wayne, where he met General Winchester, with reinforcements from Ohio and Kentucky, in all about two thousand men. Winchester ranked Harrison, and the latter finding himself superseded, was about to retire. The President, however, restored him to his original command, and he continued his march northward. **Sept.** In the latter part of this month he was at Fort Defiance. Leaving his troops there, he returned to the settlements to organize and hasten up the forces designed to constitute the centre and right wing of his army. Abandoning his original plan of boldly marching on Detroit and recapturing it at once, he determined to advance in three different columns, by as many different routes, to the Miami Rapids, thence move suddenly to Brownstown, cross the river and seize Malden, which had so annoyed Hull. All along the highways and rude half-trodden paths, and skirting the banks of rivers that rolled through nothing but primeval forests from their sources to the lakes, squads of men, some mounted, some in uniform, but the most part in the rough frontiersman costume, were seen toiling northward, to avenge the disgrace of Hull. Their camp-fires lit up the wilderness by night, and their boisterous mirth filled it with echoes by day. A more motley band of soldiers were never seen swarming to battle.

CHAPTER IV.

Operations on the New York frontier — Battle of Queenstown — Death of Brock — Scott a prisoner — General Smythe's Proclamation and abortive attempts — Cursed by the army — Duel with General Porter — Retires in disgrace — Dearborn's movements and failures — Review of the campaign on the New York frontier — Character of the officers and soldiers.

While Harrison's forces were thus scattered amid the forests and settlements of Ohio and Indiana, the army along the Niagara frontier had begun to move. At this time every eye in the land was turned northward. That long chain of Mediterraneans, whose shores were fringed with hostile armies, from Sackett's Harbor to where they lost themselves in the forests of the north-west, became an object of the deepest interest. Every rumor that the wind bore across the wilderness, or that, following the chains of settlements along the rivers reached the haunts of civilization, was caught up with avidity. The discomfiture of Hull had filled every heart with trembling solicitude for the fate of our other armies. Defeat in the west, and incomprehensible delays in the east, had changed the Canadas from a weak province, to be overrun by the first invader, into a Gibraltar against which the entire strength of the nation must be hurled.

I have stated before that Dearborn, commanding the forces on the Niagara and northern frontier, instead of making a diversion in favor of Hull, by crossing the Niagara and drawing attention to himself, had been coaxed into an armistice with Provost, the English Governor, in which Hull had been left out. This armistice was asked and granted, on the ground that dispatches had been received, announcing the revocation of the orders in council. One great cause of the war being thus removed, it was hoped that peace might be restored. The result was as we have seen; the British commander immediately dispatched Brock to Malden, to capture Hull, from which successful expedition he was able to return before the armistice was broken off. General Dearborn clung to this absurd armistice, as if it were the grandest stroke of diplomacy conceivable. He carried his attachment so far as to disobey the express command of his Government, to break it off. August 24. At length, however, this nightmare ended, and preparations were made for a vigorous autumnal campaign.

The northern army, numbering between eight and ten thousand soldiers, was principally concentrated at two points. One portion was encamped near Plattsburg and Greenbush, commanded by General Dearborn, in person, the other at Lewistown, was under the direction of General Stephen Van Rensalaer, of the New York militia, while 1,500 regulars, under General

Smythe, lay at Buffalo, a few miles distant. There were a few troops stationed also at Ogdensburg, Sackett's Harbor, and Black Rock.

The discontent produced by Hull's surrender, and the loud complaints against the inaction of the northern army, together with the consciousness that something must be done to prevent the first year of war from closing in unmixed gloom, induced General Van Rensalaer to make a bold push into Canada, and by a sudden blow attempt to wrest Jamestown from the enemy, and there establish his winter quarters.

The cutting out of two English brigs[19] from under the guns of Fort Erie, by Lieutenant Elliot with some fifty volunteers, created an enthusiasm in the American camp of which General Van Rensalaer determined to avail himself.

The command of the expedition was given to his cousin, Col. Solomon Van Rensalaer, a brave and chivalric officer, who on the 13th of October, at the head of three hundred militia, accompanied by Col. Chrystie with three hundred regular troops, prepared to cross the river. It wanted still an hour to daylight when the two columns stood in battle array on the shore. Through carelessness, or inability to obtain them, there were not sufficient boats to take all over at once, and they were compelled to cross in detachments. The boat which carried Col. Chrystie being badly managed, was swept away by the current, and finally compelled to re-land on the American shore. This gallant officer was wounded while thus drifting in the stream, yet soon after he made another attempt to cross, and succeeding, led his troops nobly until the close of the action.

Col. Van Rensalaer having effected a landing, formed on the shore and marched forward. The whole force at this time did not exceed one hundred men. These, however, were led up the bank where they halted to wait the junction of the other troops that kept arriving, a few boat loads at a time. But daylight now having dawned, the exposed position of this detachment rendered it a fair mark for the enemy, who immediately opened their fire upon it. In a few minutes every commissioned officer was either killed or wounded. Col. Van Rensalaer finding that the bank of the river afforded very little shelter, determined with the handful under him to storm the heights. But he had now received four wounds, and was compelled to surrender the command to Captains Ogilvie and Wool,[20] who gallantly moved forward, and carried the fort and heights. The enemy were driven into a strong stone house, from which they made two unsuccessful attempts to recover the ground they had lost. Brock, flushed with the easy victory he had gained over Hull, rallied them by his presence, and while attempting to lead on the grenadiers of the 49th, fell mortally wounded. This for a time gave the Americans undisturbed possession of the heights, and great efforts were made to bring over the other troops. General Van Rensalaer, after the fall of his cousin, crossed and took the command, but hastening back to urge on the embarkation of the militia, it devolved on General Wadsworth.

Daylight had seen this brave little band form on the shores of the river under a galling fire—the morning sun glittered on their bayonets from the heights of Queenstown, and the victory seemed won. The day so gloriously begun would have closed in brighter effulgence, had not the militia on the farther side refused to cross over to the assistance of their hard-pressed comrades. A stone house near the bank defended by two light pieces of artillery, still played on the boats that attempted to cross, and the Americans on the Canada side, having no heavy artillery, were unable to take it. The firing from this, and soon after the appearance of a large body of Indians on the field of battle, so frightened the militia, that neither entreaties nor threats could induce them to embark. Through utter want of orderly management, half of the twenty boats had been destroyed or lost; still it was not the lack of means of transportation that held them back, but *conscientious scruples about invading an enemy's territory.* Attempting to mask their cowardice under this ridiculous plea, they stood and saw the dangers thicken around their comrades who had relied on their support, without making a single effort to save them from destruction.

Lieutenant-colonel Scott by a forced march through mud and rain, had arrived at Lewistown with his regiment at four o'clock in the morning, just as the troops were embarking. He begged permission to take part in the expedition, but the arrangements having all been made, his request was denied. He therefore planted his guns on the shore and opened his fire on the enemy. But seeing how small a proportion of the troops were got across, and perceiving also the peril of Van Rensalaer's detachment, his young and gallant heart could not allow him to remain an idle spectator, and taking one piece of artillery he jumped into a boat with his adjutant Roach, and pushed for the opposite shore. Wadsworth immediately gave the command of the troops to him, and his chivalric bearing and enthusiastic language soon animated every heart with new courage. Six feet five inches in height and in full uniform, he presented a conspicuous mark for the enemy and a rallying point to the troops. Had his regiment been with him, Queenstown would have been a second Chippewa.

Considerable reinforcements, however, had arrived, swelling the number to six hundred, of whom three hundred and fifty were regular troops. These, Scott, assisted by the cool and skillful Capt. Zitten, soon placed in the most commanding positions, and waited for further reinforcements. Just before, a body of five hundred Indians, whom the firing had suddenly collected, joined the beaten light troops of the English. Encouraged by this accession of strength, the latter moved again to the assault, but were driven back in confusion. Still the enemy kept up a desultory engagement. On one occasion, the Indians, issuing suddenly from the forest, surprised a picket of militia, and following hard on their flying traces, carried consternation into that part of the line. Scott, who was in the rear, showing the men how to unspike a gun, hearing the tumult, hastened to the front, and rallying a few platoons, scattered those wild warriors with a single blow. But while the day was wearing away in this doubtful manner, a more formidable foe appeared on the field. General Sheaffe, commanding at Fort George, had heard the firing in the morning; and a little later the news of the death of Brock was brought him. His forces were immediately put in motion, and soon after midday the little band that had from day dawn bravely breasted the storm, saw from the heights they had so bravely won, a column eight hundred and fifty strong, approaching the scene of combat—not in haste or confusion, but with the slow and measured tread of disciplined troops. These few hundred Americans watched its progress with undaunted hearts, and turned to catch the outlines of their own advancing regiments, but not a bayonet was moving to their help. At this critical moment news arrived of the shameful mutiny that had broken out on the opposite shore. The entreaties of Van Rensalaer, and the noble example of Wadsworth, and the increasing peril of their comrades, were wholly unavailing—not a soul would stir. This sealed the fate of the American detachment. A few hundred, sustained by only one piece of artillery against the thirteen hundred of the enemy—their number when the junction of the advancing column with the remaining troops and the Indian allies should be effected—constituted hopeless odds. General Van Rensalaer, from the opposite shore, saw this, and sent word to Wadsworth to retreat at once, and he would send every boat he could lay hands on to receive the fugitives. He, however, left everything to the judgment of the latter. Colonels Chrystie and Scott, of the regulars, and Mead, Strahan, and Allen of the militia, and officers Ogilvie, Wool, Totten, and Gibson McChesney, and others, presented a noble yet sorrowful group, as they took council over this message of the commander-in-chief. Their case was evidently a hopeless one, yet they could not make up their minds to retreat. Col. Scott, mounting a log in front of his troops, harangued them in a strain worthy of the days of chivalry. He told them their condition was desperate, but that Hull's surrender must be redeemed. "Let us then die," he exclaimed, "arms in hand. Our country demands the sacrifice. The example will not be lost. The blood of the slain will make heroes of the living. Those who follow will avenge our fall, and our country's wrongs. Who dare to stand?" A loud "ALL!" rang sternly along the line.[21] In the mean time Gen. Sheaffe had arrived, but instead of advancing immediately to the attack, slowly marched his column the whole length of the

American line, then countermarched it, as if to make sure that the little band in front of him was the only force he had to overcome. All saw at a glance that resistance was useless, and retreat almost hopeless. The latter, however, was resolved upon, but the moment the order was given to retire, the whole broke in disorderly flight towards the river. To their dismay, no boats were there to receive them, and a flag of truce was therefore sent to the enemy. The messenger, however, never returned; another and another shared the same fate. At last Scott tied a white handkerchief to his sword, and accompanied by Captains Totten and Gibson, crept under one of the precipices, down the river, till he arrived where a gentle slope gave an easy ascent, when the three made a push for the road, which led from the valley to the heights. On the way they were met by Indians, who firing on them, rushed forward with their tomahawks, to kill them. They would soon have shared the fate of the other messengers, but for the timely arrival of a British officer, with some soldiers who took them to Gen. Sheaffe, to whom Scott surrendered his whole force. Two hundred and ninety-three were all that survived of the brave band who had struggled so long and so nobly for victory. Several hundred militia, however, were found concealed along the shore, who had crossed over, but skulked away in the confusion.

The entire loss of the Americans in this unfortunate expedition, killed and captured, was about one thousand men.

General Van Rensalaer, disgusted with the conduct of the militia, soon after sent in his resignation.

Brock was buried the following day "under one of the bastions of Fort George," and at the request of Scott, then a prisoner, minute guns were fired from Fort Niagara during the funeral ceremonies. Above the dull distant roar of the cataract, the minute guns of friends and foes pealed over the dead, as with shrouded banners the slowly marching column bore him to his last resting place. Cannon that but a few hours before had been exploding in angry strife on each other, now joined their peaceful echoes over his grave. Such an act was characteristic of Scott, who fierce and fearless in battle, was chivalrous and kind in all his feelings.

While a prisoner in an inn at Niagara, Scott was told that some one wished to see the "tall American." He immediately passed through into the entry, when to his astonishment he saw standing before him two savage Indian chiefs, the same who had attempted to kill him when he surrendered himself a prisoner of war. They wished to look on the man at whom they had so often fired with a deliberate aim. In broken English, and by gestures, they inquired where he was hit, for they believed it impossible that out of fifteen or twenty shots not one had taken effect. The elder chief, named Jacobs, a tall, powerful savage, became furious at Scott's asserting that not a ball had touched him, and seizing his shoulders rudely, turned him round to examine his back. The young and fiery Colonel did not like to have such freedom taken with his person by a savage, and hurling him fiercely aside, exclaimed, "Off, villain, you fired like a squaw." "We kill you now," was the quick and startling reply, as knives and tomahawks gleamed in their hands. Scott was not a man to beg or run, though either would have been preferable to taking his chances against these armed savages. Luckily for him, the swords of the American officers who had been taken prisoners, were stacked under the staircase beside which he was standing. Quick as thought he snatched up the largest, a long sabre, and the next moment it glittered unsheathed above his head. One leap backward, to get scope for play, and he stood towering even above the gigantic chieftain, who glared in savage hate upon him. The Indians were in the wider part of the hall, between the foot of the stairs and the door, while Scott stood farther in where it was narrower. The former, therefore, could not get in the rear, and were compelled to face their enemy. They manœuvred to close, but at every turn that sabre flashed in their eyes. The moment they should come to blows, one, they knew, was sure to die, and although it was equally certain that Scott would fall under the knife of the survivor before he could regain his position, yet neither Indian seemed anxious to be the sacrifice. While they thus stood watching each other, a British officer chanced to enter, and on beholding the terrific tableau, cried out, "The guard," and at the same instant seized the tallest chief by the arm and presented a cocked pistol to his head. The next moment the blade of Scott quivered over the head of the other savage, to protect his deliverer. In a few seconds the guards entered with levelled bayonets, and the two chieftains were secured. One of them was the son of Brant, of revolutionary notoriety.

The prisoners were all taken to Quebec, whence they were sent in a cartel to Boston. As they were about to sail, Scott, who was in the cabin of the transport, hearing a noise on deck, went up to ascertain the cause, and found that the British officers were separating the Irishmen, to exclude them from mercy due to the other prisoners, and have them taken to England and tried for treason. Twenty-three had thus been set apart when he arrived. Indignant at this outrage, he peremptorily ordered the rest of the men to keep silent and not answer a question of any kind, so that neither by their replies or voice they could give any evidence of the place of their birth. He then turned to the doomed twenty-three, and denounced the act of the officers, and swore most solemnly that if a hair of their heads was touched, he would avenge it, even if he was compelled to refuse quarter in battle.

Soon after he reached Boston, he was sent to Washington, and in a short time was exchanged. He then drew up a report of the whole affair to the Secretary of War, and it was presented the same day to Congress. The result was the passage of an act of retaliation (March 3d, 1813.)

Nov. 10.

General Van Rensalaer having resigned his commission, making the second general disposed of since the commencement of hostilities, the command on the Niagara frontier devolved on General Smythe, who issued a proclamation to the "men of New York," which was of itself a sufficient guarantee that he would soon follow Hull into worse than oblivion. In it, after speaking of the failure of the former expedition, he said, "Valor had been conspicuous, but the nation unfortunate in the selection of some of those directing it"——"the commanders were popular men, destitute alike of theory and experience in the art of war." "In a few days," said he, "the troops under my command will plant the American standard in Canada to conquer or die." He called on all those desirous of honor or fame, to rally to his standard. He was not one of the incompetent generals whose plans failed through ignorance. Portions of his proclamations, however, were well adapted to rouse the military spirit of the state, and in less than three weeks he had nearly five thousand men under his command. His orders from the Secretary of War, were, not to attempt an invasion with "less than three thousand combatants," and with sufficient boats to carry the whole over together.

Seventy boats and a large number of scows having been collected at Black Rock, he issued his orders for the troops to be in readiness early on the morning of the 28th of November, to cross over and attack the enemy.

Previous to the main movement, however, he sent over two detachments, one under Colonel Bœstler, and the other under Captain King—the former to destroy a bridge five miles below Fort Erie, in order to cut off the communication between it and Chippewa, while the latter, with a hundred and fifty regular troops and seventy seamen, was to carry the "Red House," and storm the British batteries on the shore.

The boats pushed off at midnight, and were soon struggling in the centre of the stream. Of Colonel Bœstler's seven boats, containing two hundred men, only three reached the Canada shore. With less than half his force he advanced and easily routed the guard, but hearing that a British reinforcement was marching up, he retreated without destroying the bridge, and re-embarked his men. Captain King started with ten boats, but six of them were scattered in the darkness, and only four reached the point of attack. Among these, however, were the seventy seamen. The advance of the boats having been seen by the sentinels on watch, the little detachment was compelled to land under a shower of grape shot and musketry.

The sailors without waiting the order of a regular march, rushed up the bank with their boarding pikes and cutlasses, stormed the position, and carried it with loud huzzas. After securing some prisoners and tumbling two cannon and their caissons into the river, Lieutenant Angus began to look around for Captain King. The latter directing his force on the exterior batteries, carried the first by the bayonet, when the other was abandoned. The position and all the batteries being taken, the firing had ceased, and Lieutenant Angus marched his sailors, with the wounded and prisoners, to the shore to wait for Captain King, and recross the river. Finding only four boats there, and ignorant that no more had landed, he concluded that the former had already re-embarked his troops; he therefore launched these and made good his retreat to the American shore. In a short time Captain King arrived, and to his amazement found all the boats gone. After a short search, however, he discovered two belonging to the enemy, in which he despatched the prisoners he had taken, and as many of his men as they would hold. He remained behind with the remainder of his detachment, and was soon after compelled to surrender himself prisoner of war.

On the return of Bœstler and Angus without Captain King and the rest of the detachment, Colonel Winder volunteered to go in search of them.

But, as he approached the opposite shore, he found all the batteries re-established, which opened their fire upon him, compelling him to return with the loss of six killed and twenty-six wounded. In fact his own boat was the only one that touched land at all—the others being carried down by the force of the stream.

Through some unaccountable delay, the main body, to which the two detachments sent off at midnight were designed as an advance guard, did not embark till twelve o'clock next day. But at length two thousand men under

General Porter, were got on board, while General Tannehill's volunteers and M'Clure's regiment were drawn up on the shore ready to follow. As if on purpose to give his adversary time for ample preparation, thus imitating the fatal examples of Dearborn and Hull, Smythe kept his men paraded on the beach in full view of the Canada shore, till late in the afternoon. He then, instead of giving the anxiously expected order to advance, commanded the whole to debark. Indignation and rage at this vacillating, pusillanimous conduct seized the entire army, and curses and loud denunciations were heard on every side. General Porter boldly and openly accused his commander of cowardice. The latter, frightened at the storm he had raised, promised that another attempt should be made the next day. It was resolved to cross at a place five miles below the navy yard, and the following day, at four o'clock, nearly the entire army was embarked. General Porter with the American colors floating from the stern of his boat, was in advance, to show that he asked no man to go where he would not lead. But when all was ready, and at the moment when every one expected to hear the signal to move forward, an order was passed along the line directing the troops to be relanded, accompanied with the announcement that the invasion of Canada was for that season abandoned. A shout of wrath burst from the whole army. Many of the militia threw away their arms and started for their homes, while fierce threats against the General's life were publicly made by the remaining troops. He was branded as a coward, shot at in the streets, and without even the form of a trial, was driven in scorn and rage from the army, and chased and mobbed by an indignant people from the state he had dishonored. Before he retired, however, he made an absurd attempt to retrieve his honor by challenging General Porter to mortal combat. They met on Grand Island and exchanged shots without effect. The seconds having published the transaction in a Buffalo paper, "congratulated the public on the happy issue." In commenting on this, Ingersoll very pithily remarks, "The public would have preferred a battle in Canada."

Beginning at the extreme north-west, and continuing along the lakes to Niagara, we had met with nothing but defeat. Only one more army was left to lift the nation out of the depths of gloom by its achievements, or deepen the night in which the year 1812 was closing. General Dearborn, the commander-in-chief, had an army of three thousand regulars and as many more militia, with the power to swell his force to ten thousand if he thought proper. The plan of government to conquer Canada through Hull's invasion from Detroit, Van Rensalaer's and Smythe's from Niagara, both to be supported and their triumph secured by the advance of Dearborn, had fallen to the ground, and the latter was passing the autumn in idleness.

General Brown, who commanded the militia appointed for the defence of the eastern shore of Lake Ontario and southern shore of St. Lawrence, exhibited, at Ogdensburg, the first indications of those qualities of a great commander which afterwards developed themselves on the scene of Van Rensalaer's and Smythe's defeats and failures. Colonel Forsyth having made a successful incursion into Canada with a noble body of riflemen, twice defeating double his numbers and burning a block house with stores; the British, in retaliation, attacked Ogdensburg. On the 2d of October they commenced a cannonade from their batteries at Prescott, on the opposite side of the river. This harmless waste of ammunition was continued for two days, when it was resolved to storm the town. Six hundred men were embarked in forty boats, and under cover of the batteries, pulled steadily across the river. General Brown could collect but four hundred militia to oppose them, but having posted these judiciously, they were able to keep up such a deadly fire on the enemy that every attempt to land proved abortive, and the whole detachment was compelled to withdraw to the Canada shore.

There was, during the summer, a good deal of skirmishing along the frontier, forming interludes to the more important movements. Colonel Pike on the 19th of the same month made an incursion into Canada, surprised a body of British and Indians, and burnt a block-house. Three days after, Captain Lyon captured forty English at St. Regis, together with a stand of colors and despatches from the Governor General to an Indian tribe. The colors were taken by William M. Marcy.

Nov. 20.

Thus the autumn wore away, till at last, Dearborn seemed to awake from his torpor. Moving his army from the little town of Champlain, he forded the La Cole, and attacked and captured an English block-house. The grand movement had now commenced, and the British Governor-General prepared to meet the most serious invasion that had yet been attempted. But to his astonishment he discovered that all this display of force was to obtain possession of a guard-house, and retain it for half an hour. This feat being accomplished, General Dearborn, amid much confusion, marched his six thousand men back again, and resting on his honors soon after retired into winter quarters. After protracted delays and unaccountable inaction, he seemed at last to feel the necessity of obeying the urgent orders of the government, "*not to lose a moment in attacking the British posts in his front.*" These he had now obeyed to the letter—he had *attacked* a block-house and fled. The great tragedy had begun and ended in a farce. The surrender of Hull was an unmitigated disgrace, and the nation turned towards Niagara for relief. The failure of Van Rensalaer was not unmixed with consolation. He and the officers and men who bore the brunt of that day's battle, had shown what

American troops could do. Van Rensalaer has been charged with acting rashly, and exposing himself to discomfiture, when success would have been of no advantage. But those who suppose that a victory is fruitless, because no important position is gained, or territory is wrested from the enemy, commit a vital error. They forget that *moral* power is half, even when every thing depends on hard blows. When confidence is lost, and despondency has taken the place of courage and hope, a battle that should restore these would be a victory, at almost any sacrifice. So Van Rensalaer thought, and justly. His preparations and mode of procedure were not careful and prudent, as they should have been, exhibiting a want of thoroughness which a longer experience would have rectified; still, his plan might have succeeded but for the dastardly conduct of the militia, and a new impulse been given to the movements along the northern frontier. This cowardly behavior of his troops he could not anticipate, for they had hitherto shown no disinclination to fight. At Hull's surrender there were no indications of a craven spirit—on the contrary, the soldiers cursed their commander, and the general feeling was, that give the men a gallant leader and they would fight bravely. Van Rensalaer knew that his troops would not fail through reluctance on his part to lead them to battle, and it was enough to break his noble heart, as he stood bleeding from four wounds, to see them refuse to come to his rescue.

General Smythe's conduct admits of no apology. His excuse for countermanding his last order, after the troops had embarked, is groundless. He says that his orders were strict, not to attempt an invasion of Canada with less than three thousand men, and that he but fifteen hundred. Yet in his last attempt all but some two hundred of his troops were actually embarked, when he commanded them to re-land. He was either not aware how many soldiers composed his army until he counted them as they lay off in their boats, ready to pull for the opposite shore, or he knew it before. If the latter be true, why all this display, designed to eventuate in nothing? On the other hand, the confession of ignorance is still worse. This much is clear, all these difficulties and objections could not have occurred to him for the first time when he saw the army drawn up on shore or afloat. The excuse, if honest, is worse than the act itself.

Aug. 1.

Dearborn's inactivity furnished less salient points of criticism, but it was fully as culpable as Smythe's failure. In the first place, he received orders from the Secretary of War to make a diversion in favor of *Hull at Niagara and Kingston, as soon as possible.* His position might have been such that no blame could attach to him for not making such diversion, but nothing could warrant him in entering into an armistice with the enemy, in which Hull was excluded. If he assumed such a responsibility in the hope that peace would be secured, he was bound to make as one of the first conditions, that no reinforcements should be sent to Malden and Detroit. One such act is sufficient to cause the removal of a commander, for he can never be an equal match against a shrewd and energetic enemy. Prevost wrote to Gen. Brock: "*I consider it* most fortunate that I have been able to prosecute this object of Government, (the armistice,) *without interfering with your operations on the Detroit. I have sent you men, money, and stores of all kinds.*"[22]

One cannot read this letter without feeling chagrin that the Senior Major-General of the American army could be so easily overreached.

In the second place, his delay in breaking off this armistice when peremptorily ordered by government, was clearly reprehensible, while the fact that with an army of six thousand men under his immediate command, he accomplished absolutely nothing, is incontrovertible proof of his inefficiency as a commander. The isle of Aux Noix was considered the key of Central Canada, and this he could have taken at any moment and held for future operations; yet he went into winter quarters without having struck a blow.

The troops, regular and militia, under his general direction, amounted in the latter part of September to thirteen thousand men. Six thousand three hundred were stationed along the Niagara, two thousand two hundred at Sackett's Harbor, and five thousand on Lake Champlain. To oppose this formidable force, Sir George Provost had not more than three thousand troops,[23] and yet not even a battle had been fought, if we except that of Van Rensalaer's detachment, while instead of gaining we had lost both fortresses and territory.

One naturally inquires what could be the cause of such a complete failure where success was deemed certain. In the first place, there was not a man in the cabinet fit to carry out a campaign, however well planned. The sudden concentration of so large a force on our northern frontier, before reinforcements could arrive from England, was a wise movement, and ought to have accomplished its purpose. But there the wisdom ended, and vacillation and doubt took the place of promptness, energy and daring.

In the second place, inefficient commanders were placed at the head of our armies. Both Dearborn and Hull had been gallant officers in the Revolution, but they were wholly unaccustomed to a separate command, and while imitating the caution of their great exemplar, exhibited none of his energy and daring. They remembered his Fabian inactivity, but they forgot the overwhelming reasons that produced it, and forgot, also, Trenton, Princeton and Monmouth.

In the third place, the militia were undisciplined and could not be relied upon. The insubordination, unmilitary conduct, and recklessness of rules which force a commander into extreme caution, lest his semblance of an army should be annihilated, are not known to the persons who coolly criticise him at a distance. These things are doubtless an ample excuse for much that is unsparingly condemned. Hence it is unjust to pronounce judgment on this or that action, because it might apparently have been avoided, unless those actions and the declarations of their author contradict each other, or stand condemned by every interpretation of military rules.

In the commencement of the war we had neither an army nor generals that could be trusted. The troops lacked confidence in their leaders, and the latter had no confidence in their troops. Such mutual distrust can result in nothing but failure. Our commanders were in an embarrassing position, but they ought to have been aware that to *fight* their way out was the only mode of escape left them. Battles make soldiers and develop generals. In the tumult and dangers of a fierce fight, the cool yet daring officers, fertile in resources, fierce in the onset, and stubborn and unconquered in retreat, are revealed, and soon men are found who will follow where they lead, even into hopeless combat. A spirit of emulation and valor succeeds timidity and distrust.

The administration at this period was surrounded with great and perplexing difficulties. With but the germ of a military academy, efficient officers were scarce. The establishment of the school at West Point was one of the wisest acts ever performed by this government, and the attempt, a few years since, to destroy it, one of the most unscrupulous, reckless and dangerous ever put forth by ignorant demagogues. Our volunteers and militia have confidence in men bred to the profession of arms. They yield them ready obedience—submit to rigid discipline—while the method and skill with which everything is conducted, impart confidence and steadiness. A country like ours will never submit to the expense and danger of a large standing army, nor do we need it if we can keep well supplied with military schools. A few West Point officers on the Canada frontier would have brought the campaign of 1812 to a different close.

CHAPTER V.

THE NAVY.

The Cabinet resolves to shut up our ships of war in port — Remonstrance of Captains Bainbridge and Stuart — Rodgers ordered to sea — Feeling of the crews — Chase of the Belvidere — Narrow escape of the Constitution from an English fleet — Cruise of the Essex — Action between the Constitution and Guerriere — Effect of the Victory in England and the United States — United States takes the Macedonian — Lieutenant Hamilton carries the captured colors to Washington — Presented to Mrs. Madison in a ball-room — The Argus — Action between the Wasp and Frolic — Constitution captures the Java — Hornet takes the Peacock — Effect of these Victories abroad.

Having gone through the first campaigns on the Canadian frontier, I leave for awhile the army of Harrison, swallowed up in the forests of Ohio and surrounded by the gloom of a northern winter, toiling its way towards Malden, and turn with a feeling of relief to the conduct of our little navy during the summer that had passed.

As I stated before, our naval force amounted to but nine frigates and a few sloops of war, while Great Britain had a hundred ships of the line in commission, and more than a thousand vessels in all, bearing the royal flag. Added to this stupendous difference in the number of ships, was the moral power attached to the universally acknowledged superiority of the British navy. England was recognized mistress of the seas. The fleets of Spain, France and Holland had one after another submitted to her sway, and fresh with still greater laurels won under Nelson, her navy was looked upon as irresistible. A naval contest on our part, therefore, was not dreamed of, and hence arose the determination on the part of the Administration at Washington, to convert our frigates into mere floating batteries for the protection of harbors. But it must be remembered, weak as our navy appeared, it was stronger at the declaration of war than the whole British force on our coast. We had ships enough to blockade Halifax and Bermuda, and bear undisputed sway until reinforcements could be sent across the Atlantic. Our privateers in the revolution—the conduct of our ships in the Bay of Tripoli had given evidence of what could be done, and the determination of the Cabinet, therefore, to lay up the ships of war before their metal had been tested—to leave the waters around our coast vexed with British cruisers, when at least for six weeks we could have kept them clear of the enemy, and in all probability captured their entire squadron on the American station, is another painful evidence of the utter incapacity of the administration to carry on the war. If, in anticipation of hostilities, our whole fleet had been collected and put in such order that it could have sailed at an hour's notice, results would have been accomplished far greater than those which followed.

Against our nine frigates, the President, United States, and Constellation, of the first class, the Congress, Constitution, and the Chesapeake of the second, the Essex, Adams, Boston and New York,[24] together with several smaller vessels, there were on the Halifax station but five frigates and some smaller vessels. The Africa, sixty-four, was the only two decker on our coast, in active service. The Halifax station could have been reinforced by the other two stations, the Jamaica and Leeward Island, but not within a month, which would have given us an opportunity of cutting them up in detail. England, at this time, was so occupied with the momentous affairs in Europe, that she kept her fleets on the eastern board of the Atlantic, and ignorant of our naval strength, supposed the ships on the Halifax station more than a match for the whole American navy. Had the British fleet on this coast been captured, and an alliance offensive and defensive formed with France, we should have struck the maritime power of England a blow from which she never would have recovered. But the outcries of the Federalists filled the administration with as much dread of French alliance, as it entertained of the naval power of England.

Not only was the American Government innocent of all such plans for the navy, but it did not even provide for the merchantmen which might be approaching the American coast, and liable to be captured by the most contemptible cruiser that sailed unmolested along our shores. No nation ever before had the opportunity of doing so much with small means, as circumstances placed in the hands of the American Government at the commencement of the war, and threw it away so foolishly, so unpardonably.

The insane project to lay up the American ships in harbor, was defeated by two naval officers, to whom the nation owes perpetual gratitude. Captains Bainbridge and Stewart were at Washington when the subject was under discussion, and being shown the written orders to Commodore Rodgers, to keep his fleet in the harbor of New York, as a part of its defence, they sought an interview with the Secretary of the Navy, and boldly remonstrated against this death-blow to the navy. "If laid up in war, who would support it in peace?" Although told that the thing was settled, so far as regarded the fleet in New York Bay, they appealed with still greater urgency, and in the true spirit of their profession, declared that the American commanders were capable of taking care of their own ships; nay, in noble enthusiasm asserted, that eight times out of ten, an American frigate would capture an antagonist of equal metal.

The secretary was moved by their appeal, backed as it was with solid argument, and took them to see the President. They made to him the same statements which had so deeply impressed the Secretary of the Navy. Moreover, they promised *victories*, a dream which had never visited the brain of a member of the cabinet. "Eight times out of ten," said they, "with equal force we can hardly fail—our men are better men, and better disciplined; our midshipmen are not mere boys, only fit to carry orders, but young men capable of reflection and action. Our guns are sighted, which is an improvement of our own the English know nothing of. While we can fire cannon with as sure an aim as musketry, or almost rifles, striking twice out of every three shots, they must fire at random, without sight of their object or regard to the undulations of the sea, shooting over our heads, seldom hulling us or even hitting our decks. We may be captured, and probably shall be, even after taking prizes from them, because their numbers are so much greater than ours. But the American flag will never be dishonored, seldom if ever struck to equal force."[25] The President, as well as the Secretary of the Navy, was swept away by the arguments and gallant spirit of those officers, and suddenly remembered the daring and success of the few ships of war and the privateersmen during the Revolution.

Seeing their advantage, these officers pressed it with redoubled energy, until the President called a meeting of the cabinet to consult on the matter. But Mr. Gallatin, to whose sagacity and foresight all paid the most profound deference, treated the project as absurd. He had studied European affairs too much, and the rising genius of this country too little. Like many other wise statesmen, he could not introduce into the elements from which he drew his conclusions, the gallant spirit, lofty enthusiasm and indomitable courage, which then pervaded our little navy. He saw only the tremendous maritime preponderance against us, and hence, with all his patriotism and wisdom, acted as a perpetual clog to the government till he was sent abroad, and his counsels could no longer influence the cabinet.

But his advice that all maritime efforts should be confined to privateers, prevailed, and Bainbridge and Stewart were told that the decision which had been made respecting the national ships, could not be changed. Undaunted by their repulse, they spent nearly the whole night after this resolve had been made known to them, in drawing up a remonstrance to the President. Having witnessed the effect of their personal appeal to him, they determined to address him once more by letter.

The language of that address was not softened by well rounded periods, but plain and direct, placed the subject in its true aspect before Mr. Madison, and put on him as Chief Magistrate of the Union, the responsibility of keeping the navy from its legitimate field of action. When this joint communication was laid before the Secretary of the Navy, he objected to it as too strong and stern to present to the President, and advised them to modify its language. They refused to do so, and Mr. Madison instead of being offended at their plainness of speech, took upon himself the responsibility of acting independent of his cabinet, and assured them the vessels should be ordered to sea. No one can tell the joy of these brave men, when they found the navy they loved so well, was not to be dishonored, and elate with pride, determined that the flag they had so long carried over the sea, should never be struck but with honor.

The naval officers knew that the country reposed no confidence in its marine force, and Captains Bainbridge and Stewart, anticipating the doom they had struggled so noble to avert, had determined to go to sea in a privateer which the latter had purchased.[26] With a band of hardy seamen about them, and each serving in rotation as captain and first officer, they resolved to claim the right of the American flag to the high seas.[27]

At this time there were in the port of New York, the President, forty-four; Essex, thirty-two; and Hornet, eighteen; to which, on the 21st of June, were added the United States, forty-four; Congress, thirty-eight; and Argus, sixteen, all ready to sail in an hour's notice, with the exception of the Essex, which was repairing her rigging and restowing her hold. As soon as the President had determined to send the vessels to sea, this squadron was put under the command of Commodore Rogers, and he ordered to get under way at once, and intercept a large fleet of Jamaica men which were reported to have sailed, and by this time should be off the American coast. An hour after Commodore Rogers received his orders, he was leading his squadron down the Bay, and soon his canvas disappeared in the distance.

From the joy that pervaded this little squadron, as the sails were given to the wind, one would have supposed it was going to witness a grand regatta, instead of to unequal and deadly strife with an enemy. In the gallant hearts that trod those decks, existed none of the timidity and distrust that weighed down the government. There was not merely the determination of brave men entering on a desperate conflict, but the buoyancy of confidence, the joy of those who were to wipe out with their heavy broadsides the imputations cast on them by their own countrymen, and hush forever, with their shouts of victory, the boasting and mockery of their foe. The sailors partook of the excitement, for it was a common enemy against which they were going—the oppressor of seamen as well as the invader of national rights. Says a midshipman on board the Hornet, in his Diary: "This morning the declaration of war by the United States against Great Britain was read. *** At ten o'clock, A. M., Commodore Rodgers hove out the signal to weigh; never was anchor to the cathead sooner, nor topsail sheeted home[28] to the masthead with more dispatch, than upon the present occasion; the smallest boy on board seems anxious to meet what is now looked upon as the common tyrant of the ocean, for they had heard the woeful tales of the older tars. ** When the ship was under way, Captain Lawrence had the crew called to their quarters, and told them that if there were any amongst them who were disaffected, or one that had not rather sink than surrender to the enemy, with gun for gun, that he should be immediately and uninjured, landed and sent back in the pilot boat. The reply fore and aft was—not one." Not one hesitating voice, but instead, three hearty cheers, that made the vessel ring. With such a spirit did the first squadron put to sea, and make its first claim, at the cannon's mouth, to equal rights.

June 23.

Two days after, Rodgers discovered, at six o'clock in the morning, an English frigate to the north-east, and instantly crowded sail in pursuit. The chase led down the wind, and the President being a fast sailer when going free, soon gained on the stranger, leaving the squadron far astern. At four o'clock she got within gunshot, but the wind falling, gave the enemy the advantage, and Rodgers seeing that he no longer gained on the chase, attempted to cripple it. The first gun was pointed by the commodore himself, the shot of which struck the English frigate in the stern, and passed on into the gun-room. This was the first hostile gun fired on the sea after war was declared. The second was pointed by Lieutenant Gamble, which also struck the enemy. The third shot, directed by Rodgers himself, killed two men and wounded five others. At the fourth shot, fired by Lieutenant Gamble, the gun bursted, killing and wounding sixteen men. The Commodore was flung into the air by the explosion, and fell back on deck with such violence that his leg was broken. The enemy took heart at this unexpected accident, and opened his fire. The President, however, soon began to heave her shot again with such precision, that the British frigate was compelled to cut away her anchors, throw overboard her boats, and spring fourteen tons of water in order to lighten her. She was by these means enabled to gain on her pursuers. Commodore Rodgers finding the distance between them increasing, fired three broadsides, which falling short, he abandoned the chase. The loss of the President, in killed and wounded, was twenty-two, only six of whom were damaged by the shot of the enemy. The Belvidera, for such she was afterwards ascertained to be, reported seven killed and wounded. After repairing damages Rodgers again cruised for the Jamaica men, and at length supposing he had got in their wake, kept on until near the mouth of the English Channel, when seeing nothing of them, he returned by way of Maderia and the Western Islands to Boston. It was a barren cruise, only seven merchantmen being taken during the whole seventy days the squadron was absent.

In the mean time the report of the Belvidera, which had put into Halifax, caused the enemy to collect a fleet, which early in July was off New York, where it captured a great many American merchantmen. Among the prizes was the schooner Nautilus, the first vessel of war taken on either side. July 12. While the squadron was thus cruising off the coast, in the hope of meeting the American fleet under Rodgers, the Constitution, a forty-four, sailed from Annapolis on her way to New York. Her crew was newly shipped, a hundred men having joined her on the night before she sailed. The orders which Captain Hull, the commander, received from the Secretary of the Navy, exhibit the timidity and weakness of the Government. In the first place, after giving directions respecting the destination of the ship, he said: "I am informed that the Belvidera is in our waters, but you are not to understand me as impelling you to battle previously to your having confidence in your crew, unless attacked, or with a reasonable prospect of success, of which you are to be at your discretion the judge." In a later order he says: "If on your way thither (*i. e.* from Annapolis to New York) you should fall in with the enemy's vessel, you will be guided in your proceeding by your own judgment, bearing in mind, however, that you are not voluntarily to encounter a force superior to your own." One can imagine the smile of contempt that curled the lip of the stern commander of the Constitution, when he received this pitiful order, so well adapted in its tone and language to make timorous officers, and hence ensure defeat. The Secretary had witnessed the confidence and daring spirit of Bainbridge and Stewart, and he was afraid such men would fight, when prudence would dictate flight. But he might have known that when officers like them were once fairly out to sea, on the decks of their own ships, beneath their own flag streaming aloft, they would pay no more attention to orders like the above, than to the sighing of the wind through their cordage.

On the 17th the Constitution was out of sight of land, though still within soundings and going under easy canvas, when at two o'clock she discovered four sail in the north. At four she discovered another a little to the eastward of the first. Towards evening, the wind blowing light from the southward, the Constitution beat to quarters and cleared for action. At ten o'clock she showed the private signal, which remained unanswered; and concluding she had fallen in with a squadron of the enemy, made all sail. Just before daybreak the Guerriere, one of the fleet, sent up a rocket and fired two guns. As the light broadened over the deep, Capt. Hull, who was anxiously on the look-out, discerned seven ships closing steadily upon him. This was the squadron of Commodore Broke, consisting of the Africa 64, Guerriere 38, Shannon 38, Belvidera 36, Eolus 32, together with the captured Nautilus and a schooner. As the sun rose over the ocean and lifted the mist that lay on the water, Capt. Hull had a full view of his position. Two frigates were beating down from the north upon him, while the Africa, two frigates, a brig and schooner were following in his wake, and all with English colors flying. To increase the painful uncertainty that now hung over the fate of his vessel, the breeze which had been light all night entirely died away, and the sails flapped idly against the masts. Hull, however, resolved that his ship should not be lost, if human energy and skill could save her, and immediately sent all his boats forward to tow. But he soon found that the enemy, by putting the boats of two ships on one, were slowly closing on him. He then took all the rope he could spare and run a kedge out nearly a half a mile ahead and dropped it. The crew seized the rope, and springing to it with a will, soon made the ship walk through the water. As she came up with the kedge she overran it, and while still moving on under the headway she had obtained, another kedge was carried ahead, and the noble vessel glided away, as if by magic, from her pursuers. It was not long, however, before the enemy discovered the trick the Yankee was playing, and began also to kedge. A little air was felt at half-past seven, but at eight it fell calm again, when the vessels resorted to boats, long sweeps and the kedge. The Shannon, which was astern, having, at last, got most of the boats of the squadron on her, slowly gained on the Constitution, while the Guerriere was walking down on her larboard quarter. The prospect for the American was now gloomy enough—there was scarcely a ray of hope. The unruffled sea seemed to heave in mockery of the anguish of those whose every thought was a prayer for wind, and slowly, like the unpitying approach of death, the hostile fleet kept closing on that helpless ship. One more hour like the last, would bring her under the guns of two frigates. Still, there was not a craven heart within those ribs of oak. Each man, as he looked sternly on his comrade, read in his face the determination to fight while a gun was left. Hull, chafing at his desperate position, resolved to close fiercely with the first vessel that approached; and judging from his after conduct, he would have made wild work with his antagonist. The men in the boats strove nobly, but it was a contest of mere physical strength, in which there was not the least hope of success. But adverse fate seemed at last to relent, and a light breeze sprung up from the southward. Hull no sooner saw it approaching on the water than he ordered the sails to be trimmed, and the moment the vessel felt its gentle pressure, she was brought up into the wind—the boats fell alongside and were hoisted to their davits or swung, just clear of the water—the men working coolly at their posts, although the shot of the Guerriere were dashing the sea into spray around them.

But in an hour it again fell nearly calm, and the boats were once more put on. The crew strove to make up by effort what they lacked in force, but the Shannon steadily gained. With the exception of a little rest obtained when slight breezes struck the vessel, the men were kept incessantly at work all the day. At two o'clock, the Belvidera opened with her bow guns, to which the Constitution responded with her stern chasers. In half-an-hour, however, Captain Hull ordered the firing to cease, and the men were again ordered to the boats, and rowing and kedging were kept up till eleven at night. They were fast becoming exhausted under the tremendous strain that had been put upon them since early in the morning, when to their great relief a breeze sprung up, and every sail that would draw was set. It lasted, however, only for an hour. At midnight, it was calm again; but the crews of both vessels had been overtasked, and no boats were sent out. In the morning, Captain Hull discovered that some of the vessels had gained on him, and four frigates were within long gun shot. It was now apparent that the least unfavorable change would settle the fate of the Constitution. The officers had snatched a little sleep at their posts, and were ready to defend their flag to the last. It was a lovely summer morning, and as the orb of day slowly rolled into view, it lighted up a scene of thrilling interest and transcendant beauty. The ocean lay slumbering in majestic repose, reflecting from its unruffled bosom the cloudless sky. A light breeze was fanning the sea, and every stitch of canvas that would draw was set. All the vessels had now got on the same tack, the gallant American leading the van. "The five frigates were clouds of canvas from their trucks to the water," as slowly and proudly they swept along the deep. The Constitution looked back on her eager pursuers, each eye on her decks watching the relative speed of the vessels, and each heart praying for wind. But, at noon, it again fell calm, when the Belvidera was found to be two miles and a half astern, the next frigate three miles distant, and the others still farther to leeward. This was a great gain on the position of the day before, and with a steady breeze, there would be no doubt of the issue. About half-past twelve, a light wind sprung up, and although it kept unsteady during the afternoon, it was evident the Constitution was walking away from her pursuers. Every sail was tended, and every rope watched with scrupulous care, that showed the American frigate to be a thorough man of war. The day which had been so beautiful threatened a stormy close, for a heavy squall was rising out of the southern sea. Captain Hull narrowly watched its approach, with every man at the clew lines. Just before it struck the ship, the order was given, and the vessel was stripped of her canvas as by a single blow. The British vessels began to take in sail without waiting for the near approach of the squall. As soon as the strength of the gale had been felt, the Constitution was again put under a press of canvas, and bowing gracefully, as if in gratitude to the rising sea, she flung the foam joyfully from her bows, and was soon rushing through the water at the rate of eleven knots an hour. When the rain cloud had passed, and an observation of the enemy's ships could be obtained, they were far astern, and with the last rays of the setting sun, the Constitution bade farewell to her pursuers. It was gallantly and gloriously done.

Cool and steady action on the part of the commander, met by corresponding conduct on the part of the officers and crew, thorough seamanship exhibited in every manœuvre she attempted, saved the noble vessel from capture. What a contrast does this conduct of the nephew, thus surrounded by a superior force and beset with apparently insurmountable difficulties, present to that of the uncle at Detroit. In the one, desperate circumstances produced great effort, in the other none at all. One with no thought of surrendering, while a spar was left standing, the other meekly laying down his arms without firing a shot. Shortly after, the Constitution arrived in Boston.

Previous to the sailing of this vessel from Annapolis, the Essex, under Capt. Porter, having been got ready for sea at New York, started on a cruise to the southward. Making several prizes of merchantmen, she again stood to the southward, when she fell in with a fleet of British transports, convoyed by a frigate and bomb vessel. She endeavored to get along side of the former, but one of the transports which Capt. Porter had spoken, threatening to make signal to the other vessels, he was obliged to take possession of her. To accomplish this, as the prize had a hundred and fifty soldiers aboard, consumed so much time that the rest of the fleet escaped.

The Essex having disguised herself as a merchant man continued her cruise, and in a few days discovered a strange sail, which, deceived by her appearance, boldly attacked her. The latter having got the enemy in close range, knocked out her ports, which had been closed, and poured in her broadsides. This sudden metamorphosis and tremendous firing completely stunned the stranger, and he immediately hauled down his colors. The prize proved to be the ship Alert, mounting twenty-two eighteen-pound carronades. This was the first British war vessel taken by an American cruiser.

Captain Porter having converted the Alert into a cartel, sent her with the prisoners into St. John's. The English Admiral, at Newfoundland, remonstrated against this course, as it deprived the British of the chances of recapture before entering an American port. He however could not well refuse to carry out the arrangements which the Captain of the Alert had entered into.

The Essex, after an unsuccessful cruise and some narrow escapes, finally reached the Delaware, where she replenished her stores.

THE CONSTITUTION AND GUERRIERE.

On the 28th of July an order was sent from the Secretary of the Navy, to Capt. Hull, at Boston, to deliver up the Constitution to Commodore Bainbridge, and take charge of the frigate Constellation. Aug. 2. But fortunately for him and the navy, just before this order reached him he had again set sail, and was out on the deep, where the anxieties of the department could not disturb him. Cruising eastward along the coast, he captured ten small prizes near the mouth of the St. Lawrence and burned them. In the middle of the month he recaptured an American merchantman and sent her in, and then stood to the southward. On the 19th he made a strange sail, one of the vessels that a few weeks before had pressed him so hard in the chase. When the Constitution had run down to within three miles of him, the Englishman laid his maintop sail aback, and hung out three flags, to show his willingness to engage. Capt. Dacres, the commander, surprised at the daring manner in which the stranger came down, turned to the captain of an American merchantman whom he had captured a few days before, and asked him what vessel he took that to be. The latter replied, as he handed back the glass to Dacres, that he thought from her sails she was an American. It cannot be possible, said Dacres, or he would not stand on so boldly. It was soon evident, whoever the stranger might be, he was bent on mischief. Hull prepared his vessel for action deliberately, and after putting her under close fighting canvas and sending down her royal yards, ordered the drums to beat to quarters. It was now five o'clock, and as the Constitution bore steadily down towards her antagonist, the crew gave three cheers. The English vessel was well known, for she had at one of her mast-heads a flag proudly flying, with the "Guerriere" written in large characters upon it. When the

Constitution arrived within long gun shot, the Guerriere opened her fire, now waring to bring her broadside to bear, and again to prevent being raked by the American, which slowly but steadily approached. The Englishman kept up a steady fire, for nearly an hour, to which the Constitution replied with only an occasional gun. The crew at length became excited under this inaction. The officer below had twice come on deck to report that men had been killed standing idly at their guns, and begged permission to fire; but Hull still continued to receive the enemy's broadsides in silence. The Guerriere failing to cripple the Constitution, filled and moved off with the wind free, showing that she was willing to receive her and finish the conflict in a yard-arm to yard-arm combat. The Constitution then drew slowly ahead, and the moment her bows began to lap the quarters of the Guerriere, her forward guns opened, and in a few minutes after, the welcome orders were received to pour in broadside after broadside as rapidly as possible. When she was fairly abeam, the broadsides were fired with a rapidity and power that astounded the enemy. As the old ship forged slowly ahead with her greater way, she seemed moving in flame. The mizen mast of the enemy soon fell with a crash, while her hull was riddled with shot, and her decks slippery with gore. The carnage was so awful that the blood from the wounded and mangled victims, as they were hurried into the cockpit, poured over the ladder as if it had been dashed from a bucket. As Hull passed his antagonist he wheeled short round her bows to prevent a raking fire. But in doing this he came dead into the wind—his sails were taken aback—the vessel stopped—then getting sternway, the Guerriere came up, her bows striking the former abeam. While in this position, the forward guns of the enemy exploded almost against the sides of the Constitution, setting the cabin on fire. This would have proved a serious event but for the presence of mind of the fourth lieutenant, Beekman Verplanck Hoffman, who extinguished it. As soon as the vessels got foul both crews prepared to board. The first lieutenant, Morris,[29] in the midst of a terrific fire of musketry, attempted to lash the ships together, which were thumping and grinding against each other with the heavy sea, but fell, shot through the body. M. Alwyn, the master, and Lieut. Bush of the marines, mounting the taffrail to leap on the enemy's decks were both shot down, the latter killed instantly with a bullet through the head. Finding it impossible to board under such a tremendous fire, the sails of the Constitution were filled, when the vessels slowly and reluctantly parted. As the Constitution rolled away on the heavy swell, the foremast of the Guerriere fell back against the mainmast, carrying that down in its descent, leaving the frigate a helpless wreck, "wallowing in the trough of the sea." Hull seeing that his enemy was now completely in his power, ran off a little way to secure his own masts and repair his rigging which was badly cut up. In a short time he returned, and taking up a position where he could rake the wreck of the Guerriere at every discharge, prepared to finish her. Capt. Dacres had fought his ship well, and when every spar in her was down, gallantly nailed the jack to the stump of the mizen-mast. But further resistance was impossible, and to have gone down with his flag flying, as one of the English journals declared he ought to have done, would have been a foolish and criminal act. A few more broadsides would have carried the brave crew to the bottom, and to allow his vessel to roll idly in the trough of the sea, a mere target for the guns of the American, would neither have added to his fame nor lessened the moral effect of the defeat. He therefore reluctantly struck her flag, and Lieutenant Read was sent on board to take possession.

As he stepped over the vessel's side, a disgusting scene presented itself. When the vessel struck, Captain Dacres told the crew they might go and get some refreshments, which was another mode of giving them liberty to drink. In a short time, all the petty officers and their wives, together with the sailors, were wallowing together in filth. The vessel being dismasted lay in the trough of the sea, and as she rolled backwards and forwards the water came in the ports on one side, and poured out of those on the other, mingling in a loathsome mass the motley multitude.

This vessel, as well as all the English ships, presented another striking contrast to the American. Impressment was so abhorred, that British officers were afraid of being shot down by their topmen during an engagement; and hence dared not wear their uniforms, while ours went into action with their epaulettes on, knowing that it added to their security, for every sailor would fight for his commander as he would for a comrade.

Captain Hull kept hovering around his prize during the night; and at two o'clock, "sail ho," was sent aft by the watch, when the Constitution immediately beat to quarters. The weary sailors tumbled up cheerfully at the summons, the vessel was cleared for action, and there is no doubt that if another Guerriere had closed with the Constitution, she would have been roughly handled, crippled as the latter was from her recent conflict.

After deliberating for an hour, the stranger stood off. In the morning, the Guerriere was reported to have four feet water in the hold, and was so cut up that it would be difficult to keep her afloat. The prisoners were, therefore, all removed, and the vessel set on fire. The flames leaped up the broken masts, ran along the bulwarks, and wrapped the noble wreck in a sheet of fire. As the guns became heated, they went off one after another, firing their last salute to the dying ship. At length, the fire reached the magazine, when she blew up with a tremendous explosion. A huge column of smoke arose and stood for a long time, as if petrified in the calm atmosphere, and then slowly crumbled to pieces, revealing only a few shattered planks to tell where that proud vessel had sunk. The first English frigate that ever struck its flag to an American ship of war, had gone down to the bottom of the ocean, a gloomy omen of England's future. The sea never rolled over a vessel whose fate so startled the world. It disappeared for ever, but it left its outline on the deep, never to be effaced till England and America are no more.

The loss of the Constitution was seven killed and seven wounded, while that of Guerriere was fifteen killed and sixty-four wounded, a disparity that shows with how much more precision the American had fired. It is impossible, at this period, to give an adequate idea of the excitement this victory produced. In the first place, it was fought three days after the surrender of General Hull, the uncle of the gallant captain. The mortifying, stunning news of the disaster of the North-western army met on the sea-board, the thundering shout that went up from a people delirious with delight over this naval victory. From one direction the name of Hull came loaded with execrations—from the other overwhelmed with blessings. But not only was the joy greater, arriving as the news did on the top of a disaster, but it took the nation by surprise. An American frigate had fearlessly stood up in single combat on the deep with her proud foe, and giving gun for gun, torn the crown from the "mistress of the sea." The fact that the Constitution had four guns more and a larger crew, could not prevent it from being practically an even-handed fight. The disparity of the crews was of no consequence, for it was an affair of broadsides, while the vast difference in the execution done, proved that had the relative weight of metal and the muster roll been reversed, the issue would have been the same.

Captain Hull on his return to Boston, surrendered the frigate to Bainbridge, who soon after hoisted his broad pennant on board, but did not put to sea till the 26th of October.

Oct. 12.

In the mean time, Commodore Rodgers having refitted again, started on a cruise, having the United States, forty-four, commanded by Commodore Decatur, and the Argus, sixteen, Captain Sinclair, in company. Commodore Rodgers having captured on the 17th, the British packet Swallow, with two hundred thousand dollars on board, continued his cruise to the eastward. Just before, in a heavy gale, the United States and Argus had parted company with him. The former directed her course so as to fall in the track of East Indiamen, but on Sunday morning, the 25th, she saw a large sail to the southward, which proved to be the English frigate Macedonian. After some manœuvering, the two vessels approached within a mile of each other, when the firing commenced. After the United States delivered her second broadside, she ceased manœuvering and took the same tack with her enemy, both steering free. The Macedonian, however, was to windward, and hence could make it a yard-arm-to-yard-arm combat whenever she chose. But she preferred a longer range, and the two vessels swept on, delivering their rapid broadsides within musket shot. The distance at which they kept, together with the heavy sea that was rolling, rendered the aim imperfect and protracted the conflict, so that it continued for an hour after the guns of both vessels began to bear, before any material effect was visible. The broadsides of the United States were delivered so rapidly that she was constantly enveloped in flame and smoke, and the crew of the Macedonian several times thought her on fire and cheered. Decatur, with his fine face lit up with that chivalric valor that was wont to illumine it in battle, moved amid his men with words of encouragement and praise. As the mizen-mast of the enemy went by the board, hearing a sailor say to his comrade, "Jack, we've made a brig of her;" he replied, "Take good aim, Jack, and she will soon be a sloop." Turning to a captain of the gun, he said, "Aim at the yellow streak, her spars and rigging are going fast enough, she must have a little more hulling." Soon after her fore and main top mast went over. At length, the mizen mast was cut in two by a shot, about ten feet from the deck, while with every roll of the ship the weakened foremast threatened to swell the wreck. The Englishman, perceiving that his vessel would soon become unmanageable, made an effort to close, for the purpose of boarding. But Decatur saw his advantage too plainly, to risk it in a desperate encounter, and putting on sail shot ahead. The enemy mistaking this movement for a rapid flight gave three cheers, and all the flags having come down with the spars, set a union Jack in the main rigging in token of triumph. But when the United States was seen to tack and approach, as if about to close, it was hauled down.

On this same Sabbath, while the cheers of the United States' crew rang over the deep, Napoleon was traversing in gloom the fatal, bloody field of Malo-Jaraslowitz, and with two kings and three marshals by his side, was deliberating on that retreat which was to change the face of the world.

The superiority of American gunnery, in this combat, was placed beyond dispute. It was a simple cannonade on a very rough sea. Yet the United States had but five killed and seven wounded, while out of three hundred men, the Macedonian had one hundred and four killed or wounded. So, also, the former lost her top-gallant masts, and had been hulled but a few times. It is true her rigging suffered severely, but the English frigate had almost every spar in her more or less shattered, while her hull was pierced with a hundred shot. In this, as in the former engagement between the Constitution and Guerriere, the United States carried *four more guns* than her antagonist. She was a heavier ship, but therefore a better mark, and yet the enemy's shot rarely hulled her. The decks of the latter presented a revolting spectacle. "Fragments of the dead were distributed in every direction—the decks covered with blood—one continued agonizing yell of the unhappy wounded,"[30] filled the ship.

Decatur having arrived with his prize in New London, dispatched Lieut. Hamilton, son of the Secretary of the Navy, to Washington, with an account of the victory, and the captured colors Dec. 8. Hurrying on, greeted with the acclamations of the multitude as he passed, he arrived at the capital in the evening. On that very night a ball had been given to the officers of the navy, at which Hull and Stewart and the Secretary of the Navy were present. Young Hamilton walked into the gay assemblage and delivered his message to his overjoyed father, who immediately announced it to the company. Shout after shout shook the hall—all crowded around the young lieutenant, eager to hear the incidents of the action. As he narrated how they fought and how they conquered, tears of joy and gratitude streamed from the eyes of his mother, who stood fondly gazing on him. Captured colors of the enemy decorated the room, and a delegation was sent to bring those of the Macedonia and add them to the number. Captains Stewart and Hull bore them in, and presented them, amid the loud acclamations of the throng, to the wife of the President— the band struck up an inspiring air, and intense excitement and exultation filled every bosom.

The Argus met with but little success. The seamanship of her officers was, however, tested during the cruise. She was chased three days and nights by an English squadron, and yet not only managed to escape, but having come upon an English merchantman during the chase, actually captured it in sight of the fleet, though by the time she had manned it the enemy had opened on her with his guns. Having made five prizes in all, she returned to port.

In the meanwhile the Wasp, Captain Jones, which was returning from Europe with dispatches, the time war was declared, had refitted and started on a cruise. Sailing northward to the latitude of Boston, she made a single capture and returned to the Delaware. On the 13th of October, the very day of Van Rensalaer's defeat at Queenstown, she again put to sea, and after being four days out, on the night of the 17th, made five strange sail. Not knowing their strength or character, Captain Jones deemed it prudent to keep off till daylight, when he would have a better opportunity for observing them. In the morning he discovered there were six ships under the convoy of a brig of war. Two of them were armed, but the brig deeming herself alone a match for the American, sent them all forward, and waited for the latter to approach. The sea was rough from the effects of a storm that had swept those latitudes the day before, in which Captain Jones had lost his jib boom and two of his crew. There was no manœuvering attempted in this tumultuous sea, and the Wasp surged on in dead silence, the only sound heard on her decks being the roar of the waves as they burst along her sides. She closed on her antagonist with a deadliness of purpose seldom witnessed in naval combats. She never delivered her broadside till within a hundred and eighty feet, and then with fearful effect. At first this heroism seemed doomed to a poor reward. The fire of the Frolic was incessant. Seldom had an Englishman been known to deliver such rapid broadsides. In five minutes the main topmast of the Wasp fell amid the rigging—in two minutes more the gaft and mizen top-gallant mast followed. Thus, in eight minutes from the time the vessels closed, the Wasp was so disabled that her destruction seemed almost certain. But while cut up herself so terribly aloft, she had struck with every broadside the heart of her antagonist. As she rolled on the heavy seas her guns were frequently under water, and the sailors staggered around their pieces like drunken men. Delivering her broadsides as she sunk, she hulled her antagonist at every discharge; while the latter, firing as she rose, made sad work with the rigging of the former. Jones seeing his spars and rigging so dreadfully cut up, was afraid that his vessel would become unmanageable, and therefore determined to run foul of his adversary and board. But when the vessels closed, the bows of the Frolic struck abaft the midships of the Wasp, which so swung the head of the latter around that she was enabled to throw a raking fire into the former. The order, therefore, to board was countermanded, and a fresh broadside directed to sweep her decks. In loading some of the guns, the rammers struck against the bows of the Frolic. The shot went crashing the whole length of the ship, and the crew, excited by this hand-to-hand fight, could no longer be restrained from boarding. Mr. Biddle, the first lieutenant, leaped into the rigging, followed by Lieut. Rodgers and other men, and soon gained the decks of the Frolic—but, in looking round for the enemy, they saw but three or four officers standing aft, and bleeding. None but the dead and wounded cumbered the decks. Not one was left to haul down the colors. The officers threw down their swords in token of submission, and Lieutenant Biddle, springing into the rigging, lowered the English flag with his own hand. The carnage was horrible for so small a vessel—nearly a hundred of the officers and crew being killed or wounded. The decks were literally covered with the mangled forms of men and officers. The corpses presented a ghastly appearance as they rolled from side to side with the tossing vessel, while shivered spars and masts covered the wreck, and still hanging by the ropes, swung with every lurch against its shattered hull. There can scarcely be a more mournful sight than a noble ship dismantled in mid ocean, her decks crimsoned with blood, while on every side, amid broken and rent timbers, her gallant crew dismembered and torn, are stretched in death.

The Frolic was a brig carrying in all twenty-two guns, while the Wasp, though a ship, carried but eighteen, thus making a difference in favor of the former of four guns.

The Wasp had, therefore, captured a superior force in single combat. But in this, as in the two former engagements I have detailed, the same extraordinary disparity in the respective losses of the two vessels was exhibited. While near a hundred were killed or wounded in the Frolic, there were only five killed and as many wounded in the American ship. It is not a matter of surprise that the belief became prevalent in England that our vessels were filled with Kentucky riflemen. These men had become famous for their accuracy of aim; and it was supposed we had introduced them into our navy. In no other way could they account for the awful carnage that followed every single combat of ship with ship. In all her naval history, such destructive work had never been witnessed in so short a space of time. The moment an American vessel opened her broadsides, death began to traverse the decks of her antagonist with such a rapid footstep, that men were appalled.

This was doubtless owing in a great measure to our guns being sighted, an improvement introduced by American officers, rendering the aim infinitely more accurate.

The Wasp in this engagement had been fought nobly, but her victory proved worse than a barren one to her gallant commander and crew. Scarcely had the English Jack been lowered to the Stars and Stripes, before the latter were struck to the English flag. The Poictiers an English seventy-four, soon hoved in sight and bore down on the two vessels lying to and clearing away the wreck. The Wasp endeavored to make use of her heels, but on turning out her sails, they were found completely riddled. Flight was out of the question, and both vessels surrendered. They were taken into Bermuda, where the Americans were parolled and allowed to return home.

On the 26th of October, Commodore Bainbridge left Boston, accompanied by the Hornet, with the intention of joining Captain Porter, in the Essex, and passing into the Pacific Ocean, where the British fisheries and commerce could be easily struck. Captain Lawrence, cruising southward, at length arrived at St. Salvador, where he found a British sloop of war, the Bonne Citoyenne. The latter being in a neutral port, was safe. She was superior to the Hornet, but Lawrence, determined to provoke her out to single combat, sent a challenge to her commander—Commodore Bainbridge, in the meanwhile, promising to keep out of the way. The challenge was declined, and if the fact that she had a large amount of specie on board, had been given as the reason of her refusal, the conduct of Captain Green, the commander would have been unobjectionable. But to intimate, as he did, that the frigate would interfere, after Bainbridge had pledged his word, and the American Consul offered guarantees, evinced a contemptible spirit, almost as degrading as cowardice.

Captain Lawrence determined, however, not to let the vessel go to sea without him, and he therefore blockaded the port.

The Constitution left the Hornet blockading the Bonne Citoyenne, and steered south, keeping along the coast, and on the 29th discovered two sail between her and the land, which was about thirty miles distant and in full view. One of the vessels being small, kept standing in towards the shore, while the larger one, a British frigate, the Java, of thirty-eight guns, directed her course towards the American. Bainbridge, wishing to get farther from the land, tacked and steered to the south-east for two hours, the Englishman following after. About half-past one, finding himself clear of the land, Bainbridge tacked and stood towards the stranger. At 2 o'clock the two vessels were only half a mile apart, the Englishman to windward, and showing no colors. The order to fire a shot to make the latter set his ensign being misunderstood, a whole broadside was delivered, and the battle commenced. A tremendous cannonade followed. The wind was light and the sea smooth, so that full scope was given for manœuvering and accurate aim. Bainbridge, who at the commencement of the war, had urged the President to send the national ships to sea, and was now in his first fight, felt not only the promise he had given the Secretary of the Navy weighing on him, but his responsibility as commander of the Constitution, fresh with laurels from the capture of the Guerriere.

He managed his ship with consummate skill, and not only foiled every attempt of the enemy to get a raking position, but soon obtained one himself, and delivered a broadside that swept the decks of the Java. The vessels had at length approached within pistol shot, and the effect of the rapid broadsides of the Constitution delivered so closely and on that smooth sea, could be heard in the rending timbers of the enemy's ship. Bainbridge, in the mean time, received a musket ball in his thigh. He however still walked the quarter deck, watching every movement of his antagonist, and the effect of every broadside. In a few minutes later, a cannon shot plunged into the wheel, shattering it in fragments, and sending a copper bolt into his leg. Crippled and bleeding— refusing even to sit down—he continued to limp over the quarter deck, watching the progress of the combat, and directing the movements, apparently unconscious of pain. The destruction of the wheel he felt to be a more serious affair than his wounded leg, for he was no longer able to give verbal orders to the helmsman. The tiller was of course worked below the second deck by ropes and tackles, where the helmsman unable to see the sails and steer accordingly, depended entirely on orders transmitted to him. This would have been of minor consequence in a steady yard to yard-arm fight, but in the constant manœuvering of the two vessels, either to get or prevent a raking fire, it was a serious inconvenience. Still, the Constitution managed to secure this advantage in almost every evolution. The tremendous fire she kept up, so staggered the Englishman, that he resolved to run his vessel aboard at all hazards. He came stern on, and his bowsprit passed through the mizen rigging of the Constitution. The next moment, however, it was cut in two by a cannon shot, when the two vessels parted. At length the Constitution, after wearing twice to get the right position, threw herself fairly alongside her antagonist, and they moved on together, yard-arm and yard-arm, pouring in incessant broadsides. In a few minutes the mizen mast of the Java went over, and as her foremast had gone long before, nothing but the main mast was left standing. Her fire had now ceased, and Bainbridge, under the impression she had struck, set his sails and passed off to windward to repair damages, make his masts secure, and be ready for any new combat that might be forced on him, in a sea filled with the enemy's cruisers. After an hour spent in overhauling his ship he returned, and finding the enemy's ensign still flying, he passed directly across her bows, and was about to deliver a raking fire, when she struck. The combat lasted for more than two hours, and from the number of evolutions on both sides, was brought to a termination several miles from where it commenced. The Java was completely dismantled. Her mizen mast had been cut away close to the deck—the mainmast fell soon after the firing ceased, while nothing but a stump of the foremast, some twenty or thirty feet long, was left standing. Her bowsprit, too, was gone; in fact, every spar had been shot out of her. The Constitution, on the contrary, at the close of the long severe conflict, had every spar standing. An eighteen pound shot had made an ugly hole through her mizen mast, and another had cut a deep gash in the foremast, and a quantity of ropes swinging loose in the wind, showed that she had been in the midst of cannon balls, but she came out of the conflict as she went in, every spar erect and her royal yards across. The outward appearance of the ships did not present a more striking contrast than their decks. Those of the Java were rent and torn, and strewed with the dead. A hundred and sixty-one had been killed or wounded, while nine killed and twenty-five wounded covered the entire loss of the Constitution.

Among the prisoners taken was Lieutenant-General Hislop, with his staff, on his way to Bombay, as Governor. They were all treated with that kindness and generosity which ever characterizes a truly brave man—conduct which the English, in the very very few opportunities offered them, did not generally reciprocate.

The severe wounds of Commodore Bainbridge could not force him to leave the deck, even after the action was over. In his anxiety for his ship and the prize, and care of the wounded and prisoners, he forgot his sufferings, keeping his feet till eleven o'clock at night. These eight hours of constant exertion increased the inflammation to an alarming degree, and well nigh cost him his life.

It was a proud day for him; he had redeemed his pledge to the government, and added another wreath to the laurels that already crowned the American navy.

The Constitution lay by the Java for two or three days, in order that the wounded might be removed with care and safety. When this was accomplished, the latter vessel being so completely riddled that it would be impossible to get her into an American port, was blown up. Our gunners fired with too accurate an aim; they so destroyed the vessels of the enemy, that they could not be secured as prizes.

The Constitution was carried into St. Salvador, where her arrival did not improve the prospect before the Bonne Citoyenne, should she venture to break a lance with the Hornet. She was apparently preparing to go to sea that night, with the intention of avoiding her antagonist if convenient, and fighting her if necessary. The capture of the Java, however, produced a change in her plans, and she took eighteen days longer to reflect on the subject.

Commodore Bainbridge dismissed the private passengers found on board the Java, without regarding them as prisoners of war, while all the others were released on their parol. Governor Hislop presented him with an elegant sword, as a token of his esteem and an acknowledgment of the kindness with which he had been treated. Captain Lambert, commander of the Java, was mortally wounded, and just before his removal to the shore, Bainbridge, leaning on the shoulders of two officers, hobbled into his room to restore to him his sword. It was a touching spectacle, the wounded victor presenting to his dying antagonist, the sword he never would wield again, accompanying it with expressions of esteem and kindly hopes. Captain Lambert received it with emotion, and returned his thanks. Two days after, it was laid across his breast. It was not dishonored in its owner's hand, for his ship had been gallantly fought to the last, and surrendered only when not a sail could be set.

Bainbridge, at this time, was not quite forty years of age. Six feet in height, of commanding person, and an eye that burned like fire in battle, he moved over his quarter deck the impersonation of a hero. His noble conduct to the prisoners, won him the praise even of his enemies. An English Admiral, when told of it, shook his head, remarking, that it had an ominous look when a young commander, in a navy unaccustomed to victory, could treat his foes so like an old Spanish cavalier.[31]

The Constitution, in this engagement, carried fifty-four guns, and the Java forty-nine. On this difference of five guns, the English attempted to erect a prop to support their naval pride. The effort to prove a superiority in weight of metal and number of men, in every victorious American vessel, and the changes rung on the difference of a single gun, exhibited a sensitiveness that enhanced instead of lessened the defeats. If a battle is never to be considered equal, until both ships have the same tonnage to a pound, the same number of cannon, and the muster roll be equal to a man, it is to be feared there never will be one fought. Not only did the English allege that the Constitution was greatly superior in weight of metal, but declared that her success was owing, in a large measure, to her musketry; and yet the Java had not a spar standing at the close of the battle. Muskets do not dismantle vessels, and leave them mere hulks at the mercy of their foe.[32] The English court of enquiry appointed to investigate the subject, asked the boatswain, "if they had suffered much on the forecastle from musketry." "Yes," he very frankly replied, *"and, likewise, from round and grape."* The latter was, no doubt, true, and very probably the former.

Bainbridge returned to Boston, and resigned the command of the Constitution, which stood greatly in need of repairs.

Lawrence continued, as before stated, to blockade the Bonne Citoyenne, until the latter part of January, when a British seventy-four heaving in sight, he was compelled to run in beside his adversary. The tables were now turned upon him, and he had the prospect of seeing the man-of-war playing the part of keeper at the mouth of the port, while his own prisoner making use of this protection could pass out, and continue his voyage. This was a predicament he did not relish, and taking advantage of the night, quietly slipped out to sea, and continued his cruise. He made a few prizes, and among them a brig of ten guns, with $12,500 in specie on board. Arriving, at length, at the mouth of the Demarara river, he discovered an English brig of war, and gave chase to her. The latter running in shore, led him into such shoal water, that he deemed it prudent to haul off. He, however, did not abandon the hope of forcing the ship into an engagement, and while beating down on a different tack to get within reach of her, he discovered another brig apparently seeking to close. He immediately put the head of his vessel toward that of the stranger. Both were close on the wind, and as they continued to approach, it was evident from their course they must pass each other with their yard-arms almost touching. It was now nearly half-past five, and the lurid rays of the sun, just sinking behind the hills of the main land, flooded the two vessels as they silently closed. The moment they began to draw abeam, so that the guns bore, the firing began. When fairly abreast, the vessels were not more than fifty feet apart. The words of command and the shrieks of the wounded could be distinctly heard in either vessel, as broadside crashed against broadside. It was a stern meeting and parting. As soon as the guns ceased to bear, the Englishman wore, in order to get a raking fire on the Hornet. The latter, however, was too quick for him; he was first about, and coming down on his quarter in "a perfect blaze of fire," poured in his broadsides with such close range and destructive effect, that in ten minutes more the enemy not only struck, but hoisted a signal of distress. Mr. Shubrick being sent on board to take possession, reported that the vessel was the sloop of war, Peacock, and that she had six feet water in the hold. Every effort was made to save the prize, and to get out the wounded. Both vessels were anchored; the pumps were rigged on board the Peacock, and bailing was resorted to. The vessel, however, continued to sink, and at last went down, carrying nine of her own crew and three of the Hornet with her. Two American officers, and many more seamen came near losing their lives, in their gallant effort to save the prisoners.

The foremast of the ill-fated vessel protruded from the sea, where she went down, remaining for some time to mark the place of the battle and the victory.

The superiority of American gunnery and American seamanship was again established beyond dispute. The Hornet was slightly superior in weight of metal,[33] but she not only out-maneuvered her antagonist, but surpassed her incomparably in the effective use of her guns. The former had but one man killed and two wounded, while of the latter there were thirty-eight killed and wounded, and among them the commander. The Hornet had but a single shot in her hull, while the Peacock was so riddled that she sunk in a few minutes after the action.

The thrill of exultation that passed over the land at the announcement of the first naval victory, was alloyed by the reflection that it was but an isolated instance, and hence could hardly justify a belief in our naval superiority. But as frigate after frigate and ship after ship struck, all doubt vanished, and the nation was intoxicated with delight. The successive disasters that befel our land forces along the Canada line, could not check the outburst of enthusiasm on every side. As the news of one victory succeeding another was borne along the great channels of communication, long shouts of triumph rolled after it, and the navy from being unknown and uncared for, rose at once to be the bulwark and pride of the nation. All faces were turned to the ocean to catch the first echo of those resistless broadsides, that proudly asserted and made good the claim to "free trade and sailor's rights." Where we had been insulted and wronged the most, there we were chastising the offender with blows that astounded the world. If the American Government had been amazed at the failure of its deep laid schemes against Canada, it was no less so at the unexpected triumphs at sea. Saved from the deepest condemnation by the navy, which it had neglected—forced to fall back on its very blunders for encouragement, it could say with Hamlet—

"Let us know,
Our indiscretion sometimes serves us well
When our deep plots do pall."

But our astonishment at these successive and brilliant victories could scarcely exceed that of the old world. The British navy had been so long accustomed to victory, that a single-handed contest of an English frigate with that of any other nation, had ceased to be a matter of solicitude to her. The maritime nations of Europe had, one after another, yielded to her sway, till her flag in every sea on the globe extorted the respect and fear which the declaration, "I am a Roman citizen" did, in the proudest days of the Empire. Her invincibility on the ocean was a foregone conclusion. The victories of Napoleon stopped with the shore—even his "star" paled on the deep. His extraordinary efforts and energies could not tear from the British navy the proud title it had worn so long. His fleets, one after another, had gone down before the might of British broadsides, and the sublime sea fights of Aboukir and Trafalgar, were only corroborations of what had long been established. If this was the common feeling of the Continent it is no wonder that "the English were stunned as by the shock of an earthquake."[34] The first victory surprised them, but did not disturb their confidence. They began to discuss the causes of the unlooked for event with becoming dignity, but before the argument was concluded, another and another defeat came like successive thunder claps, till discussion gave way to alarm. The thoughtful men of England were too wise to pretend that disasters occurring in such numbers and wonderful regularity, could be the result of accident, and feared they beheld the little black cloud which the prophet saw rising over the sea, portending an approaching storm. If, in so short a time, a maritime force of only a few frigates and sloops of war could strike such deadly blows and destroy the prestige of English invincibility, what could not be done when that navy should approximate her own in strength. Some of the leading journals indulged in foolish boasting and detraction of American valor, and held up to derision those who saw portents of evil in the recent defeats. But the Times spoke the sentiments of those whose opinions were of any weight. Said the latter: "We witnessed the gloom which the event (the capture of the Guerriere) cast over high and honorable minds. We participated in the vexation and regret, and it is the first time we ever heard that the striking of the flag on the high seas to any thing like an equal force, should be regarded by Englishmen with complacency or satisfaction." *** "It is not merely that an English frigate has been taken, after what we are free to confess, may be called a brave resistance, but that it has been taken by a *new enemy*, an enemy unaccustomed to such triumphs, and likely to be rendered insolent and confident by them." Another declared: "Our maritime superiority is in fact a part of the nation's right. It has been the right of the conqueror, since men associated together in civilization, to give laws to the conquered, and is Great Britain to be driven from the proud eminence which the blood and treasures of her sons have attained for her among nations, by a piece of striped bunting flying at the masthead of a few *fir-built frigates*, manned by a handful of bastards and outlaws?"

Such were the different sentiments entertained and expressed in England at the outset, but as the war progressed, anxiety and alarm took the place of boasting.

The war vessels at length grew timorous, and lost all their desire to meet an American ship of equal rank. It was declared that our frigates were built like seventy-fours, and therefore English frigates were justified in declining a battle when offered. The awful havoc made by our fire affected the seamen also, and whenever they saw the stars and stripes flaunting from the masthead of an approaching vessel, they felt that no ordinary battle was before them. English crews had never been so cut up since the existence of her navy. In the terrific battle of the Nile, Nelson lost less than three out of one hundred, and in his attack on Copenhagen, less than four out of every hundred. In Admiral Duncan's famous action off Camperdown, the proportion was about the same as that of the Nile. In 1793, the French navy was in its glory, and the victories obtained over its single ships by English vessels were considered unparalleled. Yet in fourteen single engagements, considered the most remarkable, and in which the ships, with one exception, ranged from thirty-six guns to fifty-two, the average of killed and wounded was only seventeen per ship, while in four encounters with American vessels, the Constitution, United States and Wasp, the average was a hundred and eleven to each vessel.

Jan. 2.

This success of the navy at length roused Congress to do something in its aid, and an act was passed on the 2d of January, authorizing the President to build four seventy-fours, and six ships of forty-four guns, thus increasing the force of the navy tenfold. On the 3d of March, by another act, it authorized the building of such vessels on the lakes as was deemed necessary to their protection. Sums were also voted to the officers and crews as prize money.

CHAPTER VII.

Harrison plans a winter campaign — Advance of the army — Battle and massacre at the River Raisin — Baseness of Proctor — Promoted by his Government — Tecumseh, his character and eloquence — He stirs up the Creeks to war — Massacre at Fort Mimms — Investment of Fort Meigs — Advance of Clay's reinforcements and their destruction — Successful sortie — Flight of the besiegers — Major Croghan's gallant defence of Fort Stephenson.

The army of General Harrison, which in October was slowly pushing its way towards Malden to Detroit, soon became involved in difficulties that compelled him to abandon his original design of an autumnal campaign. The lakes being in possession of the enemy, provisions, ammunition and cannon had to be transported by land, through swamps and along forest paths which could be traced only by blazed trees, and traversed only when the ground was frozen. He therefore occupied his time in sending out detachments and hurrying up his forces, in order to be ready to advance when the frozen ground, and especially the ice along the margin of the lake would facilitate the transportation of his guns and munitions of war.

General Tupper made two attempts, first from Fort Defiance and afterwards from Fort McArthur, to dislodge the Indians at the Rapids, but failed in both. Another detachment under Col. Campbell left Franklintown in December, to attack the Indian villages on the Missisineway, which were reached on the 18th, and four out of five destroyed.

At length the column which formed the right of this army, nominally of ten thousand men, having arrived at Sandusky with the park of artillery, Gen. Harrison gave the order for the whole to move forward. In three divisions, one from Sandusky, one from Fort McArthur, and the third under General Winchester, from Fort Defiance, were to advance to the Rapids of the Maumee, there take in their supply of ordnance and provisions, and proceed at once to invest Malden. Harrison, commanding the central division, started on the 31st of December. Gen. Winchester, who had moved six miles from Fort Defiance, to Camp No. 3, did not commence his march till the 8th of January. It was a cold bitter day and the snow lay over two feet deep in the forest when that doomed column, one thousand strong, set out for the Rapids, twenty-seven miles distant. The troops, most of whom were Kentuckians, were brave and hardy, and cheerfully harnessing themselves to sledges dragged their baggage through the deep snow. Gen. Winchester was ordered to fortify himself at the Rapids and wait the arrival of the other troops. But three days after he reached the place, while constructing huts to receive the supplies on the way, and sleds for their transportation to Malden, he received an urgent request from the inhabitants of Frenchtown, a small settlement nearly forty miles distant, on the River Raisin, to come to their rescue. Feeling, however, the importance of fulfilling his orders, he gave the messengers no encouragement. But another express on the next day, and a third the day after, telling him that the whole settlement was threatened with massacre by the Indians—that only a small force of the enemy held possession of the place, and by a prompt answer to their prayer the ruin of all would be prevented, he called a council of war. Col. Allen, and other gallant officers, pleaded the cause of the helpless settlers with all the eloquence of true sympathy. They declared that the chief object of the expedition was to protect the frontiers from the merciless Indians, and that brave men spurned danger when the prayers of women and children were sounding in their ears. Jan. 20. Such appeals prevailed over the cooler and safer arguments drawn from the necessity of not damaging the success of the whole campaign by perilling one of the wings of the advancing army, and a detachment of five hundred men, under Colonel Lewis was sent forward to Presque Isle, there to await the arrival of the main column. But this officer hearing at the latter place that an advance party of French and Indians were already in possession of Frenchtown, hurried forward, and the next day in the afternoon arrived on the banks of the stream opposite the village. The river being frozen, he immediately ordered the charge to be sounded. The column advanced steadily across on the ice, and entering the village under a heavy fire of the British, forced them from their position and soon drove them to the woods, when darkness closed the combat. Two days after, General Winchester arrived with a reinforcement of two hundred and fifty men. He had sent a dispatch to Gen. Harrison, then on the Lower Sandusky, announcing his departure from his orders, and asking for reinforcements Jan. 2 . The latter sent forward a detachment of three hundred, and followed himself the same day with a corps of three hundred and sixty men. The assistance, however, came too late, for on the day before they started, the fate of Gen. Winchester's army was sealed. Gen. Proctor, at Malden, only eighteen miles distant, hearing of Col. Lewis' advance on Frenchtown, hurried down with about 1500 men and six pieces of artillery to attack him. The latter had stationed the main force behind pickets, in the form of a half circle, but the two hundred and fifty men who had arrived with Gen. Winchester were, through some strange fatuity, placed outside, four hundred yards distant, and wholly uncovered. Just as the drums beat the morning reveillé, Proctor advanced to the assault. The troops came on steadily till within range of the Kentucky rifles, when they were met by such a fierce and deadly fire that they wheeled and fled in confusion.

But, while the attack in front was thus repulsed, that on the unprotected left wing of two hundred and fifty men was, in a few minutes, completely successful. Such a preposterous position, as that to to which it was assigned, no sane man could dream of holding. Outflanked, and almost surrounded by yelling Indians, its danger was perceived when too late to remedy it. General Winchester and Colonel Lewis, however, each with a detachment of fifty men, rushed forward to the rescue, but they only swelled the disaster. Their followers were cut down and tomahawked, and they themselves captured, and taken to Proctor. The latter had paused after his attack on the pickets, for nearly one-fourth of the regular troops had fallen in that one assault, and he hesitated about exposing himself again to the deadly fire of Kentucky rifles. It is very doubtful whether he would have ventured on a second attack. He, however, represented to General Winchester, that he could easily set the town on fire, and reduce the garrison; but, in that case, he would not guarantee the lives of the soldiers, or the inhabitants from the barbarity of the Indians. General Winchester fully believing that the five hundred men, who still gazed undauntedly on the foe, must be sacrificed, agreed to a capitulation; and an officer was sent with a flag to Major Madison, on whom the command had devolved, informing him of the unconditional surrender of all the troops by his superior officer. The brave major, who did not at all look upon himself and gallant band as vanquished men, indignantly refused to obey so unworthy a summons, even from his rightful commander, and coolly told the officer, "he should do no such thing; nay, would not surrender at all, unless the side arms of the officers would be restored to them at Amhertsburg, the wounded promptly and securely transported to that post, and a guard sufficient for their safety assigned them."[35] If the British commander refused to grant these terms, he and his men would fight to the last, and, if necessary, die with their arms in their hands. This proposition, to which any officer fit to wear a sword would have cheerfully accepted, Proctor at first rejected, and yielded at last only because no other terms would be listened to. But no sooner did the garrison surrender, than in direct violation of the conditions, he gave unbridled license to the soldiers and Indians. The latter were allowed to scalp and mutilate the dead and wounded, whose bleeding corpses crimsoned the snow on every side. Proctor, fearing the approach of Harrison, made all haste to depart, and the next night reached Amhertsburg with the prisoners, who were there crowded into a "small and muddy wood yard, and exposed throughout the night to a cold and constant rain, without tents or blankets, and with only fire enough to keep them from freezing." He had brutally left the dead at French town unburied, and sixty of the wounded, who were too feeble to march, unprotected. By a great stretch of kindness, he allowed two American surgeons to remain and take care of them. He had promised to send sleds the next day, to convey them to Malden. These never arrived; but, instead, there came a party of his Indian allies, who tomahawked a portion of the wounded, and then set fire to the houses, consuming the dead and dying together, and responding to the shrieks of the suffering victims with yells and savage laughter. Captain Hart, a relative of Henry Clay, was among the number, as was also a member of Congress. Hart, and indeed a large majority of them, belonged to the most respectable families of Kentucky. One officer was scalped in presence of his friends, and with the blood streaming down his pallid features, rose on his knees, and silently and most piteously gazed on their faces. While in this position, an Indian boy was told by his father to tomahawk him. The unskilful stripling struck again and again, only producing faint groans from the sufferer, till at length the father, in showing how a blow should be planted, ended the tragedy. The secretary of General Winchester was shot while on horseback, and scalped, and his body stripped and cast into the road. The dead, to the number of two hundred, were left unburied; and, for a long time after, hogs and dogs were seen devouring the bodies, and running about crunching human skulls and arms in their teeth. Most of these facts were sworn to before a justice of the peace, and forwarded by Judge Woodward, of the supreme court of Michigan, to Colonel Proctor, with the remark, "The truth will undoubtedly eventually appear, and that unfortunate day must meet the steady and impartial eye of history." General Harrison was at the Rapids, hurrying on the reinforcements, when he heard of the catastrophe. A few days after, he dispatched Dr. M'Kechen with a flag of truce to the river Raisin, to pass thence, if possible, to Malden. Seized by the Indians and stript, he was at length taken to Captain Elliot, who kindly forwarded him to Colonel Proctor. The latter denied his mission, declaring he was a spy, and would not recognize him, in his official character, till the fifth of February. Three weeks after, he was accused of carrying on a secret correspondence with the Americans, and without the form of a trial thrown into a filthy dungeon below the surface of the ground, where he lay for a whole month, and was finally liberated, only to carry the seeds of disease, implanted by this brutal treatment, to his grave.

When the news of this horrid massacre reached Kentucky, the State was filled with mourning, for many of her noblest sons had fallen victims to the savage. The Governor and his suite were in the theatre at the time the disastrous tidings arrived in Frankfort. The play was immediately stopped, the building deserted, and the next morning a funereal sadness rested on the town, and the voice of lamentation—like that which went up from Egypt when the first born of every house was slain—arose from almost every dwelling. But amid it all there was a smothered cry for vengeance, which never ceased ringing over the State, until it was hushed in the shout of victory that rose from the battle-field of the Thames.

Language has no epithets sufficiently opprobrious with which to stamp this atrocious deed of Colonel Proctor. It combines all the inhuman elements necessary to form a perfect monster—deceit, treachery, falsehood, murder, and that refinement of cruelty which looks with derision on slow torture, and the brutality which can insult the dead. The very apologies which his countrymen made for him only blackened his character. It was said that the prisoners surrendered at discretion, and he never pledged his word for their protection—a falsehood as afterwards fully proved by the prisoners, and a statement, whether true or false, utterly useless, only to make the whole transaction complete and perfect in every part. No man who was sufficiently acquainted with honor to simulate it successfully, would have attempted to cover an act so damning with such an excuse. The annals of civilized warfare present no instance of the massacre and torture of troops who have surrendered themselves prisoners of war on a fair battle-field. An act like this, committed by a British officer on the plains of Europe, sustained only by such an apology, would cost him his head. Absolute inability, on the part of a commander to protect his captives, is the only excuse a *man* would ever offer. This Proctor had not, for his allies were under his control and he knew it. At all events he never attempted to save the prisoners. No guard was left over the wounded, as he had stipulated to do—no sleighs were sent back the next morning to fetch them to Fort Malden, as promised—no effort whatever made in their behalf. He never designed to keep his promises or fulfil his engagements—he had abandoned the dead and wounded at Frenchtown to his savage allies, as their part of the reward. Our troops frequently employed Indian tribes, but no such atrocities were ever suffered to sully the American flag. The whole transaction, from first to last, is black as night. His deceit, treachery, cruelty to officers and men, neglect of the dead and abandonment of the wounded to worse than death—his after falsehood, meanness and cupidity are all natural and necessary parts to the formation of a thoroughly base and brutal man. He was a disgrace to his profession, a disgrace to the army and to the nation which rewarded him for this act with promotion. His memory shall be kept fresh while the western hemisphere endures, and the transaction hold a prominent place in the list of dark deeds that stand recorded against the English name. Just a month from this date three American seamen went down in the Peacock, while nobly struggling to save the prisoners. A few years before, some Turkish captives, in Egypt, being paroled by Napoleon, were afterwards retaken in a desperate battle and sentenced by a council of war to be shot. Although they had forfeited their lives by the laws of all civilized nations, in thus breaking their parole, and proved by their conduct that a second pardon would simply be sending them as a reinforcement to the enemy, and though Bonaparte only carried into execution the decision of a council of war, yet for this act of his, English historians to this day heap upon him the epithets of murderer and monster; while not the mere murder, which would have been comparative kindness, but the abandonment of American prisoners to slow torture by fire and the scalping knife, was rewarded with promotion in the army.

The difficulties which our volunteers and new levies unaccustomed to such hardships, had to contend with on the western frontier, may be gathered from the march of the three hundred men dispatched to the aid of Winchester, but who did not arrive till after the massacre. Starting with twenty pieces of artillery, in a heavy snow storm, they boldly pierced the wilderness, but made the first day only a short march. The next day, a courier arrived toiling through snow and mud, ordering the artillery to advance with all speed. But under the weight of the heavy guns, the wheels sunk to their axles with every slow revolution, and it was only by dint of great effort, they were got on at all. After a weary day's march, they encamped around a blazing fire, and were just making their scanty meal, when a messenger entered the camp, stating, that Harrison had retreated from the Rapids. A portion immediately resolved to push on to his help, and snatching a few hours of repose, they, at two o'clock in the morning, tumbled up from their couch of snow, and falling into marching order, hurried forward through the gloom. To add to their discomfort and sufferings, a January rain-storm had set in, making the whole surface one yielding mass, into which they sunk sometimes to their waists. Drenched to the skin with the pelting rain, stumbling and falling at almost every step in the dissolving snow, they kept on, and at length reached the black swamp, near Portage river. This was four miles across, and was covered with a broad sheet of water as far as the eye could reach. Out of the untroubled surface rose the trunks of sickly looking and decayed trees, presenting amid the black and driving rain, a spectacle sufficient to chill and benumb the most manly heart. Ice was beneath, but of its strength, or of the depth below, no one could tell. The soldiers, however, hurried forward into the water, and though the rotten, treacherous ice under their feet would often give way, letting them down, till their farther descent was arrested by their arms; they kept intrepidly on, till, at length, the last mile was won, and weary and staggering they emerged on the farther side. Although on the whole route, there were but eight miles where they did not sink below the knee, and often to the middle, this gallant band accomplished thirty miles by night fall. Weary, dispirited and benumbed, they then encamped, and without an axe, cooking utensils, or a tent to cover them, sat down on logs, and having kindled a feeble fire made their meagre repast. They then placed two logs together to keep them from the melting snow, and lay in rows across them, exposed to the pitiless storm. Next morning, they continued their march, and effected a junction with the army.

To such hardships and exposures were the sons of gentlemen and farmers subjected, in those disheartening northern campaigns which ended only in failure.

While such scenes were transpiring in the north, there occurred one of those events which form the romance and poetry of the American wilderness. At this time, Michigan was an unbroken forest, with the exception of Detroit, and a few settlements along the line of the lakes, containing in all, but five or six thousand inhabitants. Ohio had but 300,000, while 2,000 Indians still held their lands within its limits. Thirteen thousand constituted the entire white population of Illinois. These states, which now number by millions, were then almost wholly unknown, except on the borders of the lakes and the Ohio river. All through the interior, numerous tribes of Indians roamed undisturbed, and hung, in black and threatening war clouds, around the borders of civilization. The English had succeeded in exciting many of these to hostilities against the settlers. Their efforts were aided in a masterly manner by Tecumseh, a Shawnee warrior, who had imbibed a bitter, undying hostility to the Americans. Brave, temperate, scorning a lie, and despising the spoils of war, he fought to restore his race to their ancient rights and power. Unable to cope with the Americans alone, he gladly availed himself of our declaration of war to form an alliance with the British. Lifted by native genius above the vices of savages, he also exhibited a greatness of intellect, and loftiness of character, which, in civilized life, would have led to the highest renown. Despising the petty rivalries of tribes and chiefs, he became absorbed in the grand idea of uniting all the Indian clans in one great and desperate struggle for mastery with the whites. He had succeeded in carrying out his scheme, to a great extent, throughout the North and West. Of erect, athletic frame, noble, commanding appearance, with the air of a king, and the eloquence of a Demosthenes when rousing the Greeks to arms against Philip, he went from tribe to tribe electrifying them with his appeals, and rousing them to madness by his fiery denunciations against their oppressors. His brother, the prophet, accompanied him,—a dark, subtle, cunning impostor, to whose tricks Tecumseh submitted for awhile, because they foiled the hatred and deceit of rival chiefs. As he arose before his savage audiences, his imposing manner created a feeling of awe; but when he kindled with his great subject, he seemed like one inspired. His eye flashed fire, his swarthy bosom heaved and swelled with imprisoned passion, his whole form dilated with excitement, and his strong untutored soul poured itself forth in eloquence, wild, headlong, and resistless, as the mountain torrent. Thoughts, imagery leaped from his lips in such life and vividness that the stoicism of the Indian vanished before them, and his statue-like face gleamed with passion. The people he always carried with him; but the chiefs, who feared his power over their followers, often thwarted his plans. When not addressing the clans, he was reserved, cold, and haughty. His withering sarcasm, when Proctor proposed to retreat from

Malden; his reply to the interpreter, who offering him a chair in the presence of Harrison, said, "Your father wishes you to be seated;" "My father! the sun is my father, and the earth my mother," as he stretched himself proudly on the ground, reveal a nature conscious of its greatness, and scorning the distinctions which the white man arrogated to himself.

After passing through the northern tribes, he took his brother, and went south to the Creeks, to complete the plan of a general alliance. The journey of nearly a thousand miles through the wilderness, of these two brothers,—the discussion of their deep-laid scheme at night around their camp-fire,—the day-dreams of Tecumseh, as gorgeous as ever flitted before the imagination of a Cæsar,—the savage empire destined to rise under his hand, and the greatness he would restore to his despised race, would make a grand epic. Pathless mountains and gloomy swamps were traversed; deep rivers swam, and weariness and toil endured, not for spoils or revenge, but to carry out a great idea. There is a rude, Tuscan grandeur about him, as he thus moves through the western wilderness impelled by a high purpose,—a barbaric splendor thrown about even the merciless measures he means to adopt, by the great moral scheme to which they are to be subject. His combinations exhibited the consummate general. While England occupied us along the sea-coast, he determined to sweep in one vast semi-circle from Michilimackinac to Florida upon the scattered settlements. Fires were to be kindled North and South, and West, to burn towards the centre, while civilized warfare should desolate the eastern slope of the Alleghanies. Tecumseh had seen Hull surrender, and knew that the British had been victorious all along the frontier. His prospects were brightening, and with this glorious news to back his burning eloquence, he had no doubt of exciting the Southern tribes to war. The Chickasaws and Choctaws in Mississippi, numbered over thirty thousand; the Creeks twenty-five thousand, while south of them dwelt the large and warlike tribe of the Seminoles. His chief mission was to the Creeks, from whom, on his mother's side, he was descended. This powerful clan stretched from the southern borders of Tennessee nearly to Florida. The sun in his course looked on no fairer, richer land than the country they held. Some of them had learned the arts of civilization, and, hitherto, had evinced a friendly disposition towards the whites. But British influence working through the Spanish authorities in Florida, had already prepared them for Tecumseh's visit. An alliance, offensive and defensive, had been formed between England and Spain; and the armies of the former were then in the Peninsula, endeavoring to wrest the throne from Bonaparte. The latter, therefore, was bound to assist her ally on this continent, and so lent her aid in exciting the Southern Indians to hostility.

The year before, General Wilkinson had been dispatched to take possession of a corner of Louisiana, still claimed by the Spanish. He advanced on Mobile, and seized without opposition the old fort of Condé, built in the time of Louis the XIV. He here found abundant evidence of the machinations of the Spanish and English. Runners had been sent to the Seminoles and Creeks offering arms and bribes, if they would attack the frontier settlements. But for this, Tecumseh, with all his eloquence, might have failed. Co-operating with the British agents in Florida, as he had done with Brock and Proctor in Canada, he at length saw his cherished scheme about to be fulfilled. The old and more peaceful,—those who had settled in well-built towns, with schools, and flocks, and farms about them,—opposed the war which would devastate their land, and drive them back to barbarism. But the eloquence of Tecumseh, as he spoke of the multiplied wrongs of the Indians, and their humiliation, described the glories to be won, and painted in glowing colors the victories he had gained in the North, kindled into a blaze the warlike feelings of the young; and soon ominous tidings came from the bosom of the wilderness that stretched along the Coosa and Talapoosa rivers. Having kindled the flames, he again turned his footsteps northward.

Anxiety and alarm soon spread among the white settlers, and the scattered families sought shelter in the nearest forts. Twenty-four had thus congregated at Fort Mimms, a mere block-house, situated on the Alabama, near the junction of the Tombigbee. It was garrisoned by a hundred and forty men, commanded by Major Beasely, and, with proper care, could have resisted the attacks of the savages. But the rumors of a rising among the Indians were discredited. A negro who stated he had seen them in the vicinity, was chastised for spreading a false alarm. The night preceding the massacre, the dogs growled and barked, showing that they scented Indians in the air. But all these warnings were unheeded, when suddenly, in broad midday, the savages, some seven hundred strong, made their appearance before the fort, and within thirty feet of it, before they were discovered. The gate was open, and with one terrific yell they dashed through into the outer enclosure, driving the panic-stricken soldiers into the houses within. Mounting these they set them on fire, and shot down every soul that attempted to escape. Seeing, at once, their inevitable doom, the soldiers fought with the energy of despair. Rushing madly on their destroyers, they gave blow for blow, and laid sixty of them around the burning buildings before they were completely overpowered. At last, a yell of savage triumph rose over the crackling of flames, and cries and shrieks of terrified women and children. Then followed a scene which may not be described. The wholesale butchery,—the ghastly spectacle of nearly three hundred mutilated bodies, hewed and hacked into fragments, were nothing to the inhuman indignities perpetrated on the women. Children were ripped from the maternal womb, and swung as war-clubs against the heads of the mothers, and all those horrible excesses committed, which seem the offspring of demons.

When Tecumseh reached again the British camp in Canada, he found the American army at fort Meigs. Harrison, after Winchester's defeat, instead of boldly pushing on in pursuit, had retreated. He was a brave general, but lacked the energy and promptness necessary to an efficient commander. Thus far these qualities seemed confined solely to the English officers, leaving to ours the single one of caution.

Fort Meigs was erected on the Maumee, just above where it debouches into Lake Erie. Here the army remained inactive, serving only as a barrier to the Indians, who otherwise would have fallen on the Ohio settlements, till the latter part of April. General Harrison employed the winter in getting reinforcements from Ohio and Kentucky, and did not reach the fort till the first of the month.

In the mean time, Proctor and Tecumseh had organized a large force for its reduction. On the twenty-third, the sentinel on watch reported that the boats of the enemy, in great numbers, were entering the mouth of the river. The fort, at this time, contained about a thousand men, and was well supplied with every thing necessary for a long and stout defence, while twelve hundred Kentuckians, under General Clay, were marching to its relief.

Finding the fortifications too strong to be carried by assault, Proctor sat down before them in regular siege. The light troops and Indians were thrown across the river, and heavy batteries erected on the left bank. A well-directed cannonade from the fort so annoyed the besiegers, that they were compelled to perform most of their work by night. The garrison, at first, suffered very little, except from scarcity of water. The well in the fort having dried up, they were compelled to draw their supply from the river. But the men detailed for this purpose, were constantly picked off by skulking Indians, who becoming emboldened by success gradually drew closer around the besieged; and climbing into tall trees, and concealing themselves in the thick foliage, rained their balls into the works. On the first of May, Proctor having completed his batteries, opened his fire. He sent, also, a summons to surrender, which was scornfully rejected by Harrison, who maintained a brisk cannonade for four days, when the welcome intelligence was received, that Clay with his twelve hundred Kentuckians was close at hand. Harrison determined, at once, to raise the siege, and dispatched a messenger to him, to land eight hundred men on the left bank of the river, and carry the batteries erected there by storm, and spike the guns; while the remaining four hundred should keep down the right bank towards the batteries, against which he would make a sortie from the fort. The eight hundred were placed under Colonel Dudley, who crossing the river in good order, advanced fiercely on the batteries and swept them. Flushed with the easy victory, and burning to revenge their comrades massacred at river Raisin, the men refused to halt and spike the guns, but drove furiously on after the flying troops, or turned aside to fight the Indians, who clung to the forest. In the mean time, Proctor, aroused by this unexpected onset, hastened up from his camp a mile and a half below with reinforcements, and rallied the fugitives. At this critical moment, Tecumseh also joined him, with a large body of Indians. These advancing against the disordered Kentuckians, drove them back on the river. The latter fought bravely, but discipline and numbers told too heavily against them, and but one hundred and fifty of these gallant, but imprudent men reached the farther bank in safety. Colonel Dudley while struggling nobly to repair the error they had committed in refusing to obey his orders, fell mortally wounded. The small, but disciplined band of three hundred and fifty, led by Colonel Miller, of the nineteenth infantry, against the batteries on the right bank, carried them with the bayonet, and spiking the guns returned with forty-two prisoners.

The two succeeding days, the armies remained inactive. In the mean time, the Indians began to return home in large numbers; and Proctor deserted by his savage allies, resolved to abandon the siege. Embarking his heavy ordnance and stores under a galling fire from the fort, he made a hasty and disorderly retreat down the river. The loss of the Americans during the siege, was two hundred and seventy men killed and wounded, exclusive of the destruction of a large portion of Clay's command. That of the British was much less, so that although the attack on the fort had failed, the Americans were by far the heaviest sufferers.

Harrison leaving the fort in command of Colonel Clay, repaired to Franklinton, the place appointed for the rendezvous of the regiments newly raised in Ohio and Kentucky. In the mean time, a deputation of all the friendly Indian tribes in Ohio waited on him, offering their services in the approaching conflict on the borders. They were accepted on the conditions, they should not massacre their prisoners, or wage war against women and children.

After Harrison's departure, Proctor again appeared before Fort Meigs. But finding it well garrisoned, he did not attempt another attack; but taking five hundred regulars and a horde of Indians, seven hundred in number, suddenly appeared before Fort Stephenson in Lower Sandusky. Aug. 1. Major Croghan, a young man only twenty-one years of age, held the post, with but a hundred and sixty men. He had only one cannon, a six pounder, while the fortifications having been hastily constructed, were not strong enough to resist artillery. Knowing this, and the smallness of Croghan's force, Harrison had previously ordered him to destroy the works, and retire on the approach of the enemy. But this was impossible, for Proctor took measures at once to cut off his retreat. When this was accomplished, he sent a flag demanding the immediate surrender of the place, saying, if the garrison resisted, they would be given up to massacre. This mere stripling, not old enough to be frightened, like Hull and Wilkinson, coolly replied, that when he got possession of the fort, there would be none left to massacre. River Raisin was fresh in his memory, and lay not far off; but neither the fear of Indian barbarities, nor the dark array, ten times his number, closing steadily upon him, could shake his gallant young heart. He was such stuff as heroes are made of.

This was on Sunday evening, and immediately after receiving the bold answer of Croghan, Proctor opened on the fort from his gun boats, and a howitzer on shore. The cannonading was kept up all night, lighting up the forest scenery with its fire, and knocking loudly on that feeble fort for admission. At day break, Croghan saw that the enemy had planted three sixes within two hundred and fifty yards of the fort. Against this battery, he could reply with only his single gun, whose lonely report seemed a burlesque on the whole affair. Finding that Proctor concentrated his fire against the north-western angle, he strengthened it with bags of flour and sand. The firing was kept up till late in the afternoon, when seeing that but little impression was made on the works, Proctor resolved to carry them by storm, and a column, five hundred strong, was sent against them. With undaunted heart, young Croghan saw it approach, while his little band, proud of their heroic leader, closed firmly around him, swearing to stand by him to the last. Some time previously, a ditch six feet deep and nine feet wide had been dug in front of the works, and the six pounder, loaded with slugs and grape, was now placed, so as to rake that part of it where it was conjectured the enemy would cross. Colonel Short commanded the storming column, which he led swiftly forward to the assault. As it came within range, a well directed volley of musketry staggered it for a moment, but Colonel Short rallying them, leaped first into the ditch, crying out, "Give the d—d Yankees no quarter." In a moment, the ditch was red with scarlet uniforms. At that instant, the six pounder was fired. A wild shriek followed, and when the smoke cleared away, that section of the column which had entered the ditch lay stretched on the bottom, with their leader among them. The remainder started back aghast at such sudden and swift destruction, but being rallied they again advanced, only to be swept away. All efforts to rally them the third time, were fruitless; they fled first to the woods, and then to their boats, and next morning before daybreak disappeared altogether. This garrison of striplings had behaved nobly, and notwithstanding the brutal order of the British commander to give no quarter, exhibited that humanity without which bravery is not a virtue. Moved with pity at the groans and prayers for help from those who lay wounded in the ditch, they, not daring to expose themselves outside in presence of the enemy, handed over the pickets during the night, jugs, and pails of water to allay the fever of thirst; and made a hole through which they pulled with kindly tenderness many of the wounded, and carried them to the surgeon. These men knew that, if the attack had proved successful, not one would have been left to tell how they fought, or how they fell, yet this consciousness did not deaden, for a moment, the emotions of pity. This generosity and kindness have always characterized the American soldier, from the commencement of our national existence. The merciless warfare inflicted by England through the savages during the revolution, could not make him forget his humanity; nor the haughty, insulting conduct of English officers in this second war, force him to throw aside his kind and generous feelings.

This attack closed, for the time, the efforts of Proctor to get possession of our forts, and he retired with his savage allies to Detroit. Our whole western frontier was now in a most deplorable condition. Instead of carrying the war into the enemy's country, we had been unable to protect our own borders.

Notwithstanding the repulse at Fort Meigs, the savages still hung around our settlements, making frequent and successful dashes upon them; while the powerful tribe of the Osages lying west of the Mississippi, threatened to come into Tecumseh's grand scheme, for the extermination of the whites. Forts Madison and Mason were evacuated, leaving Fort Howard, only forty miles above St. Louis, our most northern post on the Mississippi.

CHAPTER VIII.

While Harrison was pushing forward his winter campaign, Dearborn remained quietly in winter quarters, but soon as he saw the river St. Lawrence clear of ice, he prepared to renew his invasion of Canada. Armstrong having resigned the post of minister to France, was appointed Secretary of War in place of Eustis. Being an officer of distinction, it was thought he would throw more energy into the war department, than his predecessor. His plan of the campaign was simple, and if prosecuted with energy, promised success. Dearborn was to concentrate his forces at the mouth of the Niagara river, and fall successively on Kingston, York, and Fort George, thus cutting off all communication between Montreal and Upper Canada. To carry this out successfully, naval superiority on the lake, for the safe transmission of troops and ordnance, was indispensable. From the commencement of the war, the only vessel of any pretension which the United States had on lake Ontario was the Oneida, of sixteen guns, commanded by Lieutenant, afterwards Commodore Woolsey. This gallant officer managed to preserve his ship, notwithstanding the great efforts of the enemy to get possession of it, beating off, in one instance, while lying in Sackett's Harbor, six British armed vessels. At this time, a vast forest fringed the southern shore of Ontario. With the exception of here and there a clearing, Sackett's Harbor containing some half a dozen miserable houses, and Oswego not much larger, were the only settlements on the American side, while strong forts and old towns lined the Canada shore. This large body of water, the control of which was of such vast consequence to the protection of New York state, could be reached from the Hudson, two hundred miles distant, only by highways nearly impassable, except in midsummer and winter. But, whatever difficulties might attend the attempt to build and man vessels of war on those remote waters, it was evident that until it was made, all movements against Canada must prove abortive. Captain Isaac Chauncey was, therefore, ordered thither the summer previous, to take command, and build and equip vessels. 1812. He arrived in Sackett's Harbor in October, with forty carpenters, and a hundred officers and seamen. To control the lake in the mean time, he purchased and armed several American schooners. With these, he on the eighth of November set sail, and soon after chased the Royal George under the guns of the fort at Kingston, and there maintained a spirited contest for half an hour. After various skirmishes with the enemy, he at length returned to Sackett's Harbor, and spent the winter in building vessels. Nov. 26. In the mean time, the Madison, of twenty-four guns, had been completed and launched. Nine weeks before, her hull and spars were growing in the forest. By spring, when Dearborn was ready to commence operations, Chauncey had a snug little fleet under his command, composed of the Madison, Oneida, and eleven armed schooners.

It having been ascertained that three British vessels were getting ready for sea at York, it was resolved to destroy them. The original plan, therefore, of commencing the campaign by an attack on Kingston, was by the recommendation of Chauncey changed, and the former place designated as the first point of attack.

This fleet of thirteen sail could carry but 1700 men. With these Chauncey, at length, set sail, and on the twenty-fifth of April, anchored off York. Although it blew a gale from the eastward, the boats were hoisted out, and the landing of the troops under General Pike was commenced. The wind carried the boats west of the place designated, which was an open field, to a thickly wooded shore, filled with Indians and sharp shooters. Major Forsythe with a corps of rifles, in two batteaux, first approached the shore. Assailed by a shower of balls, he commanded the rowers to rest on their oars and return the fire. General Pike, who was standing on the deck of his vessel, no sooner saw this pause, than he exclaimed to his staff with an oath, "I can't stand here any longer; come, jump into the boat." Ordering the infantry to follow at once, he leaped into a boat, and with his staff was quickly rowed into the hottest of the fire. Moving steadily forward amid the enemy's balls, he landed a little distance from Forsythe. The advance boats containing the infantry reaching the shore at the same time, he put himself at the head of the first platoon he met, and ordered the whole to mount the bank and charge. Breasting the volleys that met them, the Americans with loud cheers scaled the bank, and routed the enemy. At that moment, the sound of Forsythe's bugles was heard ringing through the forest. This completed the panic, and the frightened savages, with a loud yell, fled in all directions. The landing of the remaining troops, under cover of the well directed fire of Chauncey's vessels, was successfully made. Captains Scott and Young led the van, and with the fifteenth regiment, under command of Major King, covered themselves with honor. The troops were then formed in sections, and passing through the woods, advanced towards the fort. The bridges having been destroyed over the streams that intersected the road, only one field piece and a howitzer could be carried forward to protect the head of the column, which at length came under the fire of a battery of twenty-four pounders. Captain Walworth, of the sixteenth, was ordered to advance with trailed bayonets at the charge step, and storm this battery. Moving rapidly across the intervening space, this gallant company approached to within a short distance of the guns, when at the word, "recover charge," the enemy deserted their pieces and fled. The column then continued to move on up a gentle ascent, and soon silenced the remaining battery, and took possession of the works. But just at this moment, when a flag of surrender was momentarily expected, a magazine containing five hundred barrels of powder, exploded with terrific violence. Huge stones, fragments of shivered timber, and blackened corpses were hurled heavenward together, and came back in a murderous shower on the victorious column. Forty of the enemy, and more than two hundred Americans were killed or wounded by the explosion. The army was stunned for a moment, but the band striking up Yankee Doodle, the rent column closed up with a shout, and in five minutes was ready to charge. General Pike at the time of the explosion was sitting on the stump of a tree, whither he had just removed a wounded British soldier. Crushed by the falling fragments, he together with a British sergeant, who had been taken prisoner, and Captain Nicholson, was mortally wounded. Turning to his aid, he exclaimed, "I am mortally wounded." As the surgeons and aid were bearing him from the field, he heard the loud huzzas of his troops. Turning to one of his sergeants, he with an anxious look mutely inquired what it meant. The officer replied, *"The British Union Jack is coming down and the stars are going up."* The dying hero heaved a sigh, and smiled even amid his agony. He was carried on board the commodore's ship, and the last act of his life was to make a sign, that the British flag which had been brought to him should be placed under his head.

DEATH OF PIKE.

Thus fell one of the noblest officers in the army. Kind, humane, the soul of honor and of bravery, he was made after the model of the knights of old. His father had fought in the war of the Revolution, and though too old to serve, was still an officer in the army. In a letter to his father, dated the day before the expedition, he, after stating its character, said: "Should I be the happy mortal destined to turn the scale of war—will you not rejoice, O, my father? May heaven be propitious, and smile on the cause of my country. But if we are destined to fall, may my fall be like Wolfe's—to sleep in the arms of victory." His prayer was answered, and the country mourned the loss of a gallant officer, a pure patriot, and a noble man.

Colonel Pearce, on whom the command devolved after the fall of Pike, took possession of the barracks and then advanced on the town. As he approached he was met by the officers of the Canadian militia, proposing a capitulation. This was done to produce a delay, so that the English commander, General Sheaffe, with the regulars could escape, and the vessels and military stores be destroyed. The plan was successful, the regular troops made good their retreat, one magazine of naval and military stores was burned, together with two of the vessels undergoing repairs. The third had sailed for Kingston a short time before the attack.

Owing to the explosion of the magazine the loss of the Americans was severe, amounting to three hundred killed and wounded. Notwithstanding the exasperation of the victors at the wanton, and as they supposed premeditated destruction of life, they treated the inhabitants with kindness and courtesy. Such had been the strict orders of their commander before his death. The only violence committed was the burning of the house of Parliament, and this was owing, doubtless, to the fact that a scalp was found suspended over the speaker's mace. The sight of an American scalp, hanging as a trophy in a public building, would naturally exasperate soldiers, whose friends and relatives had fallen beneath the knife of the savage.[36]

The troops were at once re-embarked, for the purpose of proceeding immediately to Niagara, but owing to foul weather they were a week on the way. At length, being reinforced by troops from Sackett's Harbor and Buffalo, Dearborn, with some five thousand men, sailed for Fort George. This fort was situated on a peninsula, which it commanded. Dearborn resolved to make the landing in six divisions of boats, under cover of the fire of the armed schooners. The first division, containing five hundred men, was commanded by Winfield Scott, who volunteered for the service, followed by Colonel Porter with the field train. The gallant Perry offered to superintend the landing of the boats, which had to be effected under a heavy fire and through an ugly surf. The 27th of May, early in the morning, the debarkation began, and soon the boats, in separate divisions, were moving towards the shore. Fifteen hundred British lined the bank, which rose eight or ten feet from the water. Scott rapidly forming his men under the plunging fire of these, shouted, "Forward!" and began to scale the ascent. But, pressed by greatly superior numbers, they were at length borne struggling back. Dearborn, who was standing on the deck of Chauncey's vessel, watching the conflict through his glass, suddenly saw Scott, while waving his men on, fall heavily back down the steep. Dropping his glass he burst into tears, exclaiming: *"He is lost!—He is killed!"* The next moment, however, Scott sprang to his feet again, and shouting to his men, he with a rapid and determined step remounted the bank, and, unscathed by the volley that met him, knocked up with his sword the bayonets leveled at his breast, and stepped on the top. Crowding furiously after, the little band sent up their shout around him, on the summit. Dressing his line under the concentrated fire of the enemy, Scott then gave the signal to charge. The conflict was fierce but short; the British line was rent in twain, and the disordered ranks were driven over the field. Scott, seizing a prisoner's horse, mounted and led the pursuit.

Fort George was abandoned, and the garrison streamed after the defeated army. They, however, set fire to the train of the magazines before they left. This was told to Scott, and he instantly returned with two companies to save them. Before he could arrive, one magazine exploded, sending the fragments in every direction. A piece of timber struck him on the breast, and hurled him from his horse. Springing to his feet he shouted, "To the gate!" Rushing on the gate, they tore it from its hinges and poured in—Scott was the first to enter, and ordering the brave Captains Hindman and Stockton to extinguish the matches, he ran forward and pulled down the flag. Quickly re-mounting his horse he put himself at the head of his column and pressed fiercely after the enemy, chasing the fugitives for five miles, and halted, only because commanded to do so by Colonel Boyd, in person. He had already disobeyed two orders to stop the pursuit, and had he not been arrested by his superior officer in person, would soon have been up with the main body of the British.

The loss of the enemy in this short but spirited combat was two hundred and fifty killed and wounded and one hundred prisoners, while that of the Americans was only seventy-two.

The British army, under Gen. Vincent, retreated towards Burlington Heights, followed soon after by General Winder, with eight hundred men.

But while Chauncey and Dearborn were thus destroying the forts on the Niagara, Sir George Provost made a sudden descent on Sackett's Harbor. The protection of this place was of vital importance to us. Here was our naval depôt—here our ship yard with vessels on the stocks, and in fact, this was the only available port on the lake for the construction and rendezvous of a fleet. Yet the garrison left to protect it consisted of only two hundred and fifty dragoons under Lieutenant Colonel Backus, Lieutenant Fanning's artillery, two hundred invalid soldiers and a few seamen, making in all some five hundred men. Two days after the capture of Fort George, the fleet of Sir James Yeo, carrying a thousand men, commanded by Provost, appeared off the harbor. Alarm guns were instantly fired and messengers dispatched to General Brown, who resided eight miles distant at Brownville, to collect the militia and hasten to the defence of the place. The year before Brown had joined the army and been appointed brigadier-general in the militia, but at the close of the campaign, being disgusted with its management and disgraceful termination, he retired to his farm. His heart, however, was in the struggle, and the courier sent from Sackett's Harbor had scarcely finished his message, before he was on his horse and galloping over the country. Rallying five or six hundred militia he hastened to the post of danger. He was one of those whom great exigences develop. Brave, prudent, resolute, and rock fast in his resolution, he was admirably fitted for a military leader, while by his daring and gallant behavior, he acquired great influence over raw troops. Acquainted with all the localities and resources of the place, he at the request of Lieutenant Backus readily assumed the command. A breastwork was hastily erected on the only spot where a landing could be effected, and the militia placed behind it. The regulars formed a second line near the barracks and public buildings, while Fanning, with the artillerists, held the fort proper, and Lieutenant Chauncey, with his men, defended the stores at Navy Point.

The night of the 28th passed in gloomy forebodings. The troops slept on their arms, and Brown and his officers passed the hours in silently and cautiously reconnoitering the shores of the lake. That little hamlet embosomed in the vast primeval forest that stretched away on either side along the water's edge and closed darkly over the solitary highway that led to the borders of civilization, presented a lonely aspect. As hour after hour dragged heavily by, every ear was bent to catch the muffled sound of the enemy's sweeps, but only the wind soughing through the tree-tops and the monotonous dash of waves on the beach disturbed the stillness of the scene. But as the long looked for dawn began to streak the water, the fleet of British boats were observed rapidly pulling towards the breastwork. Brown bade the militia reserve their fire till the enemy were within pistol shot, and then deliver it coolly and accurately. They did so, and the first volley checked the advance of the boats. After the second volley, however, the militia were seized with a sudden panic, and broke and fled. Colonel Mills, who commanded the volunteers, was shot while bravely attempting to arrest the disorder. Brown succeeded in stopping some ninety of them, whom he posted on a line with the regulars. The British having landed, formed in good order, and moved steadily forward on this little band of regulars. The latter never wavered, but maintained their ground with stubborn resolution, and as they were gradually forced back by superior numbers, took possession of the barracks, behind which they maintained a rapid and galling fire. Backus had fallen, mortally wounded, and Lieutenant Fanning was also severely wounded, but he still clung to his gun and directed its fire with wonderful accuracy. Finding the troops able to maintain their position for some time yet, Brown exhorted them to hold firm while he endeavored to rally the fugitive militia. Riding up to them, he rebuked and entreated them by turns, until, at last, when he told them how courageously and nobly the strangers were defending the homes they had basely abandoned to pillage, they promised to return and do their duty. Not daring, however, to trust men in an open attack who had just fled from a breastwork, although he solemnly swore he would cut down the first that faltered, he led them by a circuitous route along the edge of the forest, as if he designed to seize the boats and cut off the enemy's retreat. The stratagem succeeded, and the British made a rush for their boats, leaving their killed and wounded behind. Having lost, in all, between four and five hundred men, they dared not venture on a second attack, and withdrew, humbled and mortified, to the Canada shore. The American loss was about one hundred.

The successful defence of Sackett's Harbor following so quickly the capture of Forts York and George, promised well for the summer campaign. But disasters soon checked the rising hopes of the nation. General Winder, who had started in pursuit of Vincent, found, on his arrival at Forty Mile Creek, that the enemy had been reinforced. Halting here, therefore, he dispatched a messenger to Dearborn for more troops. General Chandler, with another brigade, was sent, when the whole force was put in motion, and crossing Stony Creek, arrived at night-fall, within a short distance of the British encampment. Here the army halted, preparatory to an attack the next morning. General Vincent, although greatly inferior in numbers, felt that his future success depended entirely on his retaining his present position, and, therefore, resolved to hazard a second battle. But, having, by a careful reconnoissance, discovered that the American camp guards were scattered and careless, while the whole encampment was loose and straggling, he immediately changed his plan, and determined to make a bold and furious night onset, and endeavor by one well-directed blow to break the American army in pieces. Following up this determination, he, with seven hundred men, set out at midnight, and arriving at three o'clock in the morning at the American pickets silently and adroitly captured every man before he could give the alarm. Pressing with the main column directly for the centre of the encampment, he burst with the appalling war-cry of the savage on the astonished soldiers. The artillery was surrounded, and several pieces, with one hundred men, were taken prisoners, and among them the two generals, Winder and Chandler. General Vincent having lost his column in the darkness, the second in command ignorant what course to pursue, or what to do, concluded to retreat with his trophies. The attack had been well planned and boldly carried out, and but for the blunder made by Vincent would no doubt have been completely successful. As it was the loss was nearly equal; so that the American army was still in a good condition to take the initial and advance. But the command devolving on Colonel Burns, a cavalry officer, who declared he was incompetent to direct infantry movements, a retreat was resolved upon. The army arriving at Forty Mile Creek, a messenger was despatched to Dearborn, asking for orders. General Lewis, with the sixth regiment, was immediately sent forward, with directions to engage the enemy at once. An hour after his arrival at camp the British fleet was seen slowly beating up abreast of it. A schooner was towed near the shore and opened its fire, but Lieutenant Eldridge, heaving a few hot shot into her, compelled her to withdraw. In the mean time, some vessels appearing off Fort George, Dearborn conjectured that an attack upon him was meditated, and recalled this division of the army. The boats, however, sent to bring them, were overtaken by an armed schooner, and many of them captured.

After these catastrophes Dearborn remained at Fort George an entire fortnight, wholly inactive. The British, on the other hand, made diligent use of this interval, in taking possession of mountain passes, and thus accomplished the double purpose of securing their own position and narrowing the limits of Dearborn's possessions, and destroying his communication. The latter, at length, being aroused to the danger in which these posts placed him, despatched Col. Bœstler, with six hundred men, to break up one of them, seventeen miles distant. Acting under wrong information, this small detachment arrived without molestation at Beaverdams, within two miles of the "Stone House" where the enemy had fortified themselves. But here they were suddenly surrounded by a body of British and Indians, and a conflict ensued. Believing it impossible to effect a safe retreat through the forest, pressed by such a force, Colonel Bœstler surrendered his whole detachment prisoners of war. This ended Dearborn's campaign, and his military services. Colonel Bishop, who showed great activity in carrying out the plan of the British commander, finding Fort Erie ungarrisoned, took possession of it, and crossing suddenly to Black Rock, with 250 men, drove out the militia and destroyed the guns and stores. But the news reaching Buffalo, a few regulars, together with some militia and friendly Indians hastened to the fort and expelled the invaders, killing their commander.

The successful attacks on York and Fort George had removed much of the odium with which the disasters of the previous years had covered Dearborn, and great results were expected from so brilliant an opening of the campaign. But his after inaction and efforts ending only in failure, disgusted the people and Congress. Broken down by disease and demoralized by their long camp life, the soldiers but poorly represented the vigor and energy of the republic. Dearborn, like the other generals, received all the blame that properly attached to him, together with that which belonged to the Government, and when the news of Bœstler's defeat arrived in Washington, the House of Representatives was thrown into a state of indignant excitement. Mr. Ingersoll was deputed to wait on the President and demand Dearborn's removal, as Commander-in-Chief of the Western army. The request was granted, and on the 15th of July he resigned his command. He had accomplished, literally nothing, in two campaigns, and though he was surrounded with difficulties, crippled, and rendered cautious by the indifferent and unsuitable troops under his command, yet, after making a large allowance for all, there is margin wide enough to secure his condemnation. His materials became worse instead of better under his management, and the prospects on our northern border grew gloomier the longer he held command. The energy and vigor of his younger days were gone, and the enfeebled commander of 1812 was a very different man from the daring and gallant officer of the Revolution. He had stood on the deck of his vessel and seen Pike carry York, and young Scott Fort George with mere detachments. He had witnessed the bravery of his troops under gallant officers, and it needed only energy and activity in himself to have made the army the pride of the nation.

1813.

Colonel Boyd assumed the command till the arrival of Wilkinson in September, but with the exception of some skirmishing, the summer passed away in inactivity.

The British, by capturing two American sloops that ventured into a narrow part of the lake, near the garrison of Aux Noix, obtained command of this water communication, which they held the remainder of the season.

CHAPTER IX.

SECOND SESSION OF THE TWELFTH CONGRESS.

Army bill — Quincy and Williams — Debate on the bonds of merchants given for British goods imported in contravention of the non-importation act — Debate on the bills increasing the army to 55,000 men — Williams' report — Quincy's attack — Clay's rejoinder — Randolph, Calhoun, Quincy, Lowndes and Clay — State of the Treasury.

The members of Congress, when they assembled in October, did not exchange those congratulations they promised each other at their adjournment, after declaring war. Every plan had proved abortive, every expectation been disappointed. True, the gallant little navy was left to fall back on. Its successes, however, did not reflect much credit on their sagacity, but rather by returning good for evil, had administered a severe rebuke to their neglect. The Federalists could claim the chief honor there, and make both the victories on the sea and defeats on land the grounds of attack. They had always said leave Canada alone and go to the sea, there is the proper theatre for your exploits. Results had shown the wisdom of their counsels. The army had accomplished nothing, still its skeleton ranks must be filled. A bill was therefore introduced, increasing the pay of the soldiers from six to eight dollars per month, and making their persons secure from arrest for debt, in order to tempt recruits into the service. They were allowed also to enlist either for five years or for the war. Nov. 20. A clause inserted in this bill, giving minors and apprentices, over eighteen, permission to enlist without the consent of their parents and masters, fell like a bomb-shell in the House. This was striking at the very foundation of social and domestic life—viz., parental authority—and putting a premium on disobedience and rebellion. 18 2. It furnished a new outlet for Mr. Quincy's wrath, who declared that if Congress dared apply it in New England the people would resist it, with the laws against kidnapping and stealing. He said it was odious and atrocious, unequalled, absurd, and immoral. Mr. Williams replied, that Great Britain allowed enlistments over sixteen, as did our Government in the Revolutionary War—nay, that this very clause passed in 1798, which became a law. Dec. 3. Another exciting debate sprung up relative to the bonds of the merchants for British goods lately imported in contravention of the non-importation law. This law, it will be remembered, was passed in March, 1811, in retaliation for the orders in council, and was to cease with the revocation of those orders. Before the news of the declaration of war arrived in England they were revoked, and American owners supposing the non-importation act would fall with it, immediately took in cargoes of British goods. These were allowed to depart, as well as others in process of landing, and provided with licenses to protect them against British cruisers. Thus a vast amount of merchandise arrived in the various ports of the United States during the first two or three months of the war. The non-importation act being still in force, these goods were seized as forfeited to the Government. Still many of the district judges surrendered them to the claimants on their giving bonds to the amount of their value. As under the non-importation law half the value of the forfeited goods belonged to the informer, Gallatin proposed that, as in this case there was no informer, that portion should be given to the owners, and the Government put the other half, amounting to nine millions, in the public treasury. This proposal was advocated by some and strenuously opposed by others. Dec. 30. After a vehement debate, extending through several sittings, all the penalties of the merchants were finally remitted.

Another debate, still more exciting, followed on the army bill. This bill contained provisions for raising twenty thousand men for one year, increased bounty enlistments to sixteen dollars, and appointed an officer to do all the recruiting. Dec. 27 Mr. Williams, chairman of the committee on military affairs, introduced it with an able speech. After showing that the country demanded such an augmentation of the army, making the entire regular force 55,000, and defending the increased bounty and appointment of a special officer for the recruiting service, he alluded to the disastrous issue of Hull's campaign. Said he, "there are those, perhaps, who can sneer at the disasters and misfortunes of the late campaign, and will object to this bill, saying there is no encouragement to vote additional forces, seeing that those which have been already raised have been so idly employed. It becomes us all to be equally faithful to our country, whether victorious or not; it is in times of discomfiture that the patriot's resolution and virtues are most needed. It is no matter by what party names we are distinguished, this is our country—we are children of the same family, and ought to be brothers in a common cause. The misfortune which befalls one portion should sink deep into the breasts of the others also."

Jan. 5, 1813.

Mr. Clay congratulated the committee and the nation on the report that had been made. Mr. Quincy, who saw in every proposition for replenishing the army, a project for conquering Canada, opposed the bill. Assuming that to be the object in view, he assailed it with all that sarcasm and abuse for which he was distinguished. In the first place, he said, we could not conquer Canada; in the second place, if we could, it would be a barren triumph. It would not bring peace nor be of any advantage to the country. He denounced it as cruel and barbarous, declaring it was not owing to the Government, that at that moment the bones of the Canadians were not mixed with the ashes of their habitations. Said he, "Since the invasion of the buccaneers, there is nothing like this war. We have heard great lamentations about the disgrace of our arms on the frontier. Why, sir, the disgrace of our arms on the frontier is terrestrial glory in comparison with the disgrace of the attempt! The whole atmosphere rings with the utterance, from the other side of the house, of this word, glory! glory! What glory? The glory of the tiger which lifts its jaws all foul and bloody from the bowels of his victim, and roars for his companions of the forest to come and witness his prowess and his spoils—the glory of Zenghis Khan, without his greatness—the glory of Bonaparte." He asked the members if they supposed the vagabonds who should conquer Canada would, when their aim was accomplished, heed the orders of Government. No! they would obey the "choice spirits" placed over them, who in turn would not consult spinsters and weavers, but take counsel from their leader what next they shall do. "Remember," said he, "remember, I warn you, he who plants the American standard on the walls of Quebec, plants it for himself, and will parcel it out into dukedoms, and seignorities, and counties for his followers." It was a solace to him amid all his regrets, that New England was guiltless of this war, and that she had done her utmost to hurl the wicked authors of it from their seats. That way of thinking, he said, was not peculiar to him, but was "the opinion of all the moral sense and nine-tenths of the intelligence of the section from which he came. Some of those who are here from that quarter—some of *the household troops* who lounge for what they can pick up about the Government-house will say differently—those who come here and with their families live and suck upon the heart of the treasury—toad-eaters who live on eleemosynary, ill-purchased courtesy of the palace, swallow great men's spittles, get judgships, and wonder at the fine sights, fine rooms, fine company, and most of all wonder how they themselves got here—these creatures will tell you, No—that such as I describe are not the sentiments of the people of New England. Sir, I have conversed upon the question with men of all ranks, conditions and parties in Massachusetts, men hanging over the plough and holding the spade—the twenty, thirty and fifty acre men, and their answers have uniformly been to the same effect. They have asked simply, What is the invasion for? Is it for land? We have enough. Is it for plunder? There is none there. New States? We have more than is good for us. Territory? If territory, there must be a standing army to keep it, and there must be another standing army here to watch that. These are judicious, honest, patriotic, sober men, who when their country calls, at any wise or real exigency, will start from their native soils and throw their shields over their liberties, like the soldiers of Cadmus, yet who have heard the winding of your horn for the Canadian campaign, with the same indifference they would have listened to a jews harp or the twanging of a banjo. He declared that Mr.

Madison and his cabinet had been bent on war from the outset, and their eagerness to come to blows with England evinced the disposition ascribed to the giant in the children's old play:—

'Fe, faw, fum,
I smell the blood of an Englishman,
Be he dead or be he alive
I will have some.'

He knew there were those who were ready to open on him with the old stale cry of British connection. It was not egotism to speak of what belonged to his country. It would ill become a man whose family had been two centuries settled in the State, and whose interest and connections were exclusively American, to shrink from his duty for the yelpings of those bloodhound mongrels who were kept in pay to hunt down all who opposed the court—a pack of mangy hounds, of recent importation, their backs still sore with the stripes of European castigation, and their necks marked with the check collar." Fierce and vehement, now rising into eloquence, and now descending to the coarse language of the bar-room, Mr. Quincy dealt his blows on every side—at one moment coming down on the administration with sweeping charges of dishonesty and villany, and again rushing fiercely on the solid phalanx of the war party, assailing them with scoffs and jeers and taunts, till scorn and rage gathered on their countenances.

Mr. Clay, in his urbane and gentle manner, rose to reply. He took a review of the two parties. While the administration was endeavoring to prevent war by negotiations and restrictive measures, the opposition, he said, was disgusted with the timorous policy pursued, and called for open, manly war. They declared the administration "could not be kicked into a war." "War and no restrictions, is their motto, when an embargo is laid, but the moment war is declared, the cry is restrictions but no war. They tack with every gale, displaying the colors of every party and of all nations, steady in only one unalterable purpose, to steer, if possible, into the haven of power. The charge of French influence had again and again been made, which should be met in only one manner—by giving it the lie direct. The opposition had also amused themselves by heaping every vile epithet which the English language afforded on Bonaparte. He had been compared to every monster and beast, from that of the Revelations to the most insignificant quadruped. He said it reminded him of an obscure lady who took it into her head to converse on European affairs with an accomplished French gentleman, and railed on Napoleon, calling him the curse of mankind, a murderer and monster. The Frenchman listened to her with patience to the end, and then, in the most affable manner, replied, 'Madame, it would give my master, the Emperor, infinite pain if he knew how hardly you thought of him.' Expressing his regret that he was compelled to take some notice of Mr. Quincy in his remarks, he defended Jefferson against his attacks, and showed how absurd were all his statements and scruples respecting the invasion of Canada, by referring to the part New England took in the capture of Louisburg. He then alluded to the treasonable attitude assumed by the Federalists, denounced their hypocrisy in endeavoring to gain the adhesion of the people to their views by promising peace and commerce. But, said Mr. Clay, I will quit this unpleasant subject, I will turn from one whom no sense of decency or propriety could restrain from soiling the carpet on which he treads, to gentlemen who have not forgotten what is due to themselves, the place in which we are assembled, nor to those by whom they are opposed." He then went into a review of the causes that led to the war, to show that the government had acted with forbearance and moderation, and at length took up the subject of impressment. After proving the illegality and oppression of this right, as claimed and exercised by the English, he said, "there is no safety to us but in the rule that all who sail under the flag (not being enemies) are protected by the flag. It is impossible the country should ever forget the gallant tars who have won for us such splendid trophies. Let me suppose that the genius of Columbia should visit one of them in his oppressor's prison, and attempt to reconcile him to his wretched condition. She would say to him in the language of the gentlemen on the other side, 'Great Britain intends you no harm; she did not mean to impress you, but one of her own subjects, having taken you by mistake; I will remonstrate and try to prevail on her, by peaceable means, to release you, but I cannot, my son, fight for you.' If he did not consider this mockery he would address her judgment and say, 'You owe me my country's protection; I owe you in return, obedience; I am no British subject, I am a native of old Massachusetts, where live my aged father, my wife, my children; I have faithfully discharged my duty, will you refuse to do yours?' Appealing to her passions, he would continue, 'I lost this eye in fighting under Truxton with the Insurgente; I got this scar before Tripoli; I broke this leg on board the Constitution when the Guerriere struck.' If she remained still unmoved he would break out in the accents of mingled distress and despair,

> 'Hard, hard is my fate! once I freedom enjoyed,
>   Was as happy as happy could be!
> Oh! how hard is my fate, how galling these chains!'

I will not imagine the dreadful catastrophe to which he would be driven by an abandonment of him to his oppressor. It will not be, it cannot be, that his country will refuse him protection." This description of a poor sailor, maimed in his country's service, appealing to that country he had served so well, for protection, and rejected, cast off, abandoning himself to despair, sketched as it was with vividness and feeling, and uttered in that touching pathos for which Clay's rich and flexible voice was remarkable, went home with thrilling power to each patriotic heart, and tears were seen on the faces of members in every part of the house.

After reviewing the progress of the war, and the present attitude of England, and declaring that propositions for peace offered by the other party were futile, he drew himself to his full height, and casting his eye around the house, and pitching his voice to the note of lofty determination, closed with, "An honorable peace can be attained only by an efficient war. My plan would be to call out the ample resources of the country, give them a judicious direction, prosecute the war with the utmost vigor, strike wherever we can reach the enemy at sea or on land, and negotiate the terms of peace at Quebec or Halifax. We are told that England is a proud and lofty nation, that, disdaining to wait for danger meets it half way. Haughty as she is, we once triumphed over her, and if we do not listen to the counsels of timidity and despair, we shall again prevail. In such a cause, with the aid of Providence, we must come out crowned with success, *"but if we fail, let us fail like men, lash ourselves to our gallant tars, and expire together in one common struggle, fighting for 'Seaman's rights and Free trade.'"* Before this patriotic burst of eloquence the harsh and irritating charges and selfish objections of the opposition disappeared, like the unhealthy vapors of a morass before the fresh breath of the cool west wind.

The declaration of war consummated a revolution begun long before in Congress. The affairs of the nation were taken out of the hands of old and experienced statesmen, and placed in those of young and ardent men. Henry Clay was but thirty-five; Calhoun, thirty, and Randolph thirty-nine. Many of less note were also young men, full of hope and confidence, and jealous of their country's honor. In their first conflict with the older and more conservative members, they revealed the dawning genius and statesmanship that afterwards raised them to such high renown. The Federalists were represented also by men of great strength of intellect and forcible speakers. Quincy possessed the elements of a powerful leader, but he at times allowed his passions to override all propriety and suggestions of prudence. Vehement and fearless, he moved down on the enemy in gallant style, but, like Jackson in battle, his hostility for the time lost all magnanimity, and assumed the character of ferocity. He made the whole party opposed to him a person, and attacked it with all the malignity, scorn, invective, and jeers he would one who had grossly abused his person and assailed his honor. But there was no secresy or trickery in his movements—his followers and his foes knew where to find him, and though he often, in his intemperance, violated the rules of courtesy, and thus exposed himself to retorts that always tell against a speaker, he still was an ugly opponent to contend with. Full of energy, inflexible of purpose—aggressive, bold, and untiring—in a popular cause he would have been resistless. There were men in the Federalist party at this time capable of carrying even a bad cause if relieved from external pressure. But the impressment of American citizens, massacres in the north, and outrages along the sea coast, so aroused the national indignation, that both words and efforts became powerless before it. Like the resistless tide, which bears away both strong and weak, it hushed argument, drowned explanations, and silenced warnings, as it surged on, breaking down barriers, and sweeping away defences that seemed impregnable.

One of the most remarkable men in this Congress was John Randolph, of Roanoke, as he always wrote himself. Possessed of rare endowments, and of ample wealth, fortune had lavished on him every gift but that of sex. He was at this time exceedingly fair. Conflicts and rude jostlings with the world had not yet wrinkled and blackened his visage, soured his sensitive temper, or driven him into that misanthropy and those eccentricities which afterwards disfigured his life. He was six feet high and frail in person, but his brilliant black eye fairly dazzled the beholder, as he rose to speak, and made him forget the fragile form before him. His voice was too thin for public speaking, and when pitched high was shrill and piercing. But in common conversation it was like an exquisite instrument, on which the cunning player discoursed strange and bewitching music, and no one could escape its fascination. His first glance round the hall attracted silence, and all bent to catch the tones of that musical feminine voice. As he became excited in his harangue, his eye burned with increased lustre, while his changing countenance revealed every thought and feeling before it was uttered. So expressive was it in transmitting the transitions that passed over the soul and heart of the speaker, that they scarcely needed the assistance of language. Sometimes fearfully solemn and again highly excited; he at this time rarely indulged in that withering sarcasm which afterwards so often drew blood from his antagonist. With the delicate organization and sensibilities of a woman, joined to the thought and ambition of a man, his destiny had led him into scenes that spoiled his temper and erased some of the most beautiful features of his character. Chivalrous and fearless, he at first lent his genius to Jefferson's administration, but shrunk from the awful consequences of war when it approached.

Calhoun, one of the firmest props of the government, was his antipode in almost every particular. Though young, his face evinced no enthusiasm—his glistening eye no chivalry. With thin lips, high cheek bones, rigid, yet not strong lines in his face, an immense head of hair, his personal appearance would never have arrested the curiosity of the beholder but for his eye. This was not brilliant and radiant like Randolph's. It did not light up with valor, nor burn with indignation, nor melt with pity, but changeless as a piece of burnished steel, it had a steady, cold glitter, that fascinated for the time whomsoever it fell upon. Fixed and precise in his attitude, and moveless in his person, he poured forth his thoughts and views with a rapidity, yet distinctness, that startled one. Untrammeled at this time with those abstractions and theories which afterwards confused his reasoning faculties and gave an irrecoverable twist to his logic; he brought his cool, clear intellect to the aid of the administration, and indicated by the power and influence he soon acquired, his future greatness. No sophistry could escape him—the stroke of his cimeter cut through all complexity—and when he had done with his opponent's argument it could not have been recognized as that which, just before, looked so plausible and consistent.

Two other representatives from the same state were able friends of the administration. William Lowndes, a young man, and though not a good speaker, nor prepossessing in his appearance, carried great influence by mere weight of character, and the consistency and firmness of his political opinions. He was six feet six inches high, and slender withal; and when he rose to address the house, his unassuming and respectful manner commanded attention. Of great integrity, clear headed and consistent, a proud, bright career seemed opening before him, but death soon closed it for ever.

Mr. Cheves was chairman of committee of Ways and Means, and exhibited great ability in that station.

But the pride of the house was the young and graceful speaker, Henry Clay. Tall, and straight as a young forest tree, he was the embodiment of the finest qualities of Western character. Possessing none of the graces and learning of the schools, nor restrained in the freedom of thought and opinion by the systems and rules, with which they often fetter the most gifted genius, he poured his whole ardent soul and gallant heart into the war. The true genius, and final destiny of this republic, lie west of the Alleghanies. So there, also, will spring up our noblest American literature. Not shackled by too great reverence for the old world, educated in a freer life, and growing up under the true influences of American institutions, man there becomes a freer, a more unselfish being; his purposes are nobler, and all his instincts better.

Impelled by pure patriotism, and excited by the wrongs and insults heaped upon his country, Clay entered into those measures designed to redeem her honor, and maintain her integrity with a zeal and solicitude, that soon identified him with them. He thus unconsciously became a leader; and whether electrifying the house with his appeals, or in the intervals of the sessions of Congress traversing his state, and arousing the young men to action, exhibited the highest qualities of an orator. His stirring call to the sons of Kentucky was like the winding horn of the huntsman, to which they rallied with ardent courage and dauntless hearts. We now always associate with Clay, the scattered white locks and furrowed face, and slow, majestic movements. But, at this time, not a wrinkle seamed his youthful countenance; and lithe and active, he moved amid his companions with an elastic tread, and animated features. His rich and sonorous voice was so flexible, that it gave him great power in appealing to the passions of men. When moving to pity, it was soft and pleading as a woman's; but when rousing to indignation, or to noble and gallant deeds, it rang like the blast of a bugle. In moments of excitement, his manner became highly impassioned, his blue eye gleamed with the fire of genius, and his whole countenance beamed with emotion. Thoughts, images, illustrations leaped to his lips, and were poured forth with a prodigality and eloquence, that charmed and led captive all within reach of his voice. He loved his country well, and sung her wrongs with a pathos, that even his enemies could not withstand. When he was disheartened by our first reverses on the northern frontier, he turned to our gallant navy with a pride and affection, he maintained till his death. Madison leaned on him throughout this trying struggle, as his chief prop and stay.

Though the House, rent by the fierce spirit of faction, would often break through the bounds of decorum and order, he as speaker held the reins of power with a firm and just hand. With an easy and affable manner, that attracted every one to him, he yet had a will of iron. Under all that frankness and familiarity, there was a rock-fast heart, that never swerved from its purpose. His manner of carrying out his plans, often misled men respecting the strength of his will. He was strictly *suaviter in modo fortiter in re*. Clay, Calhoun, Randolph, and in the next Congress Webster, were striking representatives of the young country rising rapidly to greatness. Truly, "there were giants in those days."

It was estimated that the entire revenue for the ensuing year would be $12,000,000, while the expenses were calculated at $36,000,000. To make up the $24,000,000 deficit, the President was authorized to sell $16,000,000 six per cent. stock, continue outstanding the former $5,000,000 treasury notes, and raise $5,000,000 towards a new loan. But the more important business was transferred to the next Congress, which was to meet early in the spring. The two other principal acts passed this session, was one authorizing the government to occupy Mobile, and all that part of Florida ceded to the United States, with Louisiana, and the other giving it power to retaliate for the twenty-three Irishmen taken from Scott at Quebec, and sent to England to be tried for treason.

CHAPTER X.

Action between the Chesapeake and Shannon — Rejoicing in England over the victory — The Enterprise captures the Boxer — Death of Lieutenant Burrows — Daring cruise of the Argus in the English and Irish channels — Lieutenant Allen's humanity — Action with the Pelican — Death of Allen — His character.

1813.

Defeats on land had thus far been compensated by victories at sea, and to that element we ever turned with pride and confidence. Our exultation, however, was for a moment checked by the loss of the Chesapeake, within sight of our shores. This vessel had started on a cruise in February, under the command of Captain Evans. Unsuccessful in her attempts to find the enemy, and having captured but four merchantmen during the whole time of her absence, she returned to Boston with the character of an "unlucky ship," which she had borne from the outset, still more confirmed. Captain Lawrence succeeded Captain Evans in the command of her, and began to prepare for a second cruise. An English frigate, the Shannon, was lying off the harbor at the time, and her commander, Captain Broke, sent a challenge to Lawrence, to meet him in any latitude or longitude. The Chesapeake was just getting under way when this challenge arrived, and Lawrence resolved at once to accept it, though reluctantly, from the disaffected state in which he found his crew. He had joined his vessel but a few days before; the proper 1st lieutenant lay sick on shore, and the acting lieutenant was a young man unaccustomed to his position, while "there was but one other commissioned sea officer in the ship," two midshipmen acting as third and fourth lieutenants. Under these circumstances, and with a discontented, complaining crew, it was evidently unwise to hasten a combat with a ship that had long been preparing herself for such an encounter, and was, in every way, in the best possible condition. But Lawrence, brave and ambitious of renown, knowing, also, that the motives which would prompt him to avoid a combat would be misconstrued, and having but a short time before challenged an English vessel in vain, determined to run the hazard, and on the morning of the 1st of June, stood boldly out to sea. At four o'clock he overhauled the Shannon, and fired a gun, which made her heave to. The Chesapeake, now about thirty miles from land, came down under easy sail, receiving the fire of the enemy as she approached. Captain Lawrence having determined to lay the vessel alongside and make a yard-arm to yard-arm fight of it, reserved his fire until every gun bore, when he delivered a destructive broadside. The clouds of smoke as they puffed out upon the sea and rolled upward, thrilled the hearts of the hundreds of spectators that crowned the dim highlands around Boston harbor. For a few minutes the cannonading was terrific, but some of the rigging of the Chesapeake being cut to pieces one of the sails got loose and blew out, which brought the ship into the wind. Then taking sternway she backed on her enemy, and the rigging and an anchor becoming entangled, she could not get off. This, of course, exposed her to a raking fire, which swept her decks. Captain Lawrence, during the conflict, had received a wound in the leg, while several of his officers were killed. When he found that his vessel would inevitably fall aboard that of the enemy, he ordered the drums to summon the boarders. But a negro bugleman attempting to perform this duty was so frightened that he could not blow a note, and verbal orders were distributed. In the mean time, Lawrence fell mortally wounded. Carried below, his last words were "Don't give up the ship," a motto which Perry soon after carried emblazoned on his flag as he passed from his helpless, dismantled ship, through the enemy's fire, to the Niagara. With his fall ceased all efforts to carry the Shannon by boarding. The commander of the latter finding the quarter-deck guns of the Chesapeake abandoned, gave the orders to board, and the flag which had never yet been struck to anything like an equal foe, was hauled down. The destruction on board the American ship after she fell foul of the enemy was frightful. The entire battle lasted but twelve minutes, and yet in that short time a hundred and forty-six of her officers and crew were killed or wounded. The loss of the Shannon was twenty-three killed and fifty-six wounded. This victory of the British was tarnished by the brutal conduct of Lieutenant Faulkener, who took command of the prize. The testimony of the surviving officers proved him unworthy to serve under the gallant commander who had so nobly fought his ship.

The Americans had become so accustomed to naval victories that they felt great chagrin at this defeat, while the unexpected triumph, coming as it did on the top of such successive disasters, was received with the most extravagant delight in England: the Tower bells were rung, salvos of artillery fired, and praises innumerable and honors were lavished on Captain Broke. Our navy never received a greater compliment than these unwonted demonstrations of joy uttered. The state of the crew—the accidental blowing out of the sail—the neglect of officers to board—and a variety of excuses were offered to solace the American people for this defeat. There was, doubtless, much force in what was said, but the falling of a mast, or the loss of the wheel, or any casualty which renders a vessel unmanageable, and gives one or the other a decided advantage, is always liable to occur; hence, unbroken success is impossible. Occasional misfortune is a law of chance.

But during the summer and autumn our other vessels at sea continued to give a good account of themselves. The three little cruisers, Siren, Enterprise, and Vixen, were great favorites, for their gallant conduct in the bay of Tripoli. The latter was captured early in the war by an English frigate. The Siren did not go to sea till next year, when she too, after giving a British 74 a chase of eleven hours, was taken. The Enterprise was kept between Cape Ann and the Bay of Fundy, to chase off the privateers that vexed our commerce in those waters. She was a successful cruiser against these smaller vessels, capturing several and sending them into port Sept. 4. A few days before Perry's victory, this vessel left the harbor of Portland, and while sweeping out to sea discovered a strange sail close in shore. The latter immediately hoisted four British ensigns and stood on after the Enterprise. Lieutenant Burrows, the commander, kept away, and ordered a long gun forward to be brought aft and run out of one of the windows. He had but lately joined the ship, and hence was but little known by the under officers and men. The latter did not like the looks of this preparation, especially as he kept carrying on sail. They feared he had made up his mind to run, and this gun was to be used as a stern-chaser. From the moment they had seen the British ensign they were eager to close with the enemy, and the disappointment irritated them. The seamen on the forecastle stood grouped together, discussing this strange conduct on the part of their commander for awhile, and then went to their officer and begged him to go and see about it—to tell the captain they wanted to fight the British vessel, and they believed they could whip her. The latter finally went forward and spoke to the first lieutenant, who told him they need not be troubled, Mr. Burrows would soon give them fighting enough to do. This was satisfactory, and they looked cheerful again. The preparations all being made, and the land sufficiently cleared, Burrows shortened sail and bore down on the enemy. As the two vessels, approaching diagonally, came within pistol shot of each other, they delivered their broadsides, and bore away together. The Enterprise, however, drew ahead, and Burrows finding himself forward of the enemy's bows, ordered the helm down, and passing directly across his track, raked him with his long gun from the cabin window. He then waited for him to come up on the other quarter, when they again moved off alongside of each other, firing their broadsides, till at length the main-top-mast of the English vessel came down. Raking her again with his long gun, Burrows took up his station on her bows, and poured in a rapid and destructive fire.

The men serving one of the carronades being sadly reduced in numbers, and unable to manage their piece, Burrows stepped forward, and seized hold of the tackle to help them run it out. Placing his feet against the bulwark to pull with greater force, he was struck in the thigh by a shot which glanced from the bone and entered his body, inflicting a mortal, and exceedingly painful wound. He refused, however, to be carried below, and laid down on deck, resolved, though writhing in excruciating agony, to encourage his officers and men by his presence so long as life lasted.

In forty minutes from the commencement of the action the enemy ceased firing, and hailed to say he had struck. The commanding officer ordered him to haul down his flag. The latter replied they were nailed to the mast, and could not be lowered till the firing ceased. It was then stopped, when an English officer sprang on a gun, and shaking both fists at the Americans, cried, "No—no," and swore and raved, gesticulating, in the most ludicrous manner till he was ordered below. This, together with the awkward manner of lowering colors with levers and hatchets, drew peals of laughter from the American sailors.

Lieutenant Burrows lived till the sword of the English commander was placed under his head, when he murmured, "I die contented." This vessel, which proved to be the Boxer, was terribly cut up, but the number of killed was never ascertained, as they were thrown overboard fast as they fell. She had fourteen wounded, while the loss of the Americans was one killed and thirteen wounded.

After this the Enterprise, under Lieutenant Renshaw, cruised south, in company with the Rattlesnake, both having many narrow escapes from British men of war. The former captured, off the coast of Florida, the British privateer, Mars, of fourteen guns. Soon after she was chased by a frigate for three days, the latter often being within gunshot.

So hard was the brig pressed, that Lieutenant Renshaw was compelled to throw his anchors, cables, and all but one of his guns overboard. At length it fell calm, and the frigate began to hoist out her boats. The capture of the brig then seemed inevitable, but a light breeze springing up, bringing her fortunately to windward, her sails filled, and she swept joyfully away from her formidable antagonist.

Soon after Renshaw was transferred to the Rattlesnake, in which vessel he was again so hard pressed by a man of war, that he had to throw over all his guns but two. Afterwards, near the same spot, being wedged in between a British frigate and the land, he was compelled to strike his flag.

The Argus, another brig, was launched this year, and dispatched in June to France, to carry out Mr. Crawford, our newly appointed Minister to that country. Having accomplished this mission, Lieutenant Allen, the commander, steered for the coast of England, and cruised boldly in the chops of the English channel. Here and in the Irish channel, this daring commander pounced upon British merchantmen while almost entering their own ports. He was in the midst of the enemy's cruisers, and the most untiring watchfulness was demanded to avoid capture. Unable to man his prizes he set them on fire, making the Irish Channel lurid with the flames of burning vessels, and lighting up such beacon fires as England never before saw along her coast. Great astonishment was felt in Great Britain at the daring and success of this bold marauder, and vessels were sent out to capture him. But for a long time he eluded their search, leaving only smouldering ships to tell where he had been. This service was distasteful to Allen, who was ambitious of distinction, and wished for an antagonist more worthy of his attention. Determined to combine as much kindness and humanity with his duty as he could, he allowed no plundering of private property. All passengers of captured vessels were permitted to go below, and unwatched, pack up whatever they wished, and to pass unchallenged. The slightest deviation from this rule, on the part of his crew, was instantly and severely punished. This humanity, joined to his daring acts, brought back to the English the days of Robin Hood and Captain Kidd.

A cruise like this of a single brig in the Irish Channel, could not, of course, continue long. Even if she could avoid capture, the crew must in time sink under their constant and fatiguing efforts.

On the thirteenth of August, Allen captured a vessel from Oporto, loaded with wine. Towards morning he set her on fire, and by the light of her blazing spars stood away under easy sail. Soon after daylight he saw a large brig of war bearing down upon him, perfectly covered with canvas. He immediately took in sail to allow her to close, and when she came within close range gave her a broadside. As the vessels continued to approach the firing became more rapid and destructive. In four minutes Captain Allen was mortally wounded by a round shot, carrying off his leg. His officers immediately caught him up to carry him below, but he ordered them back to their posts. In a short time, however, he fainted from loss of blood and was taken away. Four minutes after, the first lieutenant, Watson, was struck in the head by a grape shot, and he too was taken below. There was then but one lieutenant left, Lieut. H. Allen, who though alone, fought his ship gallantly. But the rigging was soon so cut up that the vessel became unmanageable, and the enemy chose his own position. In about a quarter of an hour Mr. Watson was able to return on deck, when he found the brig rolling helplessly on the water, a target for the Englishman's guns. He however determined to get alongside and board, but all his efforts to do so were abortive, and he was compelled to strike his colors. His victorious adversary was the Pelican, a brig of war a fourth larger than the Argus.

Unwilling to believe that this great disparity of force was a sufficient reason for the defeat, the Americans endeavored to account for it in other ways. It was said that the sailors succeeded in smuggling wine from the brig burned a few hours before, and were not in a condition to fight—others that they were so overcome with fatigue that they nodded at their guns. Her fire was certainly much less destructive than that of other American vessels, which one of the officers on board said was owing to the powder used. Getting short of ammunition, they had taken some powder from an English vessel bound to South America. This being placed uppermost in the magazine, was used in this engagement. It was afterwards ascertained to be condemned powder, going as usual to supply South American and Mexican armies. In proof of this, it was said that the Pelican's hull was dented with shot, that had not force enough to pierce the timbers. The superiority of the English vessel in size, however, is a sufficient reason, without resorting to these explanations.[37] If any other was wanted, it would be found in the early loss of the superior officers. Such a calamity, at the outset of an engagement, will almost invariably turn an even scale. One officer cannot manage a ship, and sailors without leaders never fight well.

Captain Allen was taken ashore and placed in a hospital. As he was carried from the ship, he turned his languid eyes on the comrades of his perils and murmured, "God bless you, my lads; we shall never meet again." His conduct on the English coast furnishes a striking contrast to that of Cockburn, along our shores.[38]

CHAPTER XI.

1813.

With such a large extent of ocean and lake coast, and so vast and unprotected western and southern frontiers occupied by hostile savages, our troops were necessarily distributed over a wide surface. The northern army alone acted on the offensive—in all other sections of the country the Republic strove only to preserve its territory intact. The summer in which Dearborn's army lay inactive at Fort George, looked gloomy for the nation. Great exertions were being made to retrieve our errors, and the war in the north was carried on at an enormous expense. The conveying of provisions and arms for such a distance on pack-horses, increased immensely the price of every article. It was said that each cannon, by the time it reached Sackett's Harbor, cost a thousand dollars, while the transportation of provisions to the army of Harrison swelled them to such an exorbitant price, that the amount expended on a small detachment would now feed a whole army. The cost of building the indifferent vessels we had on Lake Ontario, was nearly two millions of dollars.

But while these vast expenditures were made for the northern army, and Harrison was gradually concentrating his troops at Fort Meigs, and Perry building his little fleet on Lake Erie, soon to send up a shout that should shake the land, and while the murmuring of the savage hordes, that stretched from Mackinaw to the Gulf of Mexico, foretold a bloody day approaching, an ominous cloud was gathering over the Atlantic sea-coast. English fleets were hovering around our harbors and threatening our cities and towns with conflagration. The year before, England could spare but few vessels or troops to carry on the war. Absorbed in the vast designs of Napoleon, who having wrested from her nearly all her allies and banded them together under his standard—Austria, Prussia, Poland, all Germany pressing after his victorious eagles as they flashed above the waters of the Niemen—was at that time advancing with a half million of men on the great northern power. If he should prove successful, England would be compelled to succumb, or with a still more overwhelming force he would next precipitate himself upon her shores. But the snow-drifts of Russia had closed over that vast and gallant host—his allies had abandoned him, and the rising of the nations around him, in his weak, exhausted condition, foretold the overthrow that soon sent him forth an exile from his throne and kingdom. Released from the anxiety that had hitherto rendered her comparatively indifferent to the war on this continent, she resolved to mete out to us a chastisement the more severe since it had been so long withheld. Irritated, too, because we had endeavored to rob her of her provinces at a moment when she was the least able to extend protection to them, she did not regard us as a common enemy, but as one who by his conduct had ceased to merit the treatment accorded in civilized warfare. The first squadron appeared in the Chesapeake in February and blockaded it. Soon after another, entered the Delaware under the command of Beresford, who attempted to land at Lewistown, but was gallantly repulsed by the militia, commanded by Colonel Davis. The town was bombarded, and though the firing was kept up for twenty hours, no impression was made upon it. In March the whole coast of the United States was declared in a state of blockade, with the exception of Rhode Island, Massachusetts, and New Hampshire. It is not known why Connecticut was not also omitted, but the invidious distinction made between the eastern and the other states grew out of the well known hostility of the former to the war. It was intended not only as a reward for their good behavior in the past, but a guerdon of better things should that hostility assume a more definite form. This intended compliment to New England was the greatest insult she ever received. It was a charge of disloyalty—the offer of a bribe for treason—the proffer of the hand of friendship, while that same hand was applying the torch to American dwellings and carrying the horrors of war to the hearth-stone and fireside.

Admiral Cockburn, especially, made his name infamous by his wanton attacks on farm houses and peaceful citizens, and the license he allowed to the brutal soldiery, who were guilty of deeds of shame and violence like those which disgraced the troops of Wellington at Badajos and St. Sebastian. After amusing himself by these predatory exercises on peasants, hen roosts, barns, and cattle, he planned the more important attack on Frenchtown, a village consisting of six dwellings and two store houses. Taking with him about five hundred marines, he set out at night, and rousing the terrified inhabitants by his cannon, landed his imposing force, burned the two store houses, after taking such of their contents as he needed—committed some petty depredations, and retired.

The American frigate, Constellation, was blockaded in the bay by this fleet, but all efforts to take her were repulsed by her brave crew.

May 3.

120

The scene of his next exploits was Havre de Grace, a thriving town, situated on the Susquehanna, about two miles from the head of the bay. He set out with his barges by night, and at daylight next morning awakened the inhabitants with the thunder of cannon and explosion of rockets in their midst. A scene of consternation and brutality followed. Frightened women and children ran shrieking through the streets, pursued by the insults and shouts of the soldiers. The houses were sacked and then set on fire. The ascending smoke and flames of the burning dwellings increased the ferocity of the men, and acts were committed, from mere wantonness, disgraceful both to the soldiers and their commanders. The work of destruction being completed, the British force was divided into three bodies—one of which was ordered to remain as guard, while the other two pierced inland, spoiling and insulting the farmers, and robbing peaceful travellers. For three days this gallant corps remained the terror and pest of the surrounding country, and then re-embarked with their booty, leaving the inhabitants to return to the ashes of their dwellings. Georgetown and Frederictown became, in turn, the prey of these marauders, and the light of burning habitations, and tears of women and children, fleeing in every direction, kindled into tenfold fury the rage of the inhabitants. A sympathetic feeling pervaded Congress, and no sooner did it assemble than Clay, the speaker, descended from the chair, and demanded an investigation of the charges brought against British soldiers and officers. These excesses, however, were but the prelude to greater and more revolting ones. Admiral Warren having arrived in the bay with reinforcements, and land troops under the command of General Beckwith, more serious movements were resolved upon. Norfolk was selected as the first point of attack. This important town was protected by two forts on either side of the Elizabeth river, between which the frigate Constellation lay at anchor. Soon after the fleet moved to the mouth of James river, and began to prepare for an attack on Craney Island, the first obstacle between it and Norfolk. Penetrating their design, Captain Tarbell landed a hundred seamen on the island, to man a fort on the north-west side, while he moved his gun boats so as to command the other channel. At day dawn on the 22d, fifty barges loaded with troops were seen pulling swiftly towards the island, to a point out of reach of the gun boats, but within range of the batteries on shore. These immediately opened their fire with such precision, that many of the boats were cut in two and sunk, and the remainder compelled to retire. An attempt from the mainland was also repulsed by the Virginia militia, under Colonel Beatty. The enemy lost in this attack between two and three hundred men, while the Americans suffered but little. Three days after the repulse at Craney Island, Admiral Cockburn, assisted by General Beckwith, made a descent on Hampton, a small fishing town by Hampton roads. The riflemen stationed there, and the militia, bravely resisted the landing, but were finally driven back by superior numbers. The place was then entered and plundered, not merely of its public stores, but private property. This little fishing town was literally sacked by the British army of twenty-five hundred men. Private houses were rifled, even the communion service of the church was carried away, while the women were subjected to the most degrading insults, and *ravished in open day*! The American army marched into Mexico over the bodies of their slain comrades, and were fired upon for a whole day from the roofs of houses after the city had surrendered, yet no such acts of violence were ever charged on them as were committed under the sanction of the British flag in this little peaceful, solitary, and defenceless village. The authorities of the different towns took up the matter—witnesses were examined, affidavits made, and the proceedings forwarded to the British Commander. The charges were denied, but they stand proved to this day, a lasting stigma on the name of Cockburn. This rear admiral in the British navy not only allowed such outrages in one instance, but repeatedly. There was a harmony in his proceedings refuting the apology of unintentional baseness. His expeditions were those of a brigand, and he changed civilized warfare into marauding, robbery, and pillage. The news of these enormities, aggravated as they passed from mouth to month, spread like wildfire amid the people. Stirring appeals were heard in every village and town. Calm reflection and reason were indignantly spurned; woman, manhood, patriotism, all cried aloud for vengeance, and the war-cry of an aroused and indignant people swelled like thunder over the land. The leaders of the anti-war faction saw with consternation this rising sympathy of the masses. It threatened, for the time, to sweep away their influence entirely. The British committed a vital error in allowing these excesses, for they harmonized the hitherto divided feelings of the people, and furnished the upholders of the war with a new and powerful argument for unity and energy. The public ear had become accustomed to the tales of impressment and charges of the invasion of neutral rights. The atrocities on the north-western frontier affected the west more than the east, where they were charged rather to the Indians than to the British Government, and were inflicted on an invading force. But a system of warfare so abhorrent to humanity, aroused into activity a spirit which gave tenfold strength to the administration.

While the Chesapeake remained blockaded, Admiral Cockburn, with a portion of the fleet, moved southward, preceded by the history of his deeds. The coasts of the Carolinas and Georgia were thrown into a state of agitation bordering on frenzy. Mrs. Gaston, wife of a member of Congress, died in convulsions from the terror inspired by this British Admiral. He, however, effected but little. Landing at Portsmouth he seized some booty and a few slaves. From the outset he had attempted to persuade the slaves to rise against their masters, and actually organized a company of blacks to aid him in his marauding expeditions.

The squadron blockading the coast north of the Chesapeake was commanded by Commodore Hardy, the reverse of Cockburn in every quality that distinguished the latter. He waged no warfare on defenceless towns, and villages, and women and children. Humane and generous, he had more cause to complain of the conduct of the excited inhabitants, than they of his. Although he landed at various places he allowed his troops to commit no violence.

The American coast, south of Cape Cod, was at length thoroughly blockaded, so that not only were our ships at home shut in port, but those endeavoring to enter from without captured, and our whole coasting trade was cut off, causing the country to feel severely the miseries of war. The Constellation remained blockaded in the Chesapeake, while the Macedonian, United States, and sloop Hornet, in endeavoring to escape from New York by the way of the Sound, were chased into New London, where they were compelled to lay inactive. In the mean time, in accordance with an act of Congress, passed in the winter, allowing half of the value of war ships to those who should destroy them by other means than armed or commissioned vessels of the United States, great ingenuity was exhibited in the construction of torpedoes. Several attempts were made to blow up the British frigates, but without success. The Plantagenet, however, riding in Lynn Haven bay, came near falling a victim to one of these missiles, which spread terror through the British fleet. After several unsuccessful efforts, Mr. Mix, to whom the torpedo was entrusted, at length succeeded in getting it near the bows of the vessel, unperceived. July 24. The "all's well" of the watch on deck had scarcely pealed over the water, when it exploded with terrific violence. A red and purple column suddenly rose fifty feet in the air, and bursting, fell like a water-spout on deck. The ship rolled heavily in the chasm, and a general rush was made for the boats, one of which was blown into the air. Commodore Hardy remonstrated against this mode of warfare, as contrary to the usages of civilized nations, and it was soon abandoned. The terror it inspired, however, made him more wary in approaching the coast. A boat-guard was kept rowing around the ships all night, and the most extraordinary precautions taken to protect them from these mysterious engines of destruction.

While our blockaded coast was thus filling Congress with alarm, and the whole land with gloom and dread, the bold and hostile attitude which Massachusetts was assuming, both deepened the general indignation and added to the embarrassments under which the administration struggled. Owing, doubtless, to the failures which marked the close of the previous year, the elections in the New England states during the early spring had terminated very satisfactorily to the Federalists. Strong was elected Governor of Massachusetts by a large majority, while both branches of the Legislature were under the control of the Federalists. In Connecticut and New Hampshire they had also triumphed, and Vermont, although her state government and delegation to Congress were Democratic, was still claimed as Federalist in the popular majority.

On the other side, New York and Pennsylvania spoke loudly for the Administration, the latter by offering to loan a million of dollars to the government, as an offset to the efforts of the Federalists to prevent the loan proposed by government being taken.

May 20.

During the summer, acting under a hostile message received from the governor, the Massachusetts Legislature drew up a remonstrance, denouncing the war as wrong and unwise, prompted by desire of conquest and love of France, rather than the wish to maintain the rights of the people. The report of a committee against the incorporation into the Union of Louisiana, as the commencement of western annexation, destined, if not arrested, to destroy the preponderance of the Eastern states, was also sustained in this remonstrance, which closed with a solemn appeal to the Searcher of all hearts for the purity of the motives which prompted it. Quincy in the House, and Otis and Loyd in the Senate, were the Federalist leaders. Not content with taking this hostile attitude to the General Government, the Legislature soon after refused to pass resolutions complimentary to Captain Lawrence for his gallant conduct in capturing the Peacock, and passed instead, the following resolution introduced by a preamble, declaring that such commendations encouraged the continuance of the war. "*Resolved*, as the sense of the Senate of Massachusetts, that in a war like the present, waged without justifiable cause, and prosecuted in a manner showing that conquest and ambition are its real motives, it is not becoming a moral people to express any approbation of military or naval exploits, which are not immediately connected with the defence of our sea-coast and soil." This was not a mere expression of feeling, but the utterance of a principle acted on from that time to the end of the war. This proud assumption of state rights and denunciation of the war when our coasts were blockaded by British cruisers and our frontiers drenched in blood, met the stern condemnation of the people throughout the land, and raised a clamor that frightened the authors of it. Party spirit had made Massachusetts mad, and blinded by her own narrow views, she wished to wrap herself up in her isolated dignity and keep forever from the great brotherhood of the Union those western territories where the hardy settler had to contend not only with the asperities of nature but a treacherous foe. That West which she then abjured has since repaid the wrong by pouring into her lap countless treasures, and furnishing homes for tens of thousands of her sons and daughters. Allowing the spirit of faction to override the feelings of nationality, she refused to rejoice in the victories of her country or sympathize in her defeats. South Carolina has since assumed a similar hostile attitude to the Union, but it yet remains to be seen whether she would not sink her private quarrels when the national rights were struck down and the country wasted by a common foe. As a state, not only repudiating the authority of the general government and the sacredness of the Union, but also refusing to stand by the republic in the hour of adversity and darkness, Massachusetts occupied at that time a preeminence in our history which it is to be hoped no other state will ever covet.

CHAPTER XII.

But while the country, torn with internal strife and wasted by external foes, looked with sad forebodings on the prospect before it, there suddenly shot forth over the western wilderness a gleam of light, like the bright hues of sunset, betokening a fairer to-morrow. Perry's brilliant victory, followed by the overthrow of Proctor a few weeks after, thrilled the land from limit to limit. On the frontier, where we had met with nothing but disgrace, and towards which the common eye turned with chagrin, we had cancelled a portion of our shame, and relieved the national bosom of a part of the load that oppressed it.

After the capture of Forts York and George, by which the river of Niagara was opened to American navigation, Captain Perry was able to take some vessels bought for the service from Black Rock into Lake Erie. The Lake at the time was in the possession of the British fleet, commanded by Captain Barclay, and Perry ran great hazard in encountering it before he could reach Presque Isle, now Erie, where the other vessels to compose his squadron had been built. He, however, reached this spacious harbor just as the English hove in sight. Having now collected his whole force he made vigorous preparations to get to sea. By the first of August he was ready to set sail, but the enemy lay off the harbor, across the mouth of which extended a bar, that he was afraid to cross under a heavy fire. To his great delight, however, the British fleet suddenly disappeared—Captain Barclay not dreaming that his adversary was ready to go to sea, having gone to the Canada shore.

Perry was at this time a mere youth, of twenty-seven years of age, but ardent, chivalrous, and full of energy and resource. From the time he arrived on the frontier, the winter previous, he had been unceasing in his efforts to obtain and equip a fleet. Materials had to be brought from Pittsburgh and Philadelphia, dragged hundreds of miles over bad roads and across unbridged streams. But after his vessels were ready for sea, he was destitute of crews. To his repeated and urgent calls for men, only promises were returned, nor did they arrive till the English had been able to finish and equip a large vessel, the Detroit, which gave them a decided preponderance. Perry was exceedingly anxious to attack the hostile fleet before it received this accession of strength, but prevented from doing this through want of men, he was at last compelled to abandon all his efforts, or take his chance with his motley, untrained crew, in an action where the superiority was manifest. He boldly resolved on the latter course, and taking advantage of Barclay's sudden departure, gave orders for the men to repair immediately on board ship, and dropped with eight of his squadron down the harbor to the bar. It was Sabbath morning, and young Perry, impressed with the great issues to himself and his country from the step he was about to take, sent his boat ashore for a clergyman, requesting him to hold religious services on board his ship. All the officers of the squadron were assembled on the deck of the Lawrence, and listened to an impressive address on the duty they owed their country. Prayer was then offered for the success of their cause. Young Perry reverently listening to the voice of prayer, as he is going forth to battle, and young Macdonough lifting his own in supplication to God, after his decks are cleared for action, furnish striking and beautiful examples to naval men.

Next morning the water being smooth, the guns of the Lawrence, the largest vessel, were taken out, and two scows placed alongside and filled till they sunk to the water's edge. Pieces of timber were then run through the forward and after ports of the vessel, and made fast by blocks to the scows. All being ready, the water was pumped out of them, and the vessel slowly rose over the bar. She stuck fast, however, on the top, and the scows had to be sunk again before she finally floated clear and moved off into deep water. The men worked all night to get this one brig over. The schooners passed easily and moored outside. The Lawrence was scarcely once more afloat before the returning fleet hove in sight. Perry immediately prepared for action. But Barclay after reconnoitering for half an hour crowded all sail and disappeared again up the lake.[39] The next day Perry sailed in pursuit, but after cruising a whole day without finding the enemy, returned to take in supplies. Aug. 12. He was about to start again, when he received information of the expected approach of a party of seamen under the command of Captain Elliot. Waiting a day or two to receive this welcome aid, he set sail for Sandusky, to put himself in communication with Gen. Harrison and the north-western army. He then returned to Malden, where the British fleet lay, and going into Put-in Bay, a haven in its vicinity, waited for the enemy to come out. Aug. 25. Here many of his crew were taken sick with fever, which at last seized him, together with the three surgeons of the squadron. He was not able to leave his cabin till the early part of September, when he received an additional reinforcement of a hundred volunteers. These troops came from Harrison's army, and were mostly Kentucky militia and soldiers from the 28th regiment of infantry, and all volunteers for the approaching battle. The Kentuckians, most of them, had never seen a square rigged vessel before, and wandered up and down examining every room and part of the ship without scruple. Dressed in their fringed linsey-woolsey hunting-shirts, with their muskets in their hands, they made a novel marine corps as ever trod the deck of a battle-ship.

Sept. 10.

On the morning of the 10th of September, it was announced that the British fleet was coming out of Malden, and Perry immediately set sail to meet it. His squadron consisted of three brigs, the Lawrence, Niagara and Caledonia, the Trippe, a sloop, and five schooners, carrying in all fifty-four guns. That of the British was composed of six vessels, mounting sixty-three guns. It was a beautiful morning, and the light breeze scarcely ruffled the surface of the water as the two squadrons, with all sails set, slowly approached each other. The weather-gauge, at first, was with the enemy, but Perry impatient to close, resolved to waive this advantage, and kept standing on, when the wind unexpectedly shifted in his favor. Captain Barclay observing this, immediately hove to, and lying with his topsails aback, waited the approach of his adversary. With all his canvass out, Perry bore slowly and steadily down before the wind. The breeze was so light that he could scarcely make two miles an hour. The shore was lined with spectators, gazing on the exciting spectacle, and watching with intense anxiety the movements of the American squadron. Not a cloud dimmed the clear blue sky over head, and the lake lay like a mirror, reflecting its beauty and its purity. Perry, in the Lawrence, led the line.

Taking out the flag which had been previously prepared, and mounting a gun-slide, he called the crew about him, and said, "My brave lads, this flag contains the last words of Captain Lawrence. Shall I hoist it?" "Aye, aye, sir," was the cheerful response. Up went the flag with a will, and as it swayed to the breeze it was greeted with loud cheers from the deck. As the rest of the squadron beheld that flag floating from the mainmast of their commander's vessel, and saw "Don't give up the ship!" was to be the signal for action, a long, loud cheer rolled down the line. The excitement spread below, and all the sick that could move, tumbled up to aid in the approaching combat. Perry then visited every gun, having a word of encouragement for each captain. Seeing some of the gallant tars who had served on board the Constitution, and many of whom now stood with handkerchiefs tied round their heads, all cleared for action, he said, "Well, boys, are you ready?" "All ready, your honor," was the quick response. "I need not say anything to you. *You* know how to beat those fellows," he added smilingly, as he passed on.

The wind was so light that it took an hour and a half, after all the preparations had been made, to reach the hostile squadron. This long interval of idleness and suspense was harder to bear than the battle itself. Every man stood silently watching the enemy's vessels, or in low and earnest tones conversed with each other, leaving requests and messages to friends in case they fell. Perry gave his last direction, in the event of his death, to Hambleton —tied weights to his public papers in order to have them ready to cast overboard if he should be defeated—read over his wife's letters for the last time, and then tore them up, so that the enemy should not see those records of the heart, and turned away, remarking, *"This is the most important day of my life."* The deep seriousness and silence that had fallen on the ship, was at last broken by the blast of a bugle that came ringing over the water from the Detroit, followed by cheers from the whole British squadron. A single gun, whose shot went skipping past the Lawrence, first uttered its stern challenge, and in a few minutes all the long guns of the enemy began to play on the American fleet. Being a mile and a half distant, Perry could not use his carronades, and he was exposed to this fire for a half an hour before he could get within range. Steering straight for the Detroit, a vessel a fourth larger than his own, he gave orders to have the schooners that lagged behind close up within half cable's length. Those orders, the last he gave during the battle, were passed by trumpet from vessel to vessel. The light wind having nearly died away, the Lawrence suffered severely before she could get near enough to open with her carronades and she had scarcely taken her position before the fire of three vessels was directed upon her. Enveloped in flame and smoke, Perry strove desperately to maintain his ground till the rest of the fleet could close, and for two hours sustained without flinching this unequal contest. The balls crashed incessantly through the sides of the ship, dismounting the guns and strewing the deck with the dead, until at length, with "every brace and bow-line shot away," she lay an unmanageable wreck on the water. But still through the smoke, as it rent before the heavy broadsides, her colors were seen flying, and still gleamed forth in the sunlight that glorious motto —*"Don't give up the ship!"* Calm and unmoved at the slaughter around him and his own desperate position, Perry gave his orders tranquilly, as though executing a manœuvre. Although in his first battle, and unaccustomed to scenes of carnage, his face gave no token of the emotions that mastered him. Advancing to assist a sailor whose gun had got out of order, he saw the poor fellow struck from his side by a twenty-four pound shot and expire without a groan. His second lieutenant fell at his feet. Lieutenant Brooks, a gay, dashing officer, of extraordinary personal beauty, while speaking cheerfully to him, was dashed by a cannon-ball to the other side of the deck and mangled in the most frightful manner. His shrieks and imploring cries to Perry to kill him and end his misery, were heard even above the roar of the guns in every part of the ship. The dying who strewed the deck would turn their eyes in mute inquiry upon their youthful commander, as if to be told they had done their duty. The living, as a sweeping shot rent huge gaps in the ranks of their companions, looked a moment into his face to read its expression, and then stepped quietly into the places left vacant.

Lieutenant Yarnall, with a red handkerchief tied round his head, and another round his neck, to staunch the blood flowing from two wounds, his nose swelled to a monstrous size, from a splinter having passed through it, disfigured and covered with gore, moved amid this terrific scene the very genius of havoc and carnage. Approaching Perry, he told him every officer in his division was killed. Others were given him, but he soon returned with the same dismal tidings. Perry then told him he must get along by himself, as he had no more to furnish him, and the gallant man went back alone to his guns. Once only did the shadow of any emotion pass over the countenance of this intrepid commander. He had a brother on board, only twelve years old. The little fellow who had had two balls pass through his hat, and been struck with splinters, was still standing by the side of his brother, stunned by the awful cannonading and carnage around him, when he suddenly fell. For a moment Perry thought he too was gone, but he had only been knocked down by a hammock, which a cannon ball had hurled against him.

BATTLE ON LAKE ERIE.

At length every gun was dismounted but one, still Perry fought with that till at last it also was knocked from the carriage. Out of the one hundred men with whom a few hours before he had gone into battle, only eighteen stood up unwounded. Looking through the smoke he saw the Niagara, apparently uncrippled, drifting out of the battle. Leaping into a boat with his young brother, he said to his remaining officer, "If a victory is to be gained, I will gain it," and standing erect, told the sailors to give way with a will. The enemy observed the movement, and immediately directed their fire upon the boat. Oars were splintered in the rowers' hands by musket balls, and the men themselves covered with spray from the round shot and grape, that smote the water on every side. Passing swiftly through the iron storm he reached the

Niagara in safety, and as the survivors of the Lawrence saw him go up the vessel's side, they gave a hearty cheer. Finding her sound and whole, Perry backed his maintop sail, and flung out his signal for close action. From vessel to vessel the answering signals went up in the sunlight, and three cheers rang over the water. He then gave his sails to the wind and bore steadily down on the centre of the enemy's line. Reserving his fire as he advanced, he passed alone through the hostile fleet, within close pistol range, wrapt in flame as he swept on. Delivering his broadsides right and left, he spread horror and death through the decks of the Detroit and Lady Prevost. Rounding to as he passed the line, he laid his vessel close to two of the enemy's ships, and poured in his rapid fire. The shrieks that rung out from the Detroit were heard even above the deafening cannonade, while the crew of the Lady Prevost, unable to stand the fire, ran below, leaving their wounded, stunned, and bewildered commander alone on deck, leaning his face on his hand, and gazing vacantly on the passing ship. The other American vessels having come up, the action at once became general. To the spectators from the shore the scene at this moment was indescribably thrilling. Far out on the calm water lay a white cloud, from out whose tortured bosom broke incessant flashes and thunder claps—the loud echoes rolling heavily away over the deep, and dying amid the silence and solitude of the forest.

An action so close and murderous could not last long, and it was soon apparent that victory inclined to the Americans, for while the enemy's fire sensibly slackened, the signal for close action was still flying from the Niagara, and from every American vessel the answering signal floated proudly in the wind. In fifteen minutes from the time the first signal was made the battle was over. A white handkerchief waved from the taffrail of the Queen Charlotte announced the surrender. The firing ceased; the smoke slowly cleared away, revealing the two fleets commingled, shattered, and torn, and strewed with dead. The loss on each side was a hundred and thirty-five killed and wounded.

Perry having secured the prisoners, returned to the Lawrence, lying a wreck in the distance, whither she had helplessly drifted. She had struck her flag before he closed with the Niagara, but it was now flying again. Not a word was spoken as he went over the vessel's side; a silent grasp of the hand was the only sign of recognition, for the deck around was covered with dismembered limbs, and brains, while the bodies of twenty officers and men lay in ghastly groups before him.

As the sun went down over the still lake his last beams looked on a mournful spectacle. Those ships stripped of their spars and canvass, looked as if they had been swept by a hurricane, while desolation covered their decks.

At twilight the seamen who had fallen on board the American fleet were committed to the deep, and the solemn burial service of the Episcopal Church read over them.

The uproar of the day had ceased and deep silence rested on the two squadrons, riding quietly at anchor, broken only by the stifled groans of the wounded, that were echoed from ship to ship. As Perry sat that night on the quarter-deck of the Lawrence, conversing with his few remaining officers, while ever and anon the moans of his brave comrades below were borne to his ear, he was solemn and subdued. The exciting scene through which he had safely passed—the heavy load taken from his heart—the reflection that his own life had been spared, and the consciousness that his little brother was slumbering sweetly and unhurt in his hammock beside him, awakened emotions of gratitude to God, and he gravely remarked, "I believe that my wife's prayers have saved me."[40]

It had been a proud day for him, and as he lay that night and thought what a change a few hours had wrought in his fortunes, feelings of exultation might well swell his bosom. Such unshaken composure—such gallant bearing—stern resolution, and steadiness and tenacity of purpose in a young man of twenty-seven, in his first battle, exhibit a marvellous strength of character, and one wonders more at him than his success.

It was a great victory, and as the news spread, bonfires, illuminations, the firing of cannon and shouts of excited multitudes announced the joy and exultation of the nation. The gallant bearing of Perry—his daring passage in an open boat through the enemy's fire to the Niagara—the motto on his flag—the manner in which he carried his vessel alone through the enemy's line, and then closed in half pistol shot—his laconic account of the victory in a letter to the Secretary of the Navy, "WE HAVE MET THE ENEMY AND THEY ARE OURS"—furnished endless themes for discussion and eulogy, and he suddenly found himself in the front rank of heroes.

The day after the battle the funeral of the officers of the two fleets took place. A little opening on the margin of the bay, a wild and solitary spot, was selected as the place of interment. It was a beautiful autumn day, not a breath of air ruffled the surface of the lake or moved the still forest that fringed that lonely clearing. The sun shone brightly down on the new-made graves, and not a sound disturbed the sabbath stillness that rested on forest and lake. The fallen officers, each in his appropriate uniform, were laid on platforms made to receive them, and placed with their hands across their breasts, in the barges. As these were rowed gently away the boats fell in behind in long procession, and the whole swept slowly and sadly towards the place of burial. The flags drooped mournfully in the still air, the dirge to which the oars kept time rose and fell in solemn strains over the water, while minute guns from the various vessels blended their impressive harmony with the scene. The day before had been one of strife and carnage, but those who had closed in mortal hate, now mourned like a band of brothers for their fallen leaders, and gathering together around the place of burial, gazed a last farewell, and firing one volley over the nameless graves, turned sadly away. There, in that wild spot, with the sullen waves to sing their perpetual dirge, they slept the sleep of the brave. They had fought gallantly, and it mattered not to them the victory or defeat, for they had gone to that still land where human strifes are forgotten, and the clangor of battle never comes.

This impressive scene occurred off the shore where the massacre of Raisin was committed, and what a striking contrast does it present to the day that succeeded the victory of Proctor. By his noble and generous conduct Perry won the esteem and love of his enemies, while Proctor by his unfeeling neglect and barbarity received the curse of all honorable men. The name of one is linked to the spot where he conquered, with blessings; that of the other with everlasting infamy and disgrace.

Harrison, after this victory, collected his army of seven thousand men, and concentrated them at Put-in Bay. Perry's fleet rode triumphant on the lake, and he offered its service to Harrison. The latter ordered the regiment of horse, one thousand strong, to proceed by land to Detroit, while the rest of the army was embarked on board the vessels and set sail for Malden. Sept. 13. Proctor commanded at the latter place, and hearing of Barclay's defeat and Harrison's advance, was seized with alarm, and dismantling and blowing up the fort, and setting on fire the navy yard, barracks and store houses, and taking with him all the horses and cattle, fled towards the Thames. The Americans followed in swift and eager pursuit. Governor Shelby, of Kentucky, though sixty-two years of age, was there with his brave Kentuckians, a volunteer, shaking his white locks with the merriest. Perry and Cass also accompanied the army, sharing in the animation and eagerness of the men. Sending a detachment across the river to drive out the hostile Indians from Detroit, Harrison, on the 30th, saw with relief the mounted column of Colonel Johnson winding along the opposite bank, announcing its approach with the stirring notes of the bugle. Resting one day to complete his preparations, he, on the 2d of October, resumed the pursuit, and soon, abandoned guns and shells, destroyed bridges, and houses and vessels on fire, revealed the haste and rage of the enemy. Proctor, after reaching the Thames, kept up the river, with the intention of striking the British posts near the head of Lake Ontario. But Harrison pressed him so closely, it soon became evident that a battle could not be avoided. On the 5th, Colonel Johnson, with his mounted Kentuckians, marching two or three miles in advance, came upon the retreating army drawn up in order of battle, on the bank of the Thames near the Moravian settlement. Proctor had taken an admirable position upon a dry strip of land, flanked by the river on the left and a swamp on the right. Here he placed his regulars, eight hundred strong, while Tecumseh with his two thousand Indian allies occupied the eastern margin of the swamp. Harrison, with his troops jaded out, encamped that night in front of the enemy. Oct. 4 After dark Proctor and Tecumseh reconnoitred together the American camp, when the latter advised a night attack. This, Proctor objected to, and strongly urged a retreat. The haughty savage spurned the proposition, and in the morning the British general finding he could not escape an engagement, resolved to give battle where he was. Thinking only of retreat he had neglected to erect a breastwork or cut a ditch in front of his position, which would have effectually prevented a cavalry attack. To ensure the complete success of this blunder, he formed his troops in open order, thus provoking a charge of horse. Oct. 5. Colonel Johnson, at his earnest request, was allowed to open the battle with his thousand mounted riflemen. But just as he was about to order the charge, he discovered that the ground was too cramped to admit of a rapid and orderly movement of the entire force, and he therefore divided it into two columns, and putting his brother, Lieutenant Colonel James Johnson, at the head of the one that was to advance on the British, he led the other against the Indians. These two battalions moved slowly forward for a short time parallel to each other, the infantry following. The column advancing on the British was checked at the first fire —the horses at the head of it recoiling. Their riders, however, quickly recovered them, and sending the rowels home, plunged with a yell of frenzy full on the British line. A few saddles were emptied, but nothing could stop that astonishing charge. Those fiery horsemen swept like a whirlwind through the panic-stricken ranks, and then wheeling, delivered their fire. Nearly five hundred rifles cracked at once, strewing the ground with men. It was a single blow, and the battle was over in that part of the field. Scarcely a minute had elapsed, and almost the entire British force was begging for quarter. A charge of cavalry with rifles only, was probably a new thing to those soldiers. Proctor, with forty men and some mounted Indians, fled at the first onset. His carriage, private papers, even his sword, were left behind, and goaded by terror he was soon lost in the distance. He remembered the massacre at Raisin, and knew if those enraged Kentuckians, whose brothers, fathers and sons he had given up to the savage, once laid hands on him they would grant him short shrift. Cruelty and cowardice are often joined together.

The other battalion not finding firm footing for the horses could not charge, and Johnson seeing that his men were being rapidly picked off, ordered them to dismount and take to the cover. Tecumseh led his men gallantly forward, and for a few minutes the conflict was sharp and bloody. Johnson was wounded in three places, yet stubbornly maintained his ground. At length Tecumseh fell, when the savages with a loud whoop, the "death halloo" of their leader, turned and fled. The death of this remarkable chieftain was worth more than a whole hostile tribe destroyed, and broke up forever the grand alliance of the Indians with the British. Not more than twenty-five hundred American troops mingled in the battle at all; of these but fifty were killed and wounded. Among the latter was Colonel Johnson, who was borne from the field in a blanket, with the blood running out at either end. Six hundred prisoners were taken, a large quantity of stores, ammunition, etc., and six pieces of artillery, among which were three captured from the British during the Revolution, and surrendered by General Hull at Detroit. The news of this important victory coming so quick on that of Perry's, filled the nation with increased confidence, and placed a cheerful countenance once more on the war party. The cloud that had hung so darkly over the land seemed lifting, and if Chauncey on Lake Ontario, and Wilkinson on the St. Lawrence, would give equally good accounts of themselves, the season would close with Canada within our grasp.

CHAPTER XIII.

1813.

While Perry and Harrison were thus reclaiming our lost ground on Lake Erie and in the north-west, Armstrong was preparing to carry out his favorite plan of a descent on Kingston and Montreal. When he accepted the post of Secretary of War, he transferred his department from Washington to Sackett's Harbor, so that he might superintend in person the progress of the campaign. In April previous, the United States had been divided into nine military districts, that portion of New York State north of the Highlands and Vermont, constituting the ninth.[41] Although Wilkinson had superseded Dearborn, as commander-in-chief of this district in July, he did not issue his first orders to the army till the 23d of August. Three days after a council of war was held at Sackett's Harbor, in which it was estimated that by the 20th of September the army would consist of nine thousand men, exclusive of militia. The garrisons at Forts George, Niagara, Oswego and Burlington, were therefore ordered to rendezvous at Grenadier Island, near Sackett's Harbor. General Wade Hampton, who had been recalled from the fifth military district to the northern frontier, encamped with his army, four thousand strong, at Plattsburg, on Lake Champlain. The plan finally adopted by the Secretary was, to have Wilkinson drop down the St. Lawrence, and without stopping to attack the English posts on the river, form a junction with General Hampton, when the two armies should march at once on Montreal. These two Generals were both Revolutionary officers, and consequently too advanced in years to carry such an expedition through with vigor and activity. Besides, a hostile feeling separated them, rendering each jealous of the other's command, which threatened to work the most serious mischief. Armstrong, however, being the friend of both, thought by acting himself as commander-in-chief, he could reconcile their differences, sufficiently to insure harmony of action. Chauncey, in the mean time, after an action with Yeo, in which both parties claimed the victory, forced his adversary to take refuge in Burlington Bay.

Sept. 28. He then wrote to Wilkinson that the lake was clear of the enemy, and reported himself ready to transport the troops down the St. Lawrence.

The greatest expectations were formed of this expedition. The people knew nothing of the quarrel between Wilkinson and Hampton, and thought only of the strength of their united force. The victories of Perry and Harrison had restored confidence—the tide of misfortune had turned, and when the junction of the two armies should take place, making in all nearly twelve thousand men, the fate of Canada, they fondly believed, would be sealed. No large British force was concentrated on the frontier, while a garrison of but six hundred held Montreal. The press, deeming Canada already won, had begun to defend its conquest. The question was no longer, *how* to take it, but to reconcile the nation to its possession.

Sept. 19. While Wilkinson was preparing to fulfill his part of the campaign, Hampton made a bold push into Canada on his own responsibility. Advancing from Plattsburg, he marched directly for St. John, but finding water scarce for his draft cattle, owing to a severe drought, he moved to the left, and next day arrived at Chateaugay Four Corners, a few miles from the Canada line. Here he was overtaken by an order from Armstrong, commanding him to remain where was, until the arrival of Wilkinson. But jealous of his rival, and wishing to achieve a victory in which the honor would not be divided, he resolved to take upon himself the responsibility of advancing alone. Several detachments of militia had augmented his force of four thousand, and he deemed himself sufficiently strong to attack Prevost, who he was told had only about two thousand ill assorted troops under him. **Oct. 21.** He therefore gave orders to march, and cutting a road for twenty-four miles through the wilderness, after five days great toil, reached the British position. Ignorant of its weakness, he dispatched Colonel Purdy at night by a circuitous route to gain the enemy's flank and rear and assail his works, while he attacked them in front. Bewildered by the darkness, and led astray by his guide, Colonel Purdy wandered through the forest, entirely ignorant of the whereabouts of the enemy or of his own. General Hampton, however, supposing that he had succeeded in his attempt, ordered General Izard to advance with the main body of the army, and as soon as firing was heard in the rear to commence the attack in front. Izard marched up his men and a skirmish ensued, when Colonel De Salaberry, the British commander, who had but a handful of regulars under him, ordered the bugles, which had been placed at some distance apart on purpose to represent a large force, to sound the charge. The ruse succeeded admirably, and a halt was ordered. The bugles brought up the lost detachment of Purdy, but suddenly assailed by a concealed body of militia, his command was thrown into disorder and broke and fled. Disconcerted by the defeat of Purdy, Hampton ordered a retreat, without making any attempt to carry the British intrenchments. A few hundred Canadian militia, with a handful of regulars, stopped this army of more than four thousand men with ten pieces of artillery, so that it was forced, with a loss of but thirty men killed, wounded and missing, to retreat twenty-four miles along the road it had cut with so much labor through the forest. Hampton, defeated by the blasts of a few bugles, took up his position again at the Four Corners, to wait further news from Wilkinson's division.

WILKINSON FLOTILLA AMID THE THOUSAND ISLES.

The latter having concentrated his troops at Grenadier Island, embarked them again the same day that Hampton advanced, against orders, towards Montreal. Three hundred boats covering the river for miles, carried the infantry and artillery, while the cavalry, five hundred strong, marched along the bank. Beaten about by storms, drenched with rain, stranded on deceitful shoals, this grand fleet of batteaux crept so slowly towards the entrance of the St. Lawrence, that the army, dispirited and disgusted, railed on its commander and the government alike. They were two weeks in reaching the river. Wilkinson, who had been recalled from New Orleans, to take charge of this expedition, was prostrated by the lake fever, which, added to the infirmities of age, rendered him wholly unfit for the position he occupied. General Lewis, his second in command, was also sick. The season was already far advanced —the autumnal storms had set in earlier than usual—everything conspired to ensure defeat; and around this wreck of a commander, tossed an army, dispirited, disgusted, and doomed to disgrace. General Brown led the advance of this army of invasion, as it started for Montreal, a hundred and eighty miles distant. Approaching French Creek, eighteen miles below Grenadier Island, it was attacked by a fleet of boats from Kingston, but repulsed them with little loss. The news of the invasion, however, spreading, the British detachment at Kingston, reinforced by the militia, followed the descending flotilla, harassing it whenever an opportunity occurred. To a beholder the force seemed adequate to secure the object contemplated, for the spectacle it presented was grand and imposing. As the head of that vast fleet came winding around the bend of the stream and swept out of view below, the long procession of boats that streamed after seemed to be endless. Scattered in picturesque groups amid the Thousand Isles, or assailed with artillery from British forts—now swallowed up in the silent forest that clothed the banks, and again slowly drifting past the scattered settlements, or shooting the long and dangerous rapids, it presented a strange and picturesque appearance. When it reached the head of the long rapids at Hamilton, twenty miles below Ogdensburg, Wilkinson ordered General Brown to advance by land and cover the passage of the boats through the narrow defiles, where the enemy had established block houses. In the mean time the cavalry had crossed over to the Canadian side and with fifteen hundred men under General Boyd, been despatched against the enemy, which was constantly harassing his rear.

Nov. 11.

General Boyd, accompanied by Generals Swartwout and Covington as volunteers, moved forward in three columns. Colonel Ripley advancing with the 21st Regiment, drove the enemy's sharp shooters from the woods, and emerged on an open space, called Chrystler's Field, and directly in front of two English regiments. Notwithstanding the disparity of numbers this gallant officer ordered a charge, which was executed with such firmness that the two regiments retired. Rallying and making a stand, they were again charged and driven back. General Covington falling fiercely on the left flank, where the artillery was posted, forced it to recoil. But at this critical moment, while bravely leading on his men, he was shot through the body. His fall disconcerted the brigade, and a shower of grape shot at the same moment scourging it severely, it retired in confusion. This restored the combat, and for more than two hours that open field was the scene of successive and most gallant charges. The front of battle wavered to and fro, and deeds of personal courage and daring were done that showed that the troops and younger officers only needed a proper commander, and they would soon give a report of themselves which would change the aspect of affairs.

At length the British retired to their camp and the Americans maintained their position on the shore, so that the flotilla passed the Saut in safety. This action has never received the praise it deserves—the disgraceful failure of the campaign having cast a shadow upon it. The British, though inferior in numbers, had greatly the advantage in having possession of a stone house in the midst of the field, from which, as from a citadel, they could keep up a constant fire, without being injured in return. The conflict was close and murderous, and the American troops gave there a foretaste of Chippewa and Lundy's Lane. Nearly one-fifth of the entire force engaged were killed or wounded; a mortality never exhibited in a drawn battle without most desperate fighting.

General Wilkinson, who lay sick in his boat, knew nothing of what was transpiring, except by report. Brown's cannon thundering amid the rapids below—the dropping fire in the rear of his flotilla, and the incessant crash of artillery and rattle of musketry in the forest, blended their echoes around him, augmenting the power of disease, and increasing that nervous anxiety, which made him long to be away from such turbulent scenes, amid occupations more befitting his age and infirmities.

The army, however, still held its course for Montreal. Young Scott, who had joined the expedition at Ogdensburg, was fifteen miles ahead, clearing, with a detachment of less than eight hundred men, the river banks as he went. Montreal was known to be feebly garrisoned, and Wilkinson had no doubt it would fall an easy conquest. He therefore sent forward to Hampton to join him at St. Regis, with provisions. Hampton, in reply, said, that his men could bring no more provisions than they wanted for their own use, and informed him, in short, that he should not cooperate with him at all, but make the best of his way back to Lake Champlain.

On receiving this astounding news, Wilkinson called a council of war, which reprobated in strong terms the conduct of Hampton, and decided that in consideration of his failure, and the lateness of the season, the march should be suspended, and the army retire to winter quarters. This was carried into effect, and Wilkinson repaired to French Mills, on Salmon river, for the winter, and Hampton to Plattsburgh. Thus, for months, an army of twelve thousand men had marched and manœuvred on the Canadian frontier without striking a single blow. Confidence in the success of this campaign had been so great, that its disgraceful issue fell like a sudden paralysis on the war party, and on the nation generally. Like Hull's defeat, it was unredeemed by a single glimmer of light. The mind had nothing to rest upon for momentary relief. The failure was so complete and total, that the advocates of the war were struck dumb, and Washington was wrapped in gloom. The Federalists, on the contrary, were strengthened. Their prognostications had proved true. The nation had concentrated its strength on Canada for two years, and yet been unable to make the least impression. A Boston paper that from the first had denounced the war, said, "Democracy has rolled herself up in weeds, and laid down for its last wallowing in the slough of disgrace."

> Now lift ye saints your heads on high,
> And shout, for your redemption's nigh.[42]

The Federalists knew their advantage and prepared to use it, for this was not a lost battle that might in a few days be retrieved; it was a lost campaign, and a whole winter must intervene before an opportunity to redeem it could occur. In that time they hoped to make the administration a hissing and a bye-word in the land. The war party looked glum and sullen in view of the long and merciless scourging which awaited it. Armstrong was loudly censured, while on Wilkinson and Hampton it poured the whole vials of its wrath. Armstrong was doubtless too much of a martinet, and could carry through a campaign on paper much better than practically; still, the one he had proposed was feasible, and ought to have succeeded. He could not be held responsible for the insubordination of officers. He however committed one great error. Aware of the hostile feeling that existed between Wilkinson and Hampton, he should have remained on the spot and acted as commander-in-chief, or else if his duties rendered his absence imperative, accepted the resignation of Wilkinson. Old and sick as the latter was, no commander could have been more inefficient than he, while the enmity between him and Hampton was certain to end in mischief. The junction of the two armies would not have prevented, but on the contrary increased it. He knew, or ought to have known, they would not act harmoniously together, and it required no prophet's vision to foretell the fate of a divided army acting on the enemy's territory. If he had remained to urge forward the expedition, and sent home Hampton for disobeying his orders, and compelled the army to form a junction with that of Wilkinson, no doubt Montreal would have fallen. But knowing, as he did from the outset, that Hampton would never harmonize with his enemy—to allow the success of the campaign to depend on their concerted action, was committing a blunder for which no apology can be made.

Wilkinson came in for more than his share of public abuse. Sickness must always cover a multitude of sins. There are very few men whose will is stronger than disease. The firmest are unstrung by it. Even Cesar, when prostrated by fever, could say:

> "Give me some drink, Titinius,
> As a sick girl."

This is especially true of men advanced in years. Age tells heavily enough on both physical and mental powers in an arduous campaign, without the additional aid of fever. Wilkinson was perfectly aware of this, and requested twice to be released from the command. Forced to retain a position he felt unequal to, his conduct was necessarily characterized by no vigor; and insubordination, disgraceful quarrels, and duels, combined to make a sorry chapter in the history of the expedition. It must be confessed, however, that for some of his conduct, age and disease are but sorry excuses, and it is pretty apparent he was in character wholly unfit for the enterprise he had undertaken. For Hampton there is no apology. His disobedience of orders in the first place should have been followed by his immediate withdrawal from the army, while his refusal to do the very thing he had been sent north to perform, was a crime next to treason. All the forts we occupied on the frontier had been emptied of their garrisons, and great expense incurred by the government to carry forward an expedition, the chief feature in which was the junction and united advance of the two armies. His resignation saved him from public disgrace. The withdrawal of our troops from Lake Ontario and

Niagara, together with the suspension of hostilities on the St. Lawrence, was followed by the capture of all the posts we had been two years in taking.

When Scott obtained permission to join Wilkinson's army, he left Fort George in the command of General McClure of the New York militia. The fort had been put in a complete state of defence by Scott, and was supposed able to repel any force that would be brought against it. Vincent, who had abandoned its investment after Proctor's overthrow, returned when he heard of Wilkinson's retreat. McClure, under the plea that his militia had left him, and that those volunteers promised could not be obtained, resolved to abandon the fort without risking a battle.

Dec. 10.

He therefore dismantled it, and then in order to deprive the enemy of shelter, set fire to the neighboring village of Newark and drove four hundred women and children forth to the fierce blasts of a northern winter. The English, who during this war rarely waited for an excuse to resort to the barbarities of savage warfare, of course retaliated with tenfold violence.

Dec. 19.

Nine days after, Fort Niagara was surprised by a party of British and Indians, under the command of Colonel Murray, and sixty of the garrison murdered in cold blood. The manner in which it was taken created a strong suspicion of treachery somewhere. The British made no secret of the premeditated attack, and the day before, General McClure issued a proclamation to the inhabitants of Niagara, Genesee and Chatauque counties, calling on them to rally to the defence of their homes and country. To this was appended a postscript, stating, "since the above was prepared, I have received intelligence from a credible inhabitant from Canada (who has just escaped from thence) that the enemy are concentrating all their forces and boats at Fort George, and have fixed *upon to-morrow night for attacking Fort Niagara* —and should they succeed they will lay waste our whole frontier." On that very "morrow night" the attack *did* take place, and yet the Commandant, Captain Leonard, was absent, having left during the evening, without entrusting the command of the post to another. The picquets were taken by surprise, and the enemy entered by the main gate, which, it is said, was found open.

It seemed at this time as if the government had carefully selected the most inefficient men in the nation to command on our frontier, in order to show what a large stock we had on hand, before those more capable and deserving could be given a place. General McClure not only fixed the *time* of the attack, but declared that the fall of the fort would be followed by the desolation of the whole frontier, (in both of which prognostications he proved an admirable prophet,) yet not a man was sent to reinforce it, no orders were issued to its commander, and no precautions taken. Had Scott been in his place, fort Niagara would have enclosed him that night—every door would have been bolted and barred, and the 27 guns it contained rained death on the assailants as they approached. McClure was right, the enemy did "lay waste the frontier." Marching on Lewistown, they burned it to the ground. Setting fire to every farm-house as they advanced, massacring many of the inhabitants, and mutilating the corpses, they burned Youngstown, the Tuscarora Indian village, and Manchester, kindling the whole frontier into a glow from the light of blazing dwellings. Eleven days after another party crossed at Grand Island, and burned Black Rock and Buffalo, leaving scarcely a house standing in the latter place. Dec. 30 At Black Rock they burned three of the schooners belonging to Perry's gallant fleet. Cruel and merciless as was this raid, it had a justification, at least in the burning of houses, on the principles of war. The destruction of Newark was a barbarous act, and in no way borne out by the orders of government, which authorized it only on the ground that the defence of the fort rendered it necessary. To fire a town, turning forth houseless and homeless women and children, because an attacking enemy might employ it as a shelter from which to make their approaches: and destroy it on the plea that it affords merely the shelter of a bivouack, after the position is abandoned, are totally different acts, nor can they be made similar by any sophistry. These outrages inflamed the passions of the inhabitants occupying the frontier to the highest degree. No epithets were too harsh when speaking of each other, and no retaliation seemed too severe. This feeling of hostility was still farther exasperated by the treatment of prisoners of war. The imprisoning of twenty Irishmen, taken at Queenstown the year before, to be tried as traitors, was no doubt a stroke of policy on the part of England, and designed to deter adopted citizens from enlisting in the army. It was announcing beforehand, that all English, Scotch and Irish taken in battle would not be regarded as ordinary prisoners of war, but as her own subjects caught in the act of revolt. Our government could not in any way recognize this arrogant claim, and twenty-three English prisoners were placed in close confinement, with the distinct pledge of the government that they should meet the fate pronounced on the Irishmen. Prevost, acting under orders, immediately shut up twice the number of American officers. Madison retorted by imprisoning an equal number of English officers. Prevost then placed in confinement all the prisoners of war; Madison did the same. The treatment of these prisoners was alike only in form, for while we showed all the leniency consistent with obedience to orders, the English, for the most part, were haughty, contemptuous, and insulting.

The Creek war commenced this year, and though the Indians were not subdued, no defeat had sullied the American arms. This, together with the capture of Detroit, summed up the amount of our successes on land for the year. York and Fort George were lost to us, while Fort Niagara, standing on our soil, was in the hands of the enemy. Such, the administration was compelled to exhibit as the results accomplished by a regular army of thirty-four thousand men, *six thousand volunteers*, and the occasional employment of *thirty thousand militia*. This report following on the heels of the disasters of the previous year, would have completely broken down the government but for the exasperated state of the nation, produced by the cruelties and atrocities of the English. Tenacity of purpose has ever been characteristic of the nation, and ever will be; disasters make us sullen and gloomy, but never incline us to submission. Armies may be beaten, but the nation, never, is a sentiment so grounded and fixed in the national heart that to question its truth excites only amazement. To deepen still more the shadows that had closed upon us, Bonaparte, at this time, was evidently in his last struggle. Although battling bravely for his throne, and exhibiting in more brilliant light than ever the splendor of his marvellous genius, yet the "star" that had led him on was already touching the horizon; and soon as his vast power should yield and fall, England would give us her undivided attention, and then our little navy, our pride and solace, would be swept from the seas.

CHAPTER XIV.

1813—1814.

Winter operations — Decatur challenges Commodore Hardy to meet the United States and Macedonian with two of his frigates — Wilkinson's second invasion of Canada — Battle of la Cole Mill — Holmes' expedition into Canada — Romantic character of our border warfare — Inroad of the British marines to Saybrook and Brockaway's Ferry.

During the autumn and winter of this year, while Congress was shaken with conflicting parties, and deeper gloom and embarrassments were gathering round the administration, reports of conflicts ever and anon came from the bosom of our northern and southern wildernesses. Wilkinson was endeavoring to redeem his failures along the St. Lawrence, and Jackson was leading his gallant little band into the fastnesses of the Creek nation. Most of the national vessels were blockaded in our harbors and rivers, but still our bold little privateers were scouring the ocean in every direction. At this time, too, a single war vessel might be seen struggling in tempestuous seas off the stormy cape, on her way to the Pacific ocean to finish in disaster the most remarkable cruise found in our naval annals. Decatur, with his squadron, lay blockaded at New London, and it was said that every attempt to get to sea was thwarted by some disaffected persons, who burned blue lights at the mouth of the river to give information of his movements to the enemy. He wrote a letter to Mr. Jones, the Secretary of the Navy, on the subject, and a proposition was made in Congress to have it investigated, but it was dismissed as of trivial importance. Irritated at his inactivity, he challenged the Endymion and Statira to meet the United States and Macedonian in single combat, offering to reduce his force till they said it equalled their own. To this Commodore Hardy at first gave his consent, but afterwards withdrew it. If the challenge had been accepted, there is little doubt but that the Chesapeake would have been signally avenged. At one time Decatur was so confident of a fight, that he addressed his crew on the subject.

Wilkinson soon after his retirement to winter quarters at French Mills, on Salmon river, resigned his command to General Izard, and proceeded to Washington to recruit his health. He here planned a winter campaign which for hardihood and boldness exceeded all his previous demonstrations. He proposed to pierce by different routes with two columns, each two thousand strong, to the St. Pierre, and sweeping the defenceless cantonments as he advanced, stop and occupy them or turn with sudden and resistless energy against the Isle Aux Noix, or go quietly back to his winter quarters again. At the same time, four thousand men were to cross the St. Lawrence, take Cornwall, fortify and hold it so as to destroy the communication between the two provinces. Nay, he proposed at one time to barrack in Kingston. The secretary, however, distrusting the feasibility of these plans, ordered him to fall back to Plattsburgh with his troops. Brown, in the mean time, was directed to take two thousand men and proceed to Sackett's Harbor, for the defence of our flotilla there, while young Scott was stationed at Buffalo.

1813.

Matters remained in this state till March, when Wilkinson resolved to erect a battery at Rouse's Point, and thus keep the enemy from Lake Champlain. The latter, penetrating the design, concentrated a force two thousand strong at La Cole Mill, three miles below the point. The early breaking up of the ice, however, had rendered the project impracticable. Still, Wilkinson resolved to attack La Cole Mill, though it does not appear what use he designed to make of the victory when gained. With four thousand men, and artillery sufficiently heavy, it was supposed, to demolish the walls of the mill, he set forth. The main road was blockaded for miles with trees that had been felled across it. He therefore, after arriving at Odletown, was compelled to take a narrow winding path only wide enough for a single sleigh, and which for three miles crept through a dense wood. With a guide who had been forced into the service to show the way, and who marched on foot between two dragoons, the advance, led by Major Forsyth and Colonel Clarke, slowly entered the wintry forest. An eighteen pounder broke down before it reached the woods, a twelve pounder lagged on the way, so as to be useless. A twelve pounder and a howitzer were got forward with great labor, for the wheels sunk into the yielding snow and mud, and thumped at almost every revolution against the trees that hemmed in the narrow path. The column was necessarily closely packed, and as it waded through the snow the fire of the concealed enemy soon opened upon it. But the two guns, what with lifting and pushing, lumbered slowly forward, and at length were placed in a position in a clearing in sight of the mill, which proved to be garrisoned by only two hundred men. The snow was a foot deep, and the panting troops, though full of courage and confidence, were brought with difficulty forward. The woods were so thick that the mill was hidden till directly upon it, and the only open space where the cannon could play unobstructed on the walls was so near, that the sharp shooters within the building could pick off the gunners with fatal rapidity. The first shots told heavily on the building, but in a short time, of the three officers who commanded the guns, two were severely wounded, and of the twenty men who served them, fourteen were dead or disabled. The troops as they came up were posted so as to prevent the escape of the garrison. Sortie after sortie was made to take the guns, but always repulsed by the American troops, who fought gallantly under their intrepid leaders. Larribee who commanded the howitzer was shot through the heart, and Macpherson who had charge of the twelve pounder, though cut by a bullet under the chin, maintained his ground till prostrated by a frightful wound in the hip. The infantry was of no avail, except to repel sorties, and stood grouped in the forest waiting till the enemy, forced by the cannonade to retreat, should uncover themselves. But it was impossible to serve the guns under the concentrated fire of two hundred muskets and rifles in such close range. Men dropped in the act of loading; in one case, after the piece was charged, but a single man remained to fire it. A portion of the garrison seeing it so unprotected, rushed forth to seize it. The single man, however, stood his ground, and as the enemy came, fired his piece. At the same time the troops in the wood poured in a volley. When the smoke cleared away but a single man was left standing. The whole column had been shot down. At length a hundred and forty or fifty having fallen and night coming on the troops were withdrawn. It was resolved to renew the attack next morning, but a rain storm set in during the night, turning the snow into a half fluid mass, and rendering a second approach impracticable. The chilled and tired army was therefore withdrawn, and Wilkinson ended at once his invasion of Canada and his military career. He retired from the army, and younger and more energetic men were appointed over it, who should lead it to victory. 1814. On the 24th of January, Brigadier-Generals Brown and Izard were promoted to the rank of Major-Generals, and later in the spring took command on our northern frontier.

While these unsuccessful plans were maturing on the St. Lawrence, Colonel Butler, commanding at Detroit, dispatched Captain Holmes with a small detachment into Canada to destroy Fort Talbot, a hundred miles inland, and what ever other "military establishments might fall in his way." Feb. 24. He had less than two hundred men and but two cannon. Pushing his way through the forests he found the road when he reached Point Au Plat, so filled with fallen trees and brushwood that his guns could not be carried forward. Leaving them therefore behind, he kept on until he ascertained that his approach was expected. Seeing that all hopes of a surprise must be abandoned, he changed his course and marched rapidly against Fort Delaware, on the Thames, occupied by the British. But when he arrived within fifteen miles of the place he was informed that his attack was expected, and that ample preparations had been made to meet it. He immediately fell back behind Twenty Mile Creek, where he had scarcely taken position, before the rangers left to protect his rear emerged on a run from the woods that covered the opposite bank, pushed fiercely by the head of the enemy's column. He immediately strengthened his position by every means in his power, and on the following morning was ready for an attack. Only a small body of the enemy, however, appeared at day break, and soon after retreated. Holmes at first suspected this to be a ruse to draw him from his position, but ascertaining from a reconnaissance that not more than sixty or seventy men composed the force, he started in pursuit. His first conjecture, however, proved true, for after marching a few miles he came upon his adversary, well posted, and expecting him. His great anxiety was now to get back to his position, and at the same time practice the very deception which had beguiled him from it. He succeeded admirably, and the British imagining his retreat to be a hasty and disorderly flight pressed after, and on coming to the creek resolved at once to attack him. Crossing the stream they ascended the opposite bank boldly, and without opposition, till within twenty yards of the top, when they were met by such a sudden and destructive volley that they broke and fled. Hiding behind trees they then kept up a harmless fire till night, when under cover of darkness they effected their retreat with the loss of nearly a hundred men, or one-third of their force, while some half dozen killed and wounded covered the loss of the Americans. This half partisan, half regular warfare, in the midst of our vast forests, combined much of the picturesque and marvellous. There was not the pomp of vast armies, nor the splendor of a great battle, but courage, skill and endurance were required, sufficient to make able commanders and veteran soldiers. The long and tedious march of a hundred miles through the snow-filled forest—the solitary block-house with its small garrison, situated in a lonely clearing, around which the leafless trees creaked and groaned in the northern blasts—the bivouack fire gleaming red through the driving storm—the paths of wild beasts crossing the wilderness in every direction, their cries of hunger mingling with the muffled sound of half frozen torrents—the war-cry of the savage and the crack of his rifle at still midnight, waking up the chilled sleepers to battle and to death—the sudden onset and the bloody hand-to-hand fight, made up the experience and history of our border warfare. Far away from the haunts of civilization, men struggled for the control of an imaginary line, and many gallant and able officers, fell ingloriously by some Indian marksman. At far intervals, stretching from the St. Lawrence to Mackinaw, the faintly heard thunder of cannon amid those vast solitudes, announced that two nations were battling for untrodden forest tracts and undisturbed sheets of water. Those tracts are now covered with towns and cities, and those sheets of water freighted with commerce. Then it was announced as a great miracle of speed, that a steamboat made four miles an hour in passing up the Ohio—now the northern lakes are ploughed with steamers, going at the rate of eighteen or twenty miles an hour, and wrapped round with railroads, over which cars are thundering with a velocity that annihilates distance, and brings into one neighborhood the remotest States.

An unsuccessful attempt on the part of the British to destroy the American vessels just launched at Vergennes, and which were to compose Macdonough's fleet, and a bold inroad of the English marines from the blockading squadron off New London, in which twenty American vessels were burned, the men pitching quoits, drinking and playing ball during the conflagration, till night, when they quietly floated down the river, constituted the other chief movements that terminated in the early spring.

CHAPTER XIV.

THIRTEENTH CONGRESS. MAY 27, 1813.

Democratic gain in Congress — Spirit in which the two parties met — Russian mediation offered and accepted, and commerce opened — State of the Treasury — Debate respecting a reporter's seat — Direct tax — Webster's resolutions — Governor Chittenden — Strange conduct of parties in New Hampshire — The embargo — England proposes peace — Commissioners appointed — Army bill — Webster's speech upon it — Sketch of him — The loan bill — Defended by Mr. Eppes — Sketch of Mr. Pickering, with his speech — Sketch of John Forsyth, and his speech — Calhoun — Grosvenor — Bill for the support of military establishments — Speech of Artemus Ward — Resolutions of Otis in the Massachusetts Senate — Repeal of the embargo — Calhoun and Webster — Strange reversal of their positions — Strength of our navy and army.

Soon after the capture of York the Thirteenth Congress assembled. By the new apportionment made the year previous, a hundred and eighty-two members had been added to the House of Representatives. One remarkable man, Randolph, had disappeared from the arena, having been defeated by Mr. Eppes, son-in-law of Jefferson. As the two great parties came together they surveyed each other's strength—prepared to close in combat with the same determination and hostile feeling that had marked the proceedings of the last session of the Twelfth Congress. In the accession of members the Federalists had made important gains, chiefly from New York, so that the House stood one hundred and twelve for the war and sixty-eight against it, and the Senate twenty-seven to nine. In the latter, however, the party lines were not so strongly drawn, and on many questions the Democrats had much less majorities than their nominal superiority would indicate. Among the new members were Pickering, who had succeeded Quincey, and Cyrus King, from Massachusetts, and Daniel Webster, from New Hampshire, Federalists. Forsyth, of Georgia, M'Lean, of Ohio, Taylor, of New York, and Findley, of Pennsylvania, were Democrats. Mr. Clay was elected speaker on the first ballot. The President's message was short, and related wholly to the war. He informed Congress that an offer of mediation had been made by the Emperor Alexander, of Russia, on the 8th of March previous—and accepted, and that Mr. Gallatin, Mr. Bayard, and Mr. Adams, had been appointed Commissioners under it, to negotiate a peace with England, and also a treaty with Russia. He expressed the belief that England would accept the mediation, whether it resulted in any settlement of difficulties or not.

The receipts into the Treasury during the six months, ending the last day of March, including sums received on account of Treasury notes and loans, amounted to $15,412,000, the expenditures to $15,920,000. A balance, however, was in the Treasury previously, so that there remained $1,857,000 unexpended. Of the loan of sixteen millions, authorized in February, one million had been paid in, and formed Feb. 18, part of the receipts mentioned, so that the remaining $15,000,000, together with $5,000,000 of Treasury notes, and $9,700,000, the sum expected from customs, sales of public lands, making in all $29,000,000, constituted the provision for the remaining nine months of the current year. To avoid the necessity of loans, which were made at rates injurious to the government, and to give a more permanent basis to the revenue, additional taxes were recommended.

The first act of Congress was the passage of a resolution, introduced by Clay, to refer that part of the message which related to the barbarous manner in which the enemy waged war to a select committee, of which Mr. Macon, of Georgia, was chairman. Mr. Eppes was made chairman of that of Ways and Means, and Calhoun of that on Foreign Affairs. The gentlemen constituting the latter were Calhoun, Grundy, Desha, Jackson of Virginia, Ingersoll, Fisk of New York, and Webster.

The extreme sensitiveness of the two parties, and the readiness with which they seized upon the most trifling matter as a bone of contention, were strikingly exhibited in some of the earliest proceedings of Congress. The reporter of the Federal Republican, the paper which had been mobbed by the Democrats at Baltimore, and was now published in Georgetown, presented a petition, asking a place to be assigned him, like that of the other reporters, and stating that the Speaker had refused to give him one. The implication was, that Mr. Clay had denied him a place on account of his politics. Mr. Clay said this was not so, that the true reason was, he had no place to give; all of those furnished by the House being pre-occupied. This statement, however, could not satisfy the members, and it was proposed to make an extra provision for the gentleman. Calhoun was opposed to the admission of any reporters. Almost the entire day was occupied in discussing this trifling affair, when such momentous questions asked the attention of Congress. It even adjourned without coming to a decision, and not until next day was it disposed of, by rejecting the prayer of the petitioner.

June 14.

Mr. Eppes, from the Committee of Ways and Means, made a report, in which, after showing that the expenditures for the next year, 1814, would exceed the revenue by $5,600,000, twelve bills were offered, one for direct taxation, another establishing the office of Commissioner of the Revenue, and others laying duties on imported salt, on licenses to retailers of liquors, on foreign merchandise, carriages, distillers of liquors, on auction sales of foreign goods and vessels, on sugars refined in the United States, on bank notes, notes of hand and certain foreign bills of exchange, and on foreign tonnage.

Mr. Webster then rose and delivered his first speech in the House, introduced by four resolutions, the purport of which were to inquire into the time, manner, &c., with the attending circumstances, in which the document, asserted to be a repeal of the Berlin and Milan decrees, was communicated to this government. Although these resolutions had their origin in Federal hostility, and were designed to sustain the old charge against the administration, of being under French influence, because it was well aware those decrees had not been repealed when it declared war against England, yet Webster carefully avoided implying it in his speech. He felt bound to offer these resolutions in justice to his constituents. A heated discussion followed their introduction, but young Webster conducted himself with great prudence and caution. At home he had made inflammable speeches against the war, but after he got out of the atmosphere of Massachusetts, and came in contact with such ardent young patriots as Clay and Calhoun, his sympathies, doubtless, were moved, and his patriotism received an impulse which went far to neutralize the views of Federalism, with which he had been inoculated. The political opponents of that war having been successively thrown overboard by the nation since its termination, much effort seems to have been made by the friends of Webster to omit entirely this portion of his life, but I have no doubt were it truly and honorably written, it would exalt his character and enhance his fame. Coming from the very furnace of Federalism—educated under the influence of men whose opinions he had been taught to venerate, and who, throwing aside their party hate, were the wisest statesmen of the land, sent to Washington on purpose to represent their views, it seems unaccountable that he, a young aspirant for fame, did not at once plunge into the arena and win reputation by crossing swords with such men as Clay and Calhoun. Standing for the first time on the field where political fame was to be won, and goaded on by attacks upon principles he had been taught to venerate, he nevertheless carefully stood aloof, and shortly after retired entirely on leave of absence. How is this strange conduct to be accounted for in one who ever after never refused to close like a lion with his foes? With his powers he would soon have been a leader of the opposition, and yet this soul, full of deep thought and slumbering fire, looked apparently cold and indifferent on the strife that was rending the nation asunder. Did not this conduct grow out of a sense of duty and of patriotism? He could not do less, as a representative of Federalism, than offer resolutions of inquiry, and without turning traitor to his constituents, he could not do more for the administration. Did not that judgment, on whose decisions the nation afterwards so implicitly relied, tell him even then that his country was right and his teachers wrong on the great question of war or no war, and did not that grand heart, which heaved like the swelling sea when he spoke of the glorious Union, even then revolt at the disloyal attitude of New England? If this be not true, then his conduct is wholly inexplicable and contradictory to his after life.

The first session of the Thirteenth Congress continued till August 2d, when it adjourned to December. In the mean time, a direct tax, amounting to $3,000,000, apportioned to the eighteen different states, was laid. A bounty of $25 was voted to privateers for every prisoner taken, and heavy penalties were placed on the use of British licenses, and provisions made to raise ten companies for the defence of the sea coast. The disasters of our northern army, during this autumn, increased the boldness of the Federalists, and a paper of Boston openly advocated the proposition for each state to take care of itself, fight its own battles, and make its own terms. Governor Chittenden of Vermont, attempted to recall a brigade of militia, appointed to garrison Burlington, during Hampton's march into Canada, on the ground it had been unconstitutionally ordered out. The commander and a part of the brigade refused, when the former was put under arrest. The Legislature of New Hampshire, in order to get rid of the democratic judges, appointed by Langdon and Plumer, abolished all the courts in the state, and constructed an entirely new system, with new judges. To this high-handed measure the democratic judges refused to submit, and held court sessions as formerly, side by side with the new judges. In those counties where the sheriff was democratic, their decision was sustained by this functionary, confusing and confounding every thing. By such measures, party spirit was inflamed to the highest pitch, dividing friends and families and societies. It became a frenzy, a madness, obliterating, in many parts of New England, all traces of former urbanity, justice, affection and courtesy. The appellation of Democrat and Federalist, applied to one or the other, converted him, in his opponent's eye, into a monster. The charge of highway robbery, rape or murder would not have been more instantaneous and direful in its effect. The Boston papers advocated the most monstrous doctrines, creating great anxiety and solicitude at Washington. But soon as the New England line was crossed, passing west and south, the feeling changed. To go from these fierce, debasing broils, into the harmonious feeling in favor of the war, was like passing from the mad struggles of a vessel amid the breakers to a quiet ship moving steadily on her way. The governors of the several states in their proclamations and messages firmly upheld the administration, and the legislatures pledged their support.

In the midst of such excitements, oppressed by the failure of Wilkinson's campaign, and dreading the use which the Federalists would make of it, Congress, according to adjournment, reassembled Dec. 6. Mr. Eppes was still continued chairman of the Committee of Ways and Means. Among the first measures was the introduction of an embargo act. Madison, in a special message, strongly recommended it, on the ground that under the present non-importation act the enemy on our shores and at a distance were constantly furnished with the supplies they needed. An illegal traffic was also carried on with foreign ports, not only exporting forbidden articles, but importing British manufactures. To stop this illicit trade in future, an act was passed in secret session, laying an embargo on all the ports of the Union. To prevent evasion, it was guarded by the most stringent provisions and heavy penalties, so that the coasting trade suffered severely. Fishermen were compelled to give bonds that they would not violate it, before they were allowed to leave port. That portion of it, however, which related to the importation of woolen, cotton, and spirits, was rejected by the House, as that prohibiting the release of goods on bonds was rejected by the Senate.

Soon after, a great excitement was caused in the country by a rumor that a British schooner, the Bramble, had arrived in Annapolis, bearing a flag of truce, and despatches of a peaceful nature to our government. Jan. 7. Seven days after, the President transmitted a message to Congress, informing it of a proposition on the part of the English government, to have commissioners appointed to negotiate a peace. This announcement was the signal for the Federalist papers to indulge in laudations of Great Britain's generosity and magnanimity. She had taken the first amicable steps, and that, too, when she was in a condition, owing to Napoleon's sinking fortunes, to direct her entire power against us. The same vessel brought the news of the disasters of Leipsic. There was, on the other hand, much distrust among the Democrats, because the offer of the Russian mediation had been coldly rejected three several times.

John Quincy Adams, and Henry Clay, and Jonathan Russel and Bayard who were already abroad, were appointed Commissioners, to whom Gallatin was soon after added, to proceed to Gottenberg. Russel, after the negotiations closed, was to remain as minister to Sweden. Jan. 19. Mr. Clay, in an eloquent address, resigned his station as Speaker of the House, and Mr. Cheves was elected in his place. Dec. One of the most exciting debates during this session of Congress arose on the introduction of resolutions by the editor of the Federal Republican, demanding an inquiry respecting a letter written by Turreau, in 1809, then Minister from France, to the Secretary of State, said to be withdrawn from the files. The disappearance of the letter was proof positive that its contents committed, in some way, the administration. A vehement debate of three days duration followed. Endless changes were rung on the old charge of French influence. At length the question was taken, and the resolutions voted down, and a simple call on the President for information substituted. This shell which had been so suddenly thrown into the House, threatening in its explosion to shatter the war party to fragments, proved a very harmless thing. Turreau, it eventually turned out, had written a letter of complaint to the Secretary of State, so overbearing in its tone, so absurd in its complaints, and so undiplomatic in every respect, that he was requested to withdraw it, which was done. In such a sensitive and excited state was party feeling at this time, that the most trivial matters became distorted and magnified into extraordinary proportions.

The army bill, providing for the filling of the ranks, the enlistment of men to serve for five years instead of twelve months, and the re-enlistment of those whose term of service had expired; and another bill authorizing a new loan of $25,000,000, was the bugle blast summoning the combatants to battle. Mr. Webster was for the first time roused. The army bill was evidently designed to provide for a third campaign against Canada. From the first, almost the entire military force of the nation had been employed in these futile invasions. The successive failures, especially the last, gave the opposition great vantage ground in declaring against the scheme altogether. They condemned it not only as an aggressive war, and therefore indefensible, but declared the acquisition of that country worse than worthless if obtained. The whole project was not only wrong in principle, but would be evil in its results, if successful.

The clause extending the term of enlistment, and authorizing the raising of new regiments, making the money bounty $124—fifty of it to be paid on an enrollment, fifty on mustering, and the remainder at the close of the war, if living, and if not to go to his heirs, was assailed with vehement opposition. Jan. 3, 1814. Mr. Webster, who had been cut short in an attack on the administration by the Speaker, on the ground that no question was before the house, now rose to speak. Carefully avoiding the asperity which distinguished his colleagues, he levelled all his force against the embargo act, and the conquest of Canada. Jan. 10. The former he denounced unjust and unequal in its bearing, and ruinous in its consequences. He called on the administration to remove it at once, as the first step towards the acquirement of a just position. He then denounced the Canadian war, to prosecute which this extraordinary bill was introduced, whose provisions if carried out would swell the regular army to sixty-six thousand troops, to say nothing of the power conferred on the President for calling out the militia for six months instead of three. Let us, he said, have only force enough on our frontier to protect it from invasion—let the slaughter of our yeomanry cease, and the fires along our northern boundary be extinguished. Already the war had cost nearly half as much as the entire struggle for independence; and said he, in conclusion, if war must be, "apply your revenue to the augmentation of your navy. That navy, in turn, may protect your commerce. Let it no longer be said that not one ship of force built by your hands since the war, floats on the ocean. Turn the current of your efforts into the channel which national sentiment has already worn broad and deep to receive it. A naval force competent to defend your coast against considerable armaments, to convoy your trade, and perhaps raise the blockade of your rivers, is not a chimera. It may be realized. If, then, the war must continue, go to the ocean. If you are seriously contending for maritime rights, go to the theatre where alone those rights can be defended. Thither every indication of your fortune points you. There the united wishes and exertions of the nation will go with you. Even our party divisions, acrimonious as they are, cease at the water's edge. They are lost in attachment to national character, on that element where that character is made respectable. In protecting naval interests by naval means, you will arm yourselves with the whole power of national sentiment, and may command the whole abundance of national resources. In time you may enable yourselves to redress injuries in the place where they may be offered, and if need be, to accompany your own flag throughout the world with the protection of your own cannon." This speech produced a marked impression on the house. Succeeding as it did, the resolutions of the Legislature of Massachusetts, refusing to compliment our naval commanders for their victories, on the ground that encouragement would be given to the war, it looked like a change in that quarter. The war was not denounced as it had ever been by the Federalist leaders—he quarrelled only with the mode of carrying it on. Nay, it implied that we had wrongs to redress at sea, and thither our force should be directed. The policy proposed in this speech should doubtless have been adopted at the commencement of the war, and might have been wise as late as 1814, but Webster did not propose it for the purpose of having it acted upon. This fine peroration was simply a safety-valve to his patriotism. He dared not—he could not uphold the war, or put his shoulders to any measures designed to carry it on with vigor. He represented a State opposed to it in principle, not in mode. Still, the language he used was so different from the other leading Federalists, that the Democrats, on the whole, did not wish to complain. Webster at this time was but thirty-one years of age, and little known except in his own vicinity. This speech, however, delivered with the fervor and eloquence which distinguished him, gave clear indications of his future greatness. Though a young man, he exhibited none of the excitement and eagerness of youth. Calm, composed, he uttered his thoughts in those ponderous sentences which ever after characterized his public addresses. Large, well made, his jet black hair parted from a forehead that lay like a marble slab above the deep and cavernous eyes; there was a solemnity, and at times almost a gloom in that extraordinary face, that awakened the interest of the beholder. There was power in his very glance, and the close compressed lip revealed a stern and unyielding character. Even at this age he looked like one apart from his fellows, with inward communings to which no one was admitted. When excited in debate, that sombre and solemn face absolutely blazed with fire, and his voice, which before had sounded sharp and unpleasant, rung like a clarion through the house. His sentences fell with the weight of Thor's hammer—indeed, every thing about him was Titanic, giving irresistible weight to his arguments.

The bill having passed the house, the other authorizing a loan of $25,000,000 and a reissue of treasury notes to the amount of $10,000,000, came up. The expenditures for the coming year were estimated at $45,000,000, to meet which the ordinary means of revenue were wholly insufficient. A violent and bitter debate arose on its presentation, which lasted three weeks. Regarded as so much money appropriated to the conquest of Canada, it met with the determined hostility of the opponents of the war. Mr. Eppes defended his bill, and went into a long and statistical account of the revenue and expenditures of the nation—showed how she could easily, in time of peace, pay off every dollar she might owe—estimated the value of the land and produce and capital of the country, and proved, as he deemed satisfactorily, that the loan combined "all the advantages of safety, profit, and a command at will of the capital invested." The long debate upon it had little to do with the bill itself, but swept the whole range of politics for the last four or five years. The history of the war was gone over—orders in council, and Berlin and Milan decrees revived with fresh vigor—the influence of Bonaparte in our councils, though now struggling for life, was charged anew on the administration. Personalities were indulged in, and the most absurd accusations made by men, who on other subjects, exhibited sound judgment and able statesmanship. Mr. Pitkin spoke a part of two days, making a frightful exhibit of expenses, and denounced the war in Canada. Pickering, with his large, powerful frame and Roman features, not belying the fearless character of the man, came down on the administration with all the power, backed by the most unquenchable hatred he was master of. A distinguished man in the Revolution, he had from that time occupied a prominent place in the political history of his country. A "Pharisee of the Pharisees" in the Essex Junto, he cherished all the intense hatred of that branch of the Federalists for the war and its supporters. Built on a grand scale, yet with a heart hard as iron towards a foe, fierce and bold, denouncing his old friend and patron, John Adams, because he did not hate France as cordially as he thought every good Christian should, having no sympathy with Washington's quiet and non-committal character, he looked upon Bonaparte and our war and its supporters, as the most monstrous births of the age. His indignation at their existence was only exceeded by his wonder that heaven, in its just wrath, did not quench all together. Probably the administration had not such a sincere and honest hater in the whole Federalist ranks. He was an honest man and possessed of most noble traits, but his feelings obscured his judgment when speaking of the war, and he gave utterance to the most extraordinary and absurd assertions. In this speech he wandered over the whole field—took bold and decided ground—advocated openly the doctrine of the right of search, as defended by our enemy—declared that our complaints were unjust—denied the statement respecting the number of impressed seamen, saying that many Americans served voluntarily on board of British cruisers—glorified England for her efforts to overthrow Napoleon, calling her the "world's last hope." Having thus defined his position so clearly, that there could be no doubt where he stood, he turned to the Speaker and looking him sternly in the face through his spectacles, and "swinging his long arm aloft," exclaimed, "I stand on a *rock* from which all Democracy—no, *not all Democracy and hell to boot* can move me—the rock of integrity and truth." Mr. Shelby and Mr. Miller followed in a similar strain, and Canada, with its disastrous campaigns, was flung so incessantly in the face of the war party, that it hated the very name. Grundy defended the bill, and Gaston, of North Carolina, opposed it. Grosvenor launched forth into a violent harangue, and was so personal and unparliamentary in his language that he was often called to order. Very little, however, was said on the merits of the bill. This served only to open the flood-gates of eloquence, which embracing every topic of the past and present, deluged for twenty days the floor of Congress. Langdon Cheves, the Speaker, though opposed to the restrictive measures of the administration, upheld the war, and defended the bill in a long and temperate speech. One of the best speeches elicited by it, was made by John Forsyth. Hitherto he had taken but little part in the debates of the House, and hence his brilliant effort took the members by surprise and arrested their attention. Handsome, graceful, fluent, with a fine voice and captivating elocution, he came down on the Federalists with sudden and unexpected power. Their unfounded assertions, unpatriotic sentiments and personal attacks had at length roused him, and as they had wandered from the question in their blind warfare, so he passed from it to repay the blows that had been so unsparingly given. Turning to the New England delegation, he charged boldly on Massachusetts the crime of fomenting treason to the State, if not intentionally, yet practically, by her legislative acts, inflammatory resolutions and violent complaints of injustice, which were the first steps towards more open hostility. "I mention them," said he, "not from fear, but to express my profound contempt for their impotent madness. Fear and interest hinder the factious spirits from executing their wishes. *If a leader* should be found bad and bold enough to try, one consolation for virtue is left, that those who raise the tempest will be the first victims of its fury." Calhoun, with his clear logic, demolished the objections that had been raised. He said they could all be reduced to two. One was, that the loan could not be had—the other, that the war was inexpedient. He declared both false, going over the ground he had been compelled so often to traverse since the commencement of the war. He took up the question of impressment—declared our war a defensive one—bore hard upon those who voted against supplies—showed that the war had liberated us from that slavish fear of England which had rested like a nightmare on the nation—and started into vigorous growth home manufactures, destined in the end to render us independent of foreign products, and furnishing us with ampler means to carry on any war that might occur in the future.

This debate might have lasted much longer but for a violent harangue of Grosvenor, full of gross personalities, discreditable to himself and insulting to the House. It was resolved to put an end to such disgraceful scenes, and the previous question was moved and carried by a majority of forty. A similar fierce conflict, however, took place soon after on the bill for the support of military establishments, in the ensuing year, and on the motion to repeal the Embargo Act. In a speech against the former, Artemus Ward opposed not only the invasion of Canada, and reiterated the old charge of subserviency to France, but openly and boldly defended England in the course she had taken; declared that impressment was in accordance with the law of nations, and that the doctrine "the flag protects all that sails under it" was untenable and false. He then went gravely into the reasons of the war, and laid down the following propositions, which he proceeded soberly to defend:—

"1st. Napoleon had an ascendancy in our councils through the fear or hopes he inspired.

"2d. The administration wished to destroy commerce, and make an agricultural and manufacturing people.

"3d. It wished to change the form of our government."

These extraordinary propositions were severally defended, and declared by himself fully proved. In reply to the charge that the Federalists were nullifiers, he pronounced it unjust and unfounded, and said that the Federalists of Massachusetts would "cling to the Union as the rock of their salvation, and will die in defence of it, *provided they have an equality of benefits.* But everything has its 'hitherto.' *There is a point beyond which submission is a crime.* God grant that we may never arrive at that point." Such language, though guarded, was significant, and justified the very charges it was designed to rebut. Coupled with the action of Massachusetts, it furnished ground for the gravest fears. Jan. 6. A motion having been introduced during the session to the effect that the Attorney-General of the United States should prosecute Governor Chittenden, of Vermont, for recalling the militia of the state from Burlington, Otis presented a resolution to the Massachusetts Senate, declaring that the State was prepared to sustain, with her whole power, the Governor of Vermont in support of his constitutional rights. |Jan. 44.| In the mean time the Legislature voted an address, denouncing the war altogether, ascribing it to hatred of the friends of Washington's policy, to the influence of foreigners, to envy and jealousy of the growing commercial states, and desire for more territory. The Pennsylvania Legislature, on the other hand, censured the conduct of both Chittenden and the Massachusetts Legislature, declaring that the State would support the General Government in meting out justice to all violators of the Constitution. |Feb. |2. New Jersey was still more enraged, and after giving utterance to her contempt and abhorrence of the "ravings of an infuriated faction, whether issuing from a legislative body, a maniac governor, or discontented and ambitious demagogues," "Resolved, that the State was ready to resist internal insurrection with the same readiness as the invasion of a foreign foe." Thus the storm of political hate raged both within and without the halls of Congress, threatening in its fury to send the waves of civil strife over the already distracted and suffering land. But there was a large party, composed of the middling classes of New England, in favor of the war. This, together with the outward pressure of the entire Union, combined to make the Federalist leaders extremely cautious in their movements. The farmer was benefitted by the war, for his produce commanded a higher price in the market, while the manufacturing interests, which the restrictive acts had forced into importance, were also advanced, thus creating a new antagonist to the Federalists. The embargo, however, pressed heavily on a large portion of the country, calling forth loud denunciations and petitions from the whole New England coast.

Fortunately for the administration, circumstances soon rendered it useless. After struggling with almost superhuman courage and endurance to repel the allies from the soil of France, Napoleon saw them at last enter Paris in triumph, and demolish with a blow the splendid structure he had reared with so much skill and labor. With the overthrow of the French Empire ended the Continental War, and of course the Orders in Council, the Berlin and Milan Decrees fell at once to the ground. The grand cause of the restrictive system having been removed, Madison sent a message to the House of Representatives, advising a repeal of the Embargo and Non-Importation Act. A bill to this effect was reported by Mr. Calhoun from the Committee on Foreign Relations. |Apr. 4| He spoke at some length on the first section, embracing the embargo, supported it on the ground of the recent changes in Europe, resulting from Bonaparte's downfall. Russia, Sweden, Germany, Denmark, Prussia, and Spain, might now be considered neutral nations, and by opening our commerce to them, we should in time, in all probability, attach them to us in common hostility to England, should she continue her maritime usurpations. This country had from the first contended for free trade, and consistency required we should allow it to neutral powers, just as we had claimed it for ourselves. In short, there was no reason for its continuance, except the plea of consistency. But he contended that a change of policy growing out of a change in the circumstances that had originated it, could not be called inconsistent. Mr. Webster replied to him, saying that he rejoiced it had fallen to his lot to be present at the funeral obsequies of the restrictive system. He felt a temperate exultation that this system, so injurious to the country and powerless in its effect on foreign nations, was about to be consigned to the tomb of the Capulets. After ridiculing the whole restrictive system, saying it was of like faith, to be acted—not deliberated on, and that no saint in the calendar had been more blindly followed than it had been by its friends, he went on to show that it was designed, originally, to cooperate with France. He denounced any system, the continuance of which depended on the condition of things in Europe. Such policy was dangerous, exposing us to all the fluctuations and changes that occurred there. If this universal application of a principle was unsound and extraordinary in a statesman, what followed was still more surprising. Speaking of the effect of the system to stimulate manufactories, he said he wished none reared in a hot-bed. Those compatible with the interests of the country should be fostered, but he wished to see no Sheffield or Birmingham in this country. He descanted largely on the evils of extensive manufactories and populous towns, and intimated strongly that any protective legislation in reference to them would be unwise. What complete summersets those two great men, Webster and Calhoun, and the sections of country they represented, have made since 1814. Then South Carolina firmly supported the union against the doctrine of state rights, and Calhoun reasoned eloquently for manufactories, against Webster, opposed to them. Years passed by, and Massachusetts, through her Webster, pleaded nobly, sublimely, for the union, against the nullifying doctrines of South Carolina, and those two men, standing on the floor of Congress, fought for the systems they had formerly opposed, and in fierce and close combat crossed swords each for the cause of the other. Webster in 1814 condemning measures that forced manufactories into existence, and afterwards pleading earnestly for a high tariff, and Calhoun at the same time defending even the embargo on the ground that it encouraged them, and afterwards fighting sternly against that tariff, are striking illustrations of the changes and fluctuations of political life. And yet there may be no inconsistency in all this. "*Tempora mutantur, et nos mutamur in illis,*" is a sound maxim. Webster, when he charged inconsistency on the administration for advising the repeal of the embargo act, after the great change in European affairs, little thought how soon he would be compelled to shelter himself behind this Latin maxim. In 1814 the interests of New England were closely allied with free commerce, and her destiny pointed towards the sea. In a few years her capital was largely invested in manufactures, and could the tariff have been made a permanent policy, all her crystal streams and dashing torrents hurrying from the mountains to the sea, would have been mines of almost exhaustless wealth. The times being changed, the dictates of true wisdom required a change of policy. There is no inconsistency so glaring and injurious as a stubborn adherence to old dogmas or systems, when events in their progress have exploded both.

Added to the acts of Congress already mentioned, the most important were those making appropriations for the support of the navy—for the building and equipment of floating batteries for the defence of the harbors and rivers of our country. The Yazoo claim was also disposed of during this session. April 18, 1814. After an ineffectual attempt to introduce a bill for the establishment of a national bank, and the transaction of some minor business, Congress adjourned to the last Monday in October.

Our naval force in service in January of this year, independent of the lake squadrons, gun-boats, etc., for harbor defences, was but seven frigates, seven sloops-of-war, four brigs, three schooners, and four other small vessels. The secretary, however, reported in February three seventy-fours and three forty-fours on the stocks, besides smaller vessels, which would make thirty-three vessels, large and small, in actual service or soon to be afloat, while thirty-one were on the lakes. The army, by law, was increased at this session to 64,759 men, while the militia of the union amounted to 719,449 men. Added to this, the president was authorized to accept the service of volunteers to the number of 10,000, their term of service not to exceed one year.

With such an imposing array of force on paper, with the increased revenue from the direct tax laid the year before, with a loan of $25,000,000, and treasury notes amounting to $10,000,000, the government prepared to enter on a third campaign.

END OF VOL. I.